A Home for the Heart

Along the way,

a land which can bring me happiness faintly appears in my mind.

Longing for, but not unreachable.

The small town,

apart the noise of big cities.

Old fragrance rose up through the air.

Under the sky with grey clouds,

buildings with roofs and spires of different colors, dazzling with grey, poi. ⌐irections,
but not messy.

From my home,

Go straight, turn left, and then go straight and turn left again,

there is a wide straight road into the distance, to an unknown place.

On this land,

Wide roads like this are not commonly seen.

A few old men are shaking fans in front of their houses.

From their eyes, you can see peace.

Peaceful sentiment would be the major mood.

Here,

there is no splendid prosperity.

Here,

there is simple meaningfulness,

like immerging breezes of the summer.

From here,

Where do I go?

Yin woke up from a nightmare. Her clothes were wet due to sweat. This was the first time in the past half a year that she again had that frightening dream. Since she moved to Altimont 4 years ago, gradually, that same nightmare went away.

The morning sunshine sprinkled into the room, on to her bed. She gazed out of the window. It was a beautiful June morning. Summer had arrived. Summers here in Altimont didn't get too warm. Even the hottest days would be a pleasant 78 degrees. *You don't need to run your air conditioner through the whole summer.* The scenery outside her window calmed her down and made her realize what scared her was just a bad dream. Lifting her forearm, she took a look at the black Swatch on her wrist. *It's 7:23 AM. Time to get up.* She stretched herself with a bit of a yawn, and then she got herself out of bed. This morning was the most ordinary of mornings, a carbon copy of yesterday morning. She, as usual, went into bathroom to prepare herself for work, showering, eliminating the foul taste of sleep in her mouth, and then washing her face, the final step of her morning ritual.

Her studio apartment was small, about 600 square feet, and without closets. Living in a larger-sized place would have made her feel a bit insecure. The sun rendered the walls of her apartment to be violet. There was a huge window on the other side of the room, with a pair of thick colorful rainbow curtains, decorated with large triangles, on each side of the window. In front of the window, there was a huge ash bed brushed gloss black. An orange sheet lay across the bed. Her wardrobe and dresser was a perfect match.

Wearing a thin white short-sleeve blouse, a pair of denim cutoff shorts and a pair of Converse tennis shoes, she eagerly walked downstairs to get her bicycle which she kept locked on the back porch. She rode her small yellow bike to work every day. There in front of the bike was a basket that gave her the room to put her bag and a bottle of diet soda. She didn't care too much about eating breakfast, so she rode directly to the location where she worked.

It was still early, and the weather outside was chilly. Breezes blew in from the south, a wind shower as she referred to it. The white English lights around the corner from her apartment were still working. From the neighborhood where she lived it was a 45 minute ride to her workplace. She enjoyed the slow pace, which gave her a better view of her small town while she rode to work.

The streets in Altimont were narrow but fairly straight, perfect for biking. There was a main road, not far from where Yin lived. She had to first get to the main road in order to get to her workplace. Along the much smaller roads to the main road, resident buildings were on the sides. It is too early that people hadn't gotten up yet, so no one was on the streets except Yin herself. In this town, people usually got up and walked outside after 8:30 AM. You couldn't use "lazy" to label them. They were just used to such a comfort. Branches of cherry trees stretched to the outside of each yard. The sunshine brought a little warmth, slanting on the roads. The period of cherry blossom already passed, yet the shadow of the branches decorated by the golden sunshine projected through, just like another period of floweriness. 7 minutes later, she arrived to the main road. Along this wide straight main road, riding for another few minutes, there was a long bridge that would cross a large peaceful river. Yin took a look down to the bridge. The water in the river was so clean, looked like a piece of mirror. Some gondolas and tiny boats anchored on the dock. No one drove them yet. The breezes got heavier on the bridge, making her feel more comfortable. After she crossed the river, she came to an open area with fewer houses or buildings, a meadow of grass and oak. Just past the river, she would find peddling difficult as she encountered a large tall hill, along the spiral roads, finally arriving at a huge complex of buildings. That was where Yin worked. The façade on each of the buildings were in different colors, mainly grey or white, with a lot of large glass windows. Each building was average 3 stories in height. There was one grey building which was quite unique. It was at the center of the complex, and was the tallest of the complex – 6 stories, with a half sphere dome of white color at the top. It was in this building where the data came from. The top of the building was used as an observatory and the complex was an astronomical station.

Yin already forgot the bad dream. She was happy as she peddled along her usual route. What made her so happy? The happiness came from feeling at ease, there was calmness in her town a simplistic way of life, not once did she ever dream of leaving the town of Altimont.

2

The complex of buildings was one of the largest astronomical station in the country. It had a long history since 1920. A few famous physicists and astronomers ever studied and did research here in their late 20s or early 30s. Tom Barton, for example, was the earliest renowned physicist who won a Nobel Prize for physics later in his life. He studied astronomical-related physics in the station from the age of 28 to 32. Then he moved to Harvard University to teach there ever since. Since then, there were a few famous astronomers and physicists came from this station. The latest one, Peter Thomas, 43, was renowned for his discovering the Ice Age of a terrestrial planet.

Yin Lin, 26, as a young woman researcher, was one of a couple woman scientists in this station. After her phD graduation of astronomy 5 years ago, she sent out a couple of hundreds of resumes and cover letters to different research institutes and universities to search for a job. There were 48 offers coming back, some offer assistant professors' jobs and a few researchers' jobs. She did some research about the jobs and the institutes and found out this offer was one of the few dream jobs she wanted. So she packed her clothes and moved to the small town almost immediately after receiving the offer, and worked here ever since.

Although the station was one of the largest station in this country with a long glory history, based on its strict policies, not many guests could have a visit inside the station, usually a few annual. Visitors had to apply on the website before their visit, not much information required. The only questions were to ask for name, address, email and phone number. However, there was an additional requirement for a 1000 words essay describing their passion for astronomy, physics or general science. Human resources would take a look at the applications and select about 8 people to come each year. Visitors who got the offer usually were very excited, not a couple of them in the history had had missed the appointment. Every time, the executive director of human resources would ask one of the researchers to introduce the station to the visitor.

Yin parked her bicycle in the parking lot, where there were many bicycles there, hoisted her bag and soda with her, then went into the front door of the complex, directly to the machine where she put her thumb inside to get a print, served to report her arrival. Then she went through the first two buildings and arrived to the 6-story building. Her office was on the 5th floor, where she could get the first-hand data from the top observatory to her daily research. She took the elevator to the 5th floor, took the key out and opened the door of her office. The air was heavy because it did not get fresh since last night. She turned on the fluorescent and opened the window to get some fresh air, then closed the door. Usually it would take a few minutes to refresh the air. She took a look at her watch again. *It was 8:50 AM.* Ten minutes advanced the beginning of work. Scientists and administration staffs worked Monday to Friday, from 9:00 AM to 11:30AM, and then it was lunch time. They finished lunch in an hour and then were back to work at around 12:30 PM. Then it was another three hours' work and the work would end at 3:30 PM each afternoon. Although the time of work was not very long, compared with works in big cities, but scientists and staffs had to pay full attention when they were at work. They had to be extremely energetic. The work would cost them a lot of energy.

Yin put her bag in the cabinet and the 1.5 liter diet soda on the desk. She pulled the decades old black leather office chair out and sat on the chair, sipping her large bottle of soda. It was just for the morning. At noon, she would go to the cafeteria on the third floor to buy another bottle. Many staffs and scientists worked in other buildings came to this cafeteria to eat lunch.

Yin was thinking what she would do today, maybe continuing working on her newest research paper, contacting publishers or going to the top floor to have some observation of the Sun. While she was thinking, a call came in.

She was hesitant to pick up the phone.

"Hello," she paused, wondering who was calling at this early time.

From the other end of the phone, a familiar voice started talking, "Hi, Lin, this is Jane Frost, from Human Resources department. How are you?"

It was Ms. Frost. Yin knew Ms. Frost for a long time since she first came to the station. Ms. Frost was the executive director for Human Resources, very intelligent and funny woman. She called Yin sometimes to talk to her but not at this early time. Why was she calling me, Yin wondered.

Yin said, "I am fine, thanks. What's up?"

"Oh, there is a visitor here in my office. He wants to take a look at the station. He was first referred to Mr. Kane. But he was sick today and could not come to the station. He just called me up this morning and told me that. I know you and Mr. Kane are friends. So I want you to take him to look around and tell him things you know. Is it ok?"

"Oh, really? Finn didn't tell me that he was sick. And...yeah... It is ok, just I was never an introducer, just would like you to know

I am inexperienced." Yin's voice was descending. For years, she put all her effort into research and not much time communicating with strangers or even classmates from her college.

"No problem, I know Lin is smart enough to do that. So now I am bringing him to your office. Just give me another 10 minutes." Ms. Jane Frost handed up the phone and turned to the guest.

3

RM Corps was a world-wide renowned Corporation, famous for its creative and leading genetic technology in application of transgenic plants and genetically modified food. Nowadays, the application was still a controversy. The mainly disputed issues are about the effect of such plants and food on the environment and health, how to label the food, government policies on how to restrict the food and so on. Many people thought eating genetically modified food may be harmful. Some others decleared the application of transgenic plants would have negative effect on the environment. Nowadays, big companies hired scientists and technicians focusing on finding out the answers for these issues. RM Corps was one of them, and the biggest one in the world. Despite its absolute leading research and technology, the main business of RM Corps was to produce and sell genetically modified organism products to many countries around the world. The headquarters of RM Corps was in New York City, USA, and a bunch of its branch companies were located in America, Europe, Canada and Asia.

The RM Corps was under the name of Richard Meier, the CEO and owner of RM Corps. Richard was born in Brooklyn, NY and a native New Yorker. He was the child of immigrants who came from German. His parents divorced when he was 5 and his mother remarried to an American and then bore his half-sister. Growing up in a middle class family, he knew the importance of independence when he was very young. After graduating from high school, he attended military. After that, when he was 26, he enrolled in Columbia University to get his bachelor's degree in Biology, with minor in chemistry and computer science. When he graduated from his undergraduate degree three years later, he took GMAT and got admitted by a good business school. He graduated from the business school at the age of 31. The same year, he got a loan from bank and started his own company, which was RM Corps.

He was 6 feet 2 inch in height. At the age of 54, he was still very young looking and extremely handsome. Despite the success in his career and his good looking, he was a low-key and private person, with modest and restrained personality. He was never reported in the press. Although, he had a weakness that made him divorce twice – he cheated on his ex-wives. He was very attractive to women. Women fell for him and he liked women. So it just happened, although he never really fell for any of them. Later on, his wives suspected him for cheating on them behind their back and questioned him. He just got tired to those questions so divorced the wives. Despite married twice, he hadn't had a child yet.

Too many competitions, he thought.

So five years ago, he considered to build up a large factory to do research and produce the most advanced products to defeat his opponents.

But where to set up the factory? Of course, in the USA. But where? After discussing the thought and practical issue in the secret meetings with management and getting advice from a dozen of lawyers and environment experts, he finally decided Altimont to be the place. Altimont was far from other towns and cities, in a relatively isolated location. The shortest distance from Altimont to the nearest town Bellington was a 3- hour drive. Not liking being reported in the media, he also wants no one to know about his newest technology, especially his competitors. *No body would know that place. It is a protection of my secret newest technologies.* Due to the very advanced research and production which might have unknown effects on environment, environment experts also recommended a more isolated location in case there was pollution, which pointed out that Altimont was really a good choice. Richard asked his most trusted subordinate Victor Dupont to buy a 200 acre land and appointed the vice president of RM Corps to work there. The factory was going to be built.

A few months ago, Richard Meier got to know Judy Kahn in a party held by his best friend, Kenneth Schmied. Judy was pretty and tall, with friendly smile. She forwardly talked to Richard, in a very nice way. Judy was in her mid 30s, divorced with one child. They started dating after that party. Richard somehow liked to keep in a marriage. A couple of months later, they were engaged and Richard booked the date for their wedding. It was in two months.

My company was always in a more important place. He thought.

So before he was getting married, he decided to go to Altimont to see the situation himself for the establishment of his factory.

And he decided to go himself this time. *I just want to be alone one more time before I get married.*

Victor Dupont booked the flight ticket to Bellington for him. From there, he would take a booked car from the small-sized airport of Bellington and then to Altimont. Victor also booked the most expensive room of the only four start hotel in Altimont for a month to make sure he had enough time to see the town of the factory and to come back to get married on time. Victor Dupont, as the most trusted subordinate of Richard Meier, concerned his boss a lot. He spent the whole night in front of the computer to look for tourist attractions Richard might go to and things Richard might do when he was in Altimont.

The second day, he reported that to his boss.

"The town is not known by many people due to its isolated location. It has beautiful scenery because I saw the pictures last night. It is quiet and peaceful." Victor proudly announced in front of his boss, as if he found something amazing, "but the most interesting location you may visit there, is an astronomical station. As far as I know, it was one of the oldest and largest astronomical station nation-wide."

Richard smiled back and said, "Oh, really? That sounds great. I love science."

Paused for a second, Victor continued, "However, in their visitor policies, there is a requirement of a 1000 word essay. What's more, they only choose around 8 people to come each year."

"That is interesting, I would love to have a visit. Please copy the website link and email to me. I am going to take a look." Richard placed his left palm on his forehead, thinking, and responded.

It took him an evening which he could initially spend with his fiancée to write the 1000 word essay. He absolutely knew a lot of knowledge about Biology and Chemistry so he could explain his love to science. Plus the logical and critical thinking he gained from business school, he wrote a very excellent and humorous essay. The website said there would be a week waiting period. So he would know the result a couple of days prior to of his trip.

4

Richard Meier handed in his application a week ago and then immerged into busy work again. He was a busy person and quite easily forgetting small details. Yet he always remembered that he was waiting for the result from the alleged largest astronomical station during the week. He questioned himself, *what is that attractive? Even if I am not admitted, what does it matter?*

A week later, on a Monday, when he had just finished a nice weekend, prepared himself for the trip and again was contributed to work, he opened his email box. *Tomorrow I will go on the trip.* When he clicked "Inbox" of his email box, there were 40 unread emails. He checked his email box every day except weekends. This weekend, he received those 40 emails. He took a quick look at the emails, most of which came from management of the company, discussing issues occurred within the company. He responded them one by one. A couple of them were advertisements. He deleted those without a second look. There came one email, within his surprise, the one he was waiting for this week – the invitation from Altimont astronomical station. He read the email carefully:

Dear Richard,

Congratulations! After reading your application, we cordially invite you to visit Altimont National Astronomical Station. You will become the 4th visitor for this year. Your appointment will be at 9:00 AM June, 15th, on a Wednesday.

If you can't make the time, please email us back as soon as possible to reschedule your appointment.

We are looking forward to see you and share our excitement and passion for science with you!
Best regard,

Jane Frost

Executive director for human resources

Altimont National Astronomical Station

The second day, Richard woke up at 6:00 AM. He went out of his house at 6:30 AM with a good spirit. His plane would take off at 8:30 AM. He was very excited. For a long time, he did not feel such excitement. Victor Dupont asked the driver of RM Corps to wait for Richard outside of his house. Then the driver took him to Laguardia Airport directly. Everything went smoothly. He went aboard the plane on time and arrived to Bellington three hours later. There, another driver waited for him outside of the airport. Michael Hernandez, whose task was to drive Richard from Bellington to Altimont and take him to wherever he wanted to go while he was there, was a resident of Altimont. Today Michael woke up an hour earlier than usual and drove his Mercedes-Benz car to Bellington Airport to pick up an important client. When he saw Richard, he greeted him politely with a big smile. Richard greeted him back with a smile and waved his hand. He thought Richard was a very nice and elegant man.

On the way to Altimont, Richard finally calmed himself down. He gazed at the scenery on the sides of the highway. There were fewer trees, but mainly farmland. Plants with dense green leaves faced the sun. A few large houses were located among farmlands. Footpaths snaked within the farmlands, from one house to the next. From a distance, it looked like a picture of houses on the green sea.

"Richard, Victor Dupont contacted me a couple of weeks ago to ask me to drive you around the town." Michael interrupted Richard's thought with a mild voice, "I am your tour guide and driver when you are in Altimont. I heard from Victor the day before yesterday that you got the opportunity to visit the astronomical station. That was hard-won. They only invite less than 10 visitors each year. You are lucky. I could never have a chance to visit there myself."

Richard took a look at Michael, who had excellent driving skills, laughing out, "yes, it's nice. I am sure it would be an excitement."

Richard wanted to know more about Altimont for setting up his factory, but of course, the plan should be a secret to Michael. He added, "Can you tell me more about Altimont?"

"Yes, sir," Michael paused, "Altimont is really a small town, I mean, compared to big city such as NYC where you come from. There are about 50000 residents living there. Most of them own lands nearby. Some have small business, opening a grocery store, retail selling. Others work in the national astronomical station."

Michael turned left from the highway, a minute later, he continued, "Not many visitors come to our town." He said it in a proud voice, "It is really a quiet and nice town. I have visited some bigger towns and cities, but I like my town the most."

Richard asked a few more questions about the town, Michael answered those questions patiently and finally they arrived in front of the four star hotel in Altimont at 3:30 PM in the center of the town.

"Sir, this is the hotel. It is a four star hotel. You will live here for the next month. You may eat in the hotel cafeteria. There are also restaurants and grocery stores nearby. I am going back to eat dinner with my family. If you need me, just give me a call. You know my number, right?" Michael turned his head back, looking at Richard.

Richard said, "yes, I have your number. Tonight I can just be alone and you don't need to come to pick me up anywhere. Tomorrow morning, however, I want to go to an address. There are people waiting me there. Can you come at 8:00 AM?"

"Of course, I will arrive on time." Michael felt a little bit curious about what Richard was going to do the next day, but he knew he should not ask for reasons.

After Michael Hernandez drove away, Richard Meier went to his hotel room. He put his luggage down, arranged his cloths and suits and suddenly felt a little bit hungry. He really didn't eat on the plane. And now it was almost 5:00 PM. Dinner time came. Yet, he was too tired to walk downstairs to buy food. He called up front desk to order a meal. Ten minutes later, the waiter sent the meal to his room. There were a dish of spaghetti, a doughnut, a dish of salmon, a fresh peach and a cup of apple juice. He brought the meal to the sofa on balcony, sat down and began to devour the food. At the same time, he was gazing at the sky.

It was late in the afternoon. Sun finally became big and red, on the edge of the sky, after fighting all day. The whole sky was illuminated to be half red, half purple. Under the sky, crowded lower buildings stretched into distance, abruptly stopped. Then there came a wood. In the farest distance, on the top of a large hill, between the skyline, there was a complex of buildings, like a majestic castle, erecting in the distance.

5

The second day, Michael Hernandez went out from his house at 7:00 AM and drove his Mercedes-Benz to the hotel parking lot, parked his car and waited in front of the big glass front door of the hotel. Michael was a driver and tour guide. Even though not many tourists would come to Altimont, he still made a good amount of money to support his family. He had his own website for people who would want to come to rent cars. He had five cars, a high-end Mecedes-Benz, a BMW, a Honda, a Nissan and a Chevrolet. Michael knew Richard was at least rich because Victor Dupont gave him double amount of the fee he asked just for more concern of Richard's needs.

At 7:55 AM, Richard went out of the front door and greeted Michael. Then they walked to parking lot to get the car. Sitting down, Richard gave Michael the address he needed to go to today. Richard knew the reason Victor Dupont chose a local driver to be his tour guide, not one from his own company, was because Victor hoped he could have a better trip and gain better knowledge about the town because Victor told Richard, after he looked up internet for information, unless constantly living here for at least three years, it was not likely to know the town well. They bought the land one year ago so no one from his company knew the town well, even though some moved here to prepare the build up of the factory after that. When Michael drove him to the address, he said, "Michael, could you come back after two hours? I need to go upstairs to meet some friends for about an hour."

"Yes, sir, may I ask when will be your visit to national astronomical station?" Michael seems interested.

Richard said, "A week later, I think. On the 15th, Wednesday."

"Ok, no problem, I will drive you there then. I will be right back in an hour." Michael turned his head back with a grin at Richard.

Richard went upstairs to an apartment to have a secret meeting with colleagues and construction worker representatives. The main purpose of the meeting is to announce some topics which would be discussed in a bigger conference held on this Friday, June 17th, on the location of the factory. On Friday, all construction workers, staffs and leaders will attend the conference and a few leaders, including Richard Meier, would give talks about the projection of building up the factory. The president of the new factory would give a speech about the importance and the status of the factory within the whole company; there was one executive director who would talk about the market of transgenic plants and genetically modified food; another would talk about the potential environment effects it would take place. Richard would give a brief talk to thank all the workers and staffs. The president of the new factory, John Jacobs, was busy preparing the Friday conference so did not attend the meeting. He had had worked with Richard for years in New York City as the vice president of RM Corps and now kept both the titles as the president of the Altimont factory and the vice president of RM Corps. He almost became the second most important person in RM Corps, next to Richard Meier and, at a younger age 40, he was expected to become the next CEO of RM Corps. The outcome of the meeting was the assurance of the date of construction. They would begin to build the factory in a month, on July, 15th.

An hour later, Michael drove Richard back to the hotel and Richard did not go out again that day and the next day due to the strain of his trip and too much concern for his business. He made phone calls to Victor Dupont and other managements in the hotel room to discuss the factory. When he did not make phone calls, he went to the balcony to look at the scenery of the town. He did not find it different. That was consistent with what Victor Dupont had told him, "If you haven't lived there long enough, you would not find out the difference." The next few days, he did not ask Michael Hernandez to come. Instead, the driver of his company drove him to the land they bought– the address of the factory, with a few important administrators of his company, to discuss the issue further. Time went by fast.

Richard really had a good sleep and when he woke up, it was the day he should visit Altimont astronomical station. He sprayed the most expensive cologne on his palms and softly rubbed around his neck and arms, got his teeth bleached, wore a yellow dress shirt and his best black suit. Michael was waiting downstairs. When Richard sat in the car, the first thing Michael said to him was, "Richard, you look great today. Today you are going to visit the national astronomical station. Are you excited?" Michael turned his head back and looked at Richard feverishly.

Richard nodded and smiled.

Then Michael started driving. The car first snaked through some small roads and finally arrived to a wide road. Along that road, crossing a river, through a wood, 20 minutes later, finally the car arrived in front of the edifice.

"It would take you up to a day to visit the station. When you finish the tour and come out, just give me a call." Michael said, pointing at the unfancied front door, "you can walk in from here. Just tell the front desk that you have an appointment today to visit the station."

Richard thanked Michael, left the car, went into the front door and told the front desk the reason of his visit. The front desk made a phone call and then brought him upstairs to the Human Resources Department and introduced him to Ms. Jane Frost, the executive director of human resources.

"Hi, Richard, nice to meet you. Unfortunately, Mr. Kane, who should guide you the trip today was sick and could not come. I am going to ask someone else to help you." Ms. Frost said. Then she made a phone call and it seemed that person agreed to bring Richard to look around.

Ms. Frost walked to the door of her office and said, "Come with me."

Then they took the elevator down to the first floor, through another building, and then took the elevator up to 5th floor. On the way, Ms. Frost told Richard, "We are going to a researcher's office. Ms. Lin will be your introducer today. She is very ambitious to become a great astronomer."

Yin Lin handed up the phone, got up from her leather chair, walked to the window and gazed out. From there, she could see the river streamed around the center of the town. The shape of the river was like a "U", or a big smile. She got a little bit nervous due to the nonconfidence and insecurity of her communication skills with strangers and the lack of practice for a long time. She was thinking where to bring the visitor to and how she should introduce the station to him to give him a better idea. Maybe she could first talk to the visitor in her office and tell him or her the overview of the station and its brief history, and after they were familiar with the way the other talked, she could bring him upstairs to the 6th floor, the observatory to let him have a view at the sun or other planets and then bring him to the third floor, the cafeteria where she usually ate lunch, to eat a meal and then we would just see what to do next. Five minutes passed, she got more nervous. *What if I got too nervous and could not speak fluently, would he or she get a bad impression about our astronomical station? No, I would not let that happen. I have to relax and try my best.* She definitely did not want herself bring the astronomical station a little bit negative impact, even if it was just over a visitor.

When she was racking her wits about different ideas and worries, "pum, pum, pum…" someone was knocking at the door.

They were coming.

6

Yin Lin awkwardly strode to the door, waited a second, and then opened the door. She first saw Ms. Frost, smiling. Hadn't let her take a look at who was behind her, Ms. Frost caught Yin's eye sight and said, "Hi, Lin, haven't seen you for a while. I heard from Mr. Kane this morning that you are working on your new research paper. Hope everything is fine with you. Oh, let me introduce the visitor to you." Ms. Frost turned her body around and let Yin see the visitor. The man standing in front of her, behind Ms. Frost, was very tall, with close cropped hair, smiling at her. He must be a nice person, Yin thought.

"This is Mr. Richard Meier, from New York City." Ms. Frost said.

New York City, the capital of the world.

"Nice... nice to meet you, Mr. Meier." Yin said awkwardly, in a light Asian accent, offering her hand to him.

Richard couldn't move his eyes from the young lady in front of him. She was slim, tall and extremely beautiful, with silky healthy skin, with silky raven shoulder-length hair. She had long skinny legs and looked extremely sexy. Richard was smiling at her and staring at her with thoughts. He offered his hand to shake hers, holding her hand, not too hardly, not to gently, but softly. He didn't say anything. He let go his hold of her hand at the same time she relaxed her hold.

Mr. Frost looked at Richard Meier with a little confusion, grinned at them both and said, "I am going back to my office. Have a wonderful time, Richard." Then she left them alone.

After Ms. Frost left, Yin looked up at Richard's face. He was still smiling nicely, making constant eye contact with her. For a moment, she felt the man, Richard Meier, was very handsome. She was shy and unconfident about her ability of communication. Now with a highly confident good looking man, she could only lower her head and look at his chest, not his eyes.

She suddenly slightly smelled something - his cologne. She inhaled slightly and knitted her brows a little bit, as the conditional responses to the smell.

He noticed this subtle detail. He was totally attracted to the young lady. He even got sexually excited.

"What's your name?" he asked friendly.

"…Yin." Yin tried to make herself sound more confident. *I can't make my feelings affect the impression of the national astronomical station.* But she still couldn't make herself look at his face. Now she was looking at his feet and the floor. She was more shy.

She said, "Mr. Meier, let's first…"

Richard could no longer control himself and his feelings. He gasped heavily and forced a sound out, trembling his legs spontaneously. He was embarrassed. Then he moved to her right hand side and then held his hands in front of his private part.

Yin took a look at his hands, couldn't figure out what he was doing, but somehow felt that he got excited might be the case. Yin never had any relationship with any men, even though she had feelings for a couple of men before. She never even touched any men. She was inexperienced in such a thing. Yet, since she was highly intelligent and had been watching a lot of romance TV series and books, she could figure out how a man would behave if he got sexually excited. She moved her head back, staring at the floor in front of her, not turning to his direction, wanting to let go the embarrassment if there was one.

She tried to make the situation looked better and relaxed, so she made her voice sound confident, "I mean, let's go upstairs to the observatory." She first wanted to invite him to her office to have a talk, but now it did not look like a good idea.

She was waiting for his response.

Richard suddenly had a strong feeling for her. Richard clapped his hands and said, in a voice like a boss made an order to his subordinate, but still in a nice way, "look at me."

Under such a "command", Yin turned her body around to his direction but stood in a little longer distance with him. She took a look at his face and then lowered her head again. He wanted to see her reaction.

"Look at me." he clapped again, put his hands out and directed Yin to look at his face. He tried to see her eyes.

When he put his hands out, Yin could see his ten fingers now, there was no ring. *He was single?* Yin suddenly felt attracted to him, even though she knew it was inappropriate under such a situation. *What am I thinking?!* She questioned herself harshly. She had ego, as a scientist, who had big dreams and spent all her effort in her career. She would not let such a thing affected her as a first-time introducer inside the place she loved the most. Yet she could not control her thoughts and feelings about the handsome man in front of her.

At the mean time, Richard stared at her gently and seriously. A thought just came up in his mind. He was not sure about his future now and he desired one thing only.

I want her.

7

Richard stared at Yin softly. His heart was going to melt. For a moment, he wanted to go ahead, hug her and kiss her.

At the mean time, Yin's heart beat fast. She stood there, looking at the floor between them, not knowing what to say or what to do. But soon, an angry feeling came up to her mind. *What is this? Why am I looking at the floor? Am I weak? Would I be defeated by this situation? Come on, I am strong. I can do it.*

So finally and abruptly, she turned her head up and made eye contact with him. Her face looked a little bit angry and words came up from her mouth like an argument was going to happen, "Mr. Meier, let's go upstairs to visit the observatory!"

Richard could sense her anger now. He stopped lingering his eyes at her, but still making constant eye contact with her, acting very professionally. He said, "Let's go upstairs now."

Yin got a bit relaxed. *The situation was finally solved.* She was happy that Richard did not add fuel to the fire. Yin smiled at Richard now and said in a soft voice, "Let's go. Just follow me."

Richard stared at her smile and walked along the corridor with her. He finally paid a little attention to the astronomical station again. Yet he still thought about how they would get together and if there was a chance with her. *Should I ask her about her phone number and email address? I will just do that later when the visit is ended.*

They walked upstairs to the 6th floor.

Finn Kane was lying on the couch with eyes closed. A bag of ice was on his forehead. A thermometer was in his mouth. He was really sick. He didn't cover himself well yesterday night with air conditioner on. Not many people used air conditioners in mid June in Altimont, but some people used them. This morning when he woke up at 7:00 AM, he found himself have a fever. He first should have gone to work and brought a visitor to look around the station. But now he really couldn't move to the station and speak clearly. He really wanted to talk to the visitor. He somehow knew the visitor was from New York City. *That is where I am from too.* Finn was born in Northern Ireland, The United Kingdom. He moved to New York City with his parents when he was only 5. Growing up in the US, he could speak both British English and a perfect American English. When he was in school, he fell in love with science and later physics, math and astronomy. Not with as big ambition as Yin's, Finn only enjoyed to be dedicated to the things he loved. He was 32 and worked in Altimont Astronomical Station for 6 years, two years earlier before Yin came. They became really good friends later. They lived not far from each other. They text chatted or phone called a few times per week in the evening time after dinner. Sometimes they met in a spot in the main road and rode bikes together to the station. He had good impression about Yin, even knowing her disadvantages. He somehow liked her. Yet he tried not to show her his interests and thoughts because she was very sensitive and would be easily uncomfortable just due to a small detail such as a constant emotional eye contact. Also, he knew she was not interested in finding a relationship.

She only loved astronomy. She was not interested in any man, at least now.

He still remembered the first time he met her. It was like yesterday.

It was a day after my birthday, a week after Yin started working in the station. My parents, concerning me a lot, traveled to Altimont to visit me on my birthday. My mother made lunch for me for tomorrow. She made my favorite British food – Steak and Guinness pie, cut it into four parts and put one piece into my plastic clear lunch box. The remaining three pieces were for the three of us on my birthday. For a year or so, I hadn't had the chance to eat food by mom. There was a British restaurant in Altimont, not far from where I lived, on the main road. It was like a small bar. I eat there a few times to remind myself of my hometown. I usually eat American food because I really like it.

My parents left the town in the second day morning. I asked them to take care and then drove my car to work with my lunch box and, when I arrived, I took the elevator to the cafeteria first and put the lunch box inside the top layer of the cooler of the refrigerator. At lunch time, I would get the lunch box and put it into the microwave oven to heat it.

Thinking about my parents' love and the delicious lunch, I worked with delight all the morning. When lunch time came, I went downstairs to the cafeteria, took my clear lunch box out and put it into the oven. Two minutes later, I took out the box and strode to a table and sat down. Just ready to eat, surprisingly, when I opened the lunch box, it turned out to be a dish of eggplant and fried small cods – Chinese food. This is not mine. Someone got the same lunch box as mine. I covered the lunch box and went back to the cooler, but could never find the other same lunch box. Someone took my food.

I searched around in the Cafeteria and finally saw that a Chinese lady was eating my lunch. I got angry and moved to her table, sat down and wanted to start an argument.

But when I saw the face of the young beautiful woman, my anger immediately disappeared. Instead, a feeling came up to my mind. She was reading a book while eating. I guess that is why she mistook my food.

"Hi, how is the lunch?" I asked, trying not to be rude.

The young woman startled, moved her eyes to me with full confusion.

A couple of seconds later, she realized she was eating another person's lunch, and probably my lunch.

"Sorry, I did not mean to…" She put down the fork and sincerely apologized, "I am so…"

"Don't say more," I interrupted her with a big smile, *"please continue to eat."*

The woman relaxed and smiled back to me, "you can eat my food. Even though not as delicious as your food, but I guess not bad. I can help you take the fishbone out."

"nice." I replied.

Then she took her lunch box and picked the fishbone out. The fishbone of the cods was very small and she picked them out carefully. Somehow I knew I liked her.

Later on, I knew her name was Yin Lin and was a new researcher in the station. From then, we became friends, and then confidants.

Thinking of that, Finn had a wish to talk to Yin. *I will call her tonight.* He took out the thermometer. The thermometer showed his temperature was 101 degree. He might need to go to the ER if the temperature went up another degree. Thinking about how he met Yin and how they became friends, He just felt asleep.

8

Yin brought Richard Meier to the 6th floor, where there were some equipments used for observation of celestial bodies. The top story, the observatory, had been the most important location of the astronomical station. Plenty of data used in a lot of influential papers published world-wide came from this observatory.

They walked through a large massive wooden door, a dark long corridor, and then another smaller massive wooden door, half the size of the first door, arriving to a dark large-sized room. Here, there were a few large astronomical telescopes, distributed throughout the whole room. Even though Richard was extremely rich, this was the first time he had a chance to observe a celestial body, especially with such a sexy woman he had much feeling for.

There was nobody else here inside the dark room.

Yin said, "Please follow me." At the same time, she walked towards a step of stairs and walked upstairs, approaching a telescope. Richard followed her closely.

Yin sat down in front of the telescope, looked into the lens and tried to adjust the buttons. She paid her full attention to adjust the telescope and almost forgot the existence of Richard for a moment. Richard sat down on another chair, close to Yin. He was still staring at her, captivated by the attitude she put into her work. Now he could even smell her fragrance from her hair and body. He couldn't control himself again, getting sexually excited. He wanted to enclasp her and cling to her skinny body. His head was getting more and more close to hers, almost touching her dark straight hair.

At this moment, Yin abruptly turned her head back. Because his face had gotten too close to her hair, her lips now touched his by accident. This was the first time her lips touched a man's lips.

Richard felt he was going to melt. His body was trembling and he was breathing more heavily. It seems Yin was captivated by this kind of feelings too and stopped moving.

Five seconds later, she moved backward her head and stood up, "sorry… Mr. Meier."

"Call me Richard." He said in a low and soft voice. Richard didn't try to kiss her longer. Firstly, all his life, except one woman Lily – his first wife, he had had never forwardly pursued any other woman. All the time, women came to him and tried to make him think they were beautiful enough. And even for Lily, he was quite sure himself the reason he pursued her was not because he loved her. So he just hadn't had the habit of forwardly expressing himself to a woman when they first met. Secondly, He actually knew a lot of people and definitely knew how people think and do things. He could sense that Yin loved her work and, since she didn't kiss him longer, she was not willing to do it, at least here. *Let me just be professional when she was at work.* However, he knew Yin had feeling for him because she didn't move back till five seconds later.

"Ri… Richard, I… I want to show you how…how the telescope works and what you can see through it," Yin tried to calm herself down and avoided talking about the embarrassment again, "from this telescope, you can see the sun. I am recently working on a research about the sunspot. Sunspot is a temporary phenomena of the sun that it looks like dark spots. I have adjusted the system to see the sunspot clearly. Now you may have a look."

Richard followed her instructions and observed through the telescope.

All the morning, till 11:30 AM, they stayed in the dark observatory room and Yin explained how the telescopes worked to Richard one by one. Haven't realized how quickly time passed, it was almost lunch time. Yin still put all her attention in explaining things to Richard. She felt extremely happy because there could be someone sharing her joyfulness about the research that no one to talk about usually.

At 11:30 AM, her phone rang. The ring was a light music played by a traditional Chinese instrument Pipa. Yin had her level ten certificate of Pipa. Level ten was the top level of playing an instrument.

Yin looked at the number calling in. It was from Finn. She picked up the phone and said, "Finn, are you getting better?"

Finn mumbled, making it hard to be heard, "I am fine. I think my fever almost goes away. I fell asleep an hour ago and just woke up. It is 11:30 AM now. Are you in the cafeteria?"

"Oh, 11:30, I am not in the cafeteria. I am in the observatory room with the visitor. A little bit busy, I will visit you after work."

She handed up the phone and was going to tell Richard lunch time came.

Not letting her saying a word first, Richard questioned her, again like a boss questioned a subordinate, "Who is he?" Richard definitely got jealous. Never in his life, he felt jealous for a woman because women he met did not want to leave him or make him leave them. *Is it your boyfriend?*

"uh… who?" She was initially confused and then realized he was talking about Finn, "ah, Finn, he is my best friend. He should initially be your introducer but he was sick. It is lunch time now, let's go to the cafeteria. Delicious food is waiting for us."

Even though hearing her saying he was just her best friend, he somehow got very jealous to a point of anger.

They went out from the observatory room, went through the two wooden doors and took elevator down to the third floor.

In the cafeteria, Richard almost spoke out the question he wanted to ask all the morning, that what Yin's phone number and email were. But he realized it was too early to ask that question. He wanted to ask her in a casual moment, not making her double think his motives. Otherwise based on his observation of her all the morning, she would probably reject to give him the details. Yin continued to explain astronomy phenomena to Richard, not giving him any chance to discuss personal lives and interests. After lunch, she brought him to look around other buildings and departments within the whole station.

At last, at 3:00 PM, she said the visit would be ended here. She brought him to the front door of the station, where he initially came in, said goodbye to him and then turned over herself starting walking back towards her office. She of course started to have strong feeling for him and did not want him go. However, she realized it was not allowed and could end up being fired, by the rules of the station, to have a relationship with any visitor, or even if to give out phone numbers or email addresses to him. Also, she kept telling herself her dream was more important than anything else and that she should never be interested in having a relationship with any man, at least not before she succeeded. Telling herself these, she just wanted to walk away and forget this man.

"Yin," Richard paused.

Yin turned herself back with hope. She was hoping that he told her that he did not want her to go away like this, but then realized he might just forget something in the station. She asked, "Did you forget something?"

"No, not really," Richard said slowly, while thinking how to speak the maybe last words with her. *If I just ask her for phone number and email address, she may just deny it. But this is the last chance.*

He exhaled deeply, "I just want you to know… I am still thinking about the things you told me today… Is it possible to ask for your phone number or email address so I can ask further information?"

"No." Yin said directly, without hesitation, "sorry about that. You may contact the station to ask for any further inquiries." Then she left Richard alone and walked inside the building.

Only one thing echoed in her mind.

Not one thing could affect my determination to my dream.

Richard stood there till her silhouette disappeared at the end of the hallway.

9

Lily Achilles was the first wife of Richard. They met each other when Richard was an undergraduate student at Columbia University. Lily was a young lady from a very rich family. Her father was the president of a nation-wide bank. When Richard met her, there were a dozen of handsome men were pursuing her. They thought up every idea to get her heart. A few men made love songs and played the guitar in front of her; one used their one-month income to buy her a LV purse; a couple of them purchased her travel. Richard also began to pursue her. Richard was a young man with an ambitious mind and determination. He knew he needed Lily, or her family's reputation. He thought up the most different but amazing way to pursue her. He wrote down diary about his love and fantasies for her, a whole year diary with 365 pages. When he handed the "book" to Lily, she moved nearly crying out. So then she agreed to date him and soon they engaged and got married.

I pursued her but I did not love her.

Richard left the astronomical station, walking down hill. He did not call Michael Hernandez. Instead, he wanted to walk alone. On the way he walked down the hill, he thought about the scenes how Yin kissed him by accident and how they spent time together the whole day. He was upset that she was not willing to give her contact information or consider dating him. He knew he loved the ego that money, women and power brought to him. But never did he feel even once that he was willing to give up the ego for a woman. He was getting old and might really need a woman who could companion him and understand him. 10 days ago, he had had thought that he finally found out a woman, his fiancée, that he try to love and could be his destination. But now he was no longer sure of it. He might never understand love. Despite of his uncertainty, something about Yin captured his heart, her beauty, her hard working or maybe her determination just like his. She just reminded him of himself when he was young.

He could sense Yin was so naïve and innocent. He could not let it go. He wanted Yin. He wanted to spend time with her, to see her hard working, to get rid of his ego.

She was his dream woman.

I would not give up. I could not live without her. I want to sleep besides her. I am falling in love.

But she totally rejected his request for her phone number and email, not giving it any space. *I would not let her reject me. I will make her believe I am the man who she should be with.*

When he walked back to the hotel room, it was 4:40 PM. He picked up the phone and dial Victor Dupont's cell phone number.

"Hi, Richard, is that you?" after two phone beeps, Victor Dupont picked up the phone.

"Yes, it is me." Richard paused without hesitation, "help me cancel the wedding and tell Judy about that now. I will talk to her later myself."

There was a moment silence.

"Richard, what happened? What changed your mind?" Victor suddenly changed his voice. He began to worry about him.

"No question, just obey the order." Richard said with composure.

Again, a moment silence came. Victor patiently asked again, "Richard, but I need to know what changed your mind and why. Can you just give me a reason? I am worried about you. I thought you loved Judy."

"No, I don't love her." Richard said in a cold voice, "I know who I love." Then he handed up the phone.

A minute later, another call came in. Richard picked up the phone and said, "hello? This is Richard Meier."

From that end, Mechael Hernandez said hospitably, "Richard, it is me, Michael. I waited for like a few hours but did not receive your call. And it is almost five o'clock. I think I need to call you and ask. I should have called you a little earlier, though."

"I am ok," Richard paused, still thinking about Yin, "I need to ask you a couple of questions. Can you come out and we eat dinner together?"

Michael said, "no problem, I know there is a great British restaurant. We can go there to eat. Can I just wait for you in front of your hotel in 30 minutes?"

After making the deal, Richard handed up the phone and prepared himself for the dinner. I took off his expensive suit and yellow shirt, took a quick shower and changed to a white T-shirt with a pair of jeans. He looked very young, like someone 35, in such an outfit.

When he went downstairs and walked to the front door of the hotel half an hour later, just as last time, he saw Michael waiting there.

Michael drove him to the British restaurant where Finn usually went. They ordered steaks, devilled kidney, bangers and mash, mashed potatos, fruit dishes and orange juice.

They talked about the weather for a little bit. Fifteen minutes later, the food came.

Michael began to ask first, "Richard, you said in the phone that you have some questions?"

Richard cut up his steak, forked one piece and put it into the black pepper sauce, "Do you know anyone from the astronomical station?"

"Of course," Michael paused, sipped a little orange juice and continued, "I know a dozen of them. The town itself was not very big, so sometimes it is quite common that people know one another, especially I do this kind of job, knowing places and people well."

Richard then said, "I want to know about one person. Do you know Yin Lin? She is a Chinese young lady, around 5 feet 6 inches in height, very skinny. She is a researcher in the station."

"Oh, yes, Yin Lin. She is quite young. I know her. Actually everyone knows her here. She is quite potential to become the next someone in astronomy and physics."

"oh, yeah, she was my introducer today. What do you know about her?" Richard was happy now because there was a hope that he could see Yin again.

"Nice. Yin Lin is from China and has lived in the states for 10 years, I believe. She got her bachelor's degree and phD in the US and then moved here to work a few years ago." Michael said with great relish, as if he knew some secrets others didn't know, "Her best friend here, Finn Kane, liked this restaurant a lot because he comes from North Ireland."

"Are they lovers?" Richard asked anxiously, putting down the fork.

"I would say so. There have been gossips saying that Finn likes Yin and they are meant to be together. There may more or less be some feelings."

"What else do you know about her?"

"Nothing more I guess, she never talked about her life in China, not even to Finn." Michael laughed out.

After dinner, Richard told Michael Hernandez that he wanted to visit Yin's apartment. Without knowing the details of the strict rules of the astronomical station, as the good manner he kept that not to ask reasons why a visitor wanted to go to a specific location, Michael Hernandez drove Richard directly to Yin's address.

There is always hope.

10

There was a meeting in the station from 3:30 PM- 5:00 PM. Usually there would be a meeting every two months. Yin had to attend the meeting so she got off work late today at 5:15 PM. After work, she rode her bike to Finn's home in a hurry. She hoped he was doing fine the whole day. On the way to his house, she bought some food and drinks for him and herself.

At around 6 o'clock, she arrived to Finn's home. She pressed the ring. A few seconds later, Finn opened the door, said hello to Yin and took the food and drinks. He walked into his home and Yin followed him.

Finn's home was pretty big, two floors, three bedrooms and two bathrooms, with living room classical British style decoration – a white artificial crystal ceiling lamp, ocean blue wall, white horizontal blind windows, cobalt blue coffee table, beige long couch and some wood furniture. There were some photos of him and his family hung on the wall. There was one in which he was with Yin in front of the astronomical station.

"How are you today?" She sat down on the couch, "I was quite busy when you called me. Didn't have time to talk longer."

"ok, I heard you said you were with the visitor. How was that?" Finn sat down next to Yin, opening one bottle of root beer.

When Finn mentioned the visitor, suddenly Yin remembered the whole day she was with Richard Meier. A delirious feeling came up. Only treating Finn as a good friend, Yin showed her excitement, "Actually, the visitor, he is very very handsome. We had a great time. I have never seen such a handsome man…"

Finn listened to Yin describing the good looking of the visitor. He was a little upset. Even though he did not show his feeling to her, to avoid her discomfort, he hoped she would find him handsome and attractive some day. Actually, Finn was also good looking, but just might not be noticed by Yin yet.

Finn pretended not to care about what she said or not to pay attention to it. After Yin finished her description, he said, pretended to be happy, "Oh, really? Sounds like you really did have a good time today."

Yin did not understand his true feeling, kept showing her huge interests for the visitor and said, "oh, yes, I think I almost fell in love with him! I never had such feeling for a man." The more she said, the more excited she was.

Hearing this, Finn got jealous and taunted her, "Do you know what love is?"

"I am not sure, but just having such a feeling that you want him to hug you and kiss you and be with you forever."

Finn laughed out, pretending he knew what love was very much, "That is not love. That is just a fantasy, a feeling or a crush. Let me tell you what love is. Love is how much you are willing to sacrifice for the other."

Yin did not understand. She opened the dinner box for Finn and herself, "anyway, let's eat dinner first. After that, you send me back home."

20 minutes later, they finished dinner. Yin threw the plastic dinner boxes in the garbage can. She gargled and then asked Finn to send her home, "We had a meeting today and I have some more work to do tonight. Let's go."

They walked from Finn's house to Yin's apartment. The sun went down from the sky. It turned dark. The weather outside was chilly, like a 60 degree. The humidity was pretty high. Wind blew them huge comfort and easiness. It was really nice walking in the quiet and safe town in this weather. Tonight, the moon was really large, hanged near the horizon. Yin cocked her head up. Looking at the peaceful starry sky, she felt life was now so peaceful and comfortable. She was not worried about anything anymore.

10 minutes later, they walked towards her apartment. Yin could now see her apartment building. It was a two story building with grey brick façade.

A dark silhouette appeared into Yin's eyesight, in front of her building. In the beginning, she did not pay attention to it. She thought it might just be someone passing by her apartment building.

From a short distance, she could now tell who he was. He was the visitor.

Richard Meier.

11

The later the time, the heavier the wind became.

Richard stood there, looking at Finn and Yin walking towards him. When they arrived in front of him, a moment of silence occupied the air.

Yin finally could not stand the silence with the mixture mood of both huge confusion and excitement, speaking out, "Richard? What brings you here?"

Richard walked a step further towards her, "Yin, I just want to tell you, I…"

Not letting him continue, with some experience in love and relationship, Finn already knew what he was going to say – this guy in front of him, Richard, was going to tell Yin he missed her. Finn interrupted him. "I am sorry, but do you know who I am?" Finn said firmly, paused for a couple of seconds, wanting to make his next "announcement" sound more influential to Richard, and then continued, "I am, her boyfriend."

Boyfriend? Yin almost laughed out, and she definitely did not want Richard misunderstand the situation due to her strong feeling towards him. She immediately said, towards Richard, "He is not my boyfriend."

Silence came again. Now Finn got a little bit angry at Yin, not because she told the truth that he hadn't become her boyfriend yet, but because she tried to explain this to Richard. *Hey, I am helping you, girl.*

Richard broke the silence, in a calm voice, "See, she said you are not her boyfriend. So do you know who I am?"

Finn got totally confused. He wanted to know who indeed Richard was and why he was in front of Yin's apartment building. He questioned, "Who are you?"

Yin wanted to tell Finn who Richard was, "he is the..."

Not letting her tell it, Richard spoke out first, "I am her husband."

What?

Haven't given time to let Finn and Yin recover from the confusion, Richard went a step further towards Yin, reached out his hand, grasped Yin's hand, pulled her over softly to attach his body, used his left arm to enclasp her, cupped her chin in the palm of his right hand and began to kiss her lips. She lifted her hands in front of her chest by instinctive reaction when Richard pulled her over. And now her hands attached Richard's chest.

Time seemed stopping there.

Richard put his tongue into her mouth, mightily stirring her tongue. At first, Yin was shy and did not know what to do due to her inexperience in such a thing. But then she began to feel comfortable and passionate. She gradually put her hands around his neck, letting his tongue dance with her tongue. Richard could not control himself again. He enclasped Yin's waist, tighter and tighter. They kissed there for a while. A few times, Richard stopped the kiss to let Yin breathe better.

When they used up all their energy, Richard stopped the kiss but still hugged Yin tightly. Yin moved her hands from his neck to his chest again and attached her head to his chest, trying to balance her breathe.

They forgot everything else.

Alongside of them, Finn could not stand watching that anymore but did not know what to do. He stood there with an empty mind, watching them passionately kissing each other, and then with anger and disappointment, he left the scene and walked back alone.

They hugged there for ten minutes. Ten minutes later, Yin recovered her mind and reminded herself that Finn was with them before. She loosed Richard's hand and turned her back over. She did not see Finn. She was a little bit confused but did not care that much. *He might just go back home since he might feel uncomfortable watching people kissing.* Yin turned her head back towards Richard. Now she looked at his eyes and found that Richard was starting at her eyes seriously.

15 seconds later, Yin broke the silence first. She said, "Ro… Richard, you said you were my husband? Why you said that?"

Richard asked her, in a calm and serious voice, "Do you love me?"

"Lo… love?" she couldn't make such a conclusion because she did not have any experience in love and relationship before, "Finn said I did not know what love is. May I answer this question later?"

Richard laughed out, acknowledging that she was innocent and naïve. He then said, "If you love me, I can then be your husband."

Yin laughed out too, "but from what I know, it takes a while before a man to become a woman's husband even if they think they love each other."

"May I stay with you tonight?"

"Stay with me? What do you mean? You want to stay in my home tonight? Or you want to sleep with me?" She was shy when she asked "or you want to sleep with me", but she needed to know. She would not allow herself to have sex with a man when they first met even if she thought she loved him.

"no, no, no, not to have sex with you. Just want to know if you welcome me to stay in your apartment tonight."

"yeah, but why?" She was curious why indeed Richard wanted to spend the whole night in her apartment, "I thought you had a place to live in the town, right?"

"That is true, but I want to spend more time with you."

Even though the answer still did not eliminate the Yin's curiosity and it seemed very odd that he wanted to spend time with her during the night, since she began to like this guy and fall for him, she nodded and agreed to let him stay in her home for tonight. She thought no man would ever talk to her like that when they just met today.

She said, "However, I have some work to do tonight. Could you spend your own time watching TV or playing the computer until I finish the work. It may take from 30 minutes to one hour and a half before I can talk to you."

"No problem." He said. "I am going to buy some wine for us. Do you want to drink?" He asked.

"Drink wine? I have no problem with that unless we will do something we are not supposed to do, if we are drunk."

"I would not allow myself to do anything that you don't like. I would not make you feel uncomfortable."

"That is fine then." She said.

"Nice, I will be back in half an hour. You may go upstairs to start your work now."

He sent Yin upstairs to her apartment and then went downstairs towards the car of Michael Hernandez. Michael stopped his car in the next street. Michael drove him to the nearest wine store to buy two dozens of wine and then was startled to know that Richard was going to spend a night in Yin's home. But he asked nothing. He stopped the car in front of Yin's home and let Richard get off and then left.

Richard cocked his head up, from the second floor, mild light was casting.

12

Finn walked back to his house. On the way back home, he lowered his head. He was very upset. A kind of bitterness occupied his mind. The scene he just saw, not only the guy forwardly kissed the woman he liked, but she somehow accepted his kiss without considering it an offense and kissed him back.

Yin was indeed a special woman, to any man. Not only she had such attractive looking and shape, delicate silky skin and beautiful hair, but she was so innocent to a point that any reasonable man would think that once she fell in love, she would have very strong and passionate love.

Finn actually knew Yin for four years. In this four years, not once did he ever express his feeling or like to her. Not even did he ever use his eyes to express his interests. He knew she was very sensitive even to a point of being paranoid, she could sense anything subtle and be easily disrupted. All people, in Altimont, knew that he liked Yin. But it seemed Yin would be the last person to know that. Even though people sometimes made fun of them two, Yin was never serious about their words or thought about their words twice. He always hoped Yin could, one day, find the goodness of him and fall in love with him. But now his hope seemed snuffed out.

He walked very slowly and finally arrived to his home. When he went inside his home, he went through the living room, walked upstairs, directly going to his bedroom and lying on the bed. He did not turn on the light in the bedroom. He only had one hope – to fall asleep and forget everything. However, this small hope could not even be achieved. He just could not fall asleep. He was thinking what the guy named Richard and Yin were doing. As long as thinking about what they were doing and might be going to do in the night, those thoughts almost drove him crazy.

Richard knocked at Yin's door. Yin opened the door, let him in and was surprised to see that he bought so much wine. She said she was not going to drink too much because she would have to work the next day. She took him to her couch and told him she would finish her work in fifteen minutes. She turned on her TV, turned the voice volume smaller and sat on the other side continuing contributing to the work.

Richard now had a chance to sense the feeling of living in this small apartment. He was not watching the TV, instead, he was looking at her stuffs in the apartment. He loved everything of hers – her bed, her window, her curtain, her dresser and her carpet - everything. This was the first time he truly wanted to pursue a woman due to his true and strong feeling. He had had never done this kind of things before, at least not from his true heart. And now impulse was telling him he had to catch this opportunity. This was the first time he felt like he was living inside a place like a home, with a woman like a beloved wife. Too much emotion came up to his mind. He wanted to be honest to this woman, tell her everything he knew and listen to her stories patiently.

Fifteen minutes passed, Yin at last finished her work. She put down the pen, arranged the materials, stood from the chair, walked to the couch and sat down on the other couch, face to face with Richard. She asked with a smile, "How was the TV?"

Richard said, "It was good, but I prefer looking at you and your apartment better."

Yin grinned at him, wanting to laugh out to express her excitement. She said, "I finally finish working. Now we can chat anything you want. By the way, tonight I sleep on the couch and you may sleep on my bed. Is that good?"

"Yes."

"You bought two dozens of wine? That is too much. I may only drink one bottle. You shouldn't drink too much, either." Surprising expression was shown on her face. She continued, "So sir, what do you want to begin the chat?"

Richard thought for ten seconds and responded, "Can you tell me more about yourself that I don't know yet? I know you are a researcher and that you love astronomy, of course."

"Yes, that is the main part. Richard, for a long time, there was nobody who I can talk to about my past and my secrets. I never told anyone in the town about those because I was accepted by the people for my present status. I feel happy when I deal with people here. I like to know some new people too all the time. I finally could get rid of my memory about my past most of the time since I was here." Yin paused, "You are a visitor to this town and will not stay long, so I guess I can tell you more. Please just keep it private about everything I tell you."

"No problem. I won't speak out a word you tell me tonight." Richard said firmly.

Getting this promise, Yin continued in a low voice, "Yesterday night, I had a scary dream. I thought I could stay away from that dream for a while because I hadn't had that dream for a few months, maybe half a year. However, it just came back last night."

A moment silence, Yin used the corkscrew to open a bottle of wine. She glugged down the wine and used the back of her hand to wipe the liquid on her mouth.

She continued, "Sometimes I drink at home a couple of bottles of wine to remind myself of my past alone. I don't know why I trust you. I may too easily to trust people. But I just want to share with you about things I will tell you tonight."

Yin began to swill the wine again.

Richard said, in a caring voice, "May you share the dream with me? I mean the one you just mentioned."

Yin said, "Can you sit down near me so I would feel a little bit of support when I speak out?"

Hearing this, Richard immediately moved to Yin's side and sat down next to her. He faced her and said, "is it ok now? Do you need me to hug you?"

"No, it is ok." Yin paused, drank the wine down and said, "It is a vague dream. They were telling me something. But when I woke up, the words were gone. I don't remember them. However, I sweated a lot when I woke up."

While she was saying, tear came out from her eyes and dropped down her cheeks.

13

Yin cried out sadly, using her right hand to cover her mouth. She looked extremely sad and depressed. After coming to this town, she gradually got rid of this kind of emotions. But it would just come back to her a few times when she was alone in her apartment. Richard had had never seen her like this the whole day, not even close. She gave him the impression that she was very positive and happy, and yet now she changed to another person that he did not know about. He suddenly felt sympathetic to her, mixing with a feeling of love. He immediately hugged her by his left arm, grasped her right hand by his right hand and fondled her hand. He knew, even though Yin was emotionally strong most of the time, at this moment, she needed his support and console.

Richard said, in a low and caring voice, "Yin, if you don't want to talk about it, let's talk about something else?" He kissed her forehead.

Yin used her left hand to grasp the bottle and started drinking again. Now she finished a bottle. She responded, "Richard, could you open another bottle for me? For a long time, I did not have a chance to speak those out. I think it will help me better if I can speak those out. But I am worried it may bore you, would it?"

Richard loosed Yin for a short moment, opened another bottle and handed it to Yin, and then hugged her tightly again. She did not stop getting depressed; on the contrary, she got even more sad and painful. Tears could not stop coming out from her eyes. Richard used his right hand to tear some tissue for her and helped her to wipe the tears on her cheeks. The first time, Richard found himself a very caring person. He enjoyed being such a caring person.

"No, not at all. Everything you talk about – it would not bore me. If you think it is going to help you, I would love to hear it." Richard stared at Yin's face with a nice smile, but looked very seriously. He knew he needed to give her a little bit positive energy and at the mean time supported whatever she said.

Yin felt a little better after seeing the smile on his face. She attached him, putting her arms around his waist and said, "Richard, you are a very nice person. Thank you so much!" Now she stopped keeping crying. It looked like she finally could calm herself down a bit. She continued, "In the dream, there were many gloomy shadows coming more and more near me. They surrounded me, leaving no air to me. They kept telling me something, which I didn't remember when I woke up. But I am sure it was some words which reminded me of my bad experience."

"What bad experience do you think you had that was related to this dream?" Richard asked, started to fondle her hand and kiss her forehead again.

Yin glugged some wine. Now she looked tipsy. She now kept saying, "Richard, very afraid, very afraid…"

Richard touched her face, her hand and her back to make her feel the support of him. He kept telling her with a very small volume, "I am here, don't be afraid…" He then asked, "Do you mind to tell me what the bad experience was that you are so afraid of?"

Yin looked at Richard's eyes again, trying to make an unconscious judgment if she trusted this man so deeply that she could tell him her past. And it seemed she had the answer. She pouted her lips, acted like a clinging vine, with shyness, and said, "Richard, I love you." Richard lingered his eyes to hers and gave her a big smile. *Then I can be your husband.* Only he knew the smile came from his heart that he had no control of it. Yin paused for a couple of seconds, enjoying the feeling coming between them, smiled back at him, laughed out and attached her whole body to his body and head to his chest. It seemed she forgot the unhappiness and fear caused by the reminding of her past because of the warmth she got from Richard.

Instead, a kind of tiredness came up to her. After all, she spent so much time and energy in work today and used up her rest energy in the kiss with Richard. She mumbled in a voice that Richard could barely hear, "I am tired, Richard. I trust you and will tell you about it. Can we just sleep tonight and we can continue it another day. I just am not in the mood now."

Richard did not say anything, still hugging her. He knew she was extremely tired and needed rest now. Very soon, Yin fell asleep. She was sleeping on his body. Richard did not move. He stared at her face, her closed eyes and her sexy lips with a feeling of content until he finally felt fatigued too. He was very surprised to see that Yin had another aspect that people didn't know about and was happy to see that she got over it most of the time. He was very curious about her past now. There was a huge responsibility he took over that he needed to understand her fear and try to heal the wound she got from her past experience. Then he just fell asleep with the mild light on and with Yin sleeping on his body.

The window was open and breezes blew inside the room from the south and brought some pleasant cool. Outside of the window, the stars and the moon were hanging on the sky, peacefully, seemed smiling at them. It looked like they were saying, "have a good night!"

14

Victor Dupont, after receiving his boss Richard Meier's phone call, thought for a while, without any other solutions, had to call up Judy Kahn, Richard's previous fiancée, to tell her that news. When Judy Kahn received the phone call from Victor, she was very startled to hear that Richard wanted to cancel the wedding which would have been held in a couple of months. She told Victor Dupont she did not believe that and was not going to let him cancel the wedding unless he told her this himself. She kept asking Victor the reasons Richard wanted to do that and that she did not believe his words. Victor could feel what she felt and did not want to say anything more to make her feel worse, and of course, he did not know anything more, so he kept telling her to calm down. Before the phone call from Victor, for a few months, She felt like she could, initially, get everything - his money, his reputation and his love, but now everything went away from her. Just like she was having a wonderful dream that she was in paradise and was extremely happy and then someone just inexorably woke her up. She loved the ego that his money and reputation could bring to her. And she was also happy to see that, at the mean time, such a rich man looked so nice too. She was not going to let him break up with her like this. She was not going to let him go and she needed to find out the reasons and solve it and gain his heart back. The most possible reason that she could think up he wanted to cancel the wedding was because he fell in love with another woman, probably younger and having a good looking and she must live in Altimont, where Richard stayed. As long as July thought up that Richard, now, was with this woman, she was angry. She pressed Richard's phone number and called him up.

Morning sunshine woke Richard up from his wonderful dream. Yin was still in a deep sleep on him. He was still hugging her. Richard didn't drink wine yesterday night so he woke up early in the morning. However, Yin drank too much. Richard took out his phone and looked up the time. It was 7:30 AM. He remembered Yin told him yesterday that she would have to work today. But he just did not want to wake her up. He wanted her to get more sleep and wake up naturally. He did not move, still letting her sleeping on his body, hugging her. Suddenly, the alarm clock of her phone rang. The phone was on the coffee table in front of the couch. He pressed to eliminate the alarm clock and then looked up the contact list of her phone. In the contact list, there was the phone number of the astronomical station. He dialed that phone number and told them that Yin Lin wanted to take off the day. They agreed. After hanging up the phone call, he was interested in searching information on her phone. He viewed her photos and texts and got an idea that she indeed did not have a boyfriend. He put her cell phone back on the coffee table, and then stared at Yin, fondled her back and her hands, waiting her to wake up herself.

At this moment, a phone call came in his phone. He pressed to eliminate the sound, not to wake Yin up. *Oh, my god. It is Judy calling.* In his life, Richard was not a coward. He knew he needed to tell Judy himself that he wanted to end their relationship and gave her a reasonable explanation. But right now, Yin was sleeping and there was no way he would let Yin know he was engaged before coming here; otherwise, she just would think he was a dishonest man and tried to lie to her. The reason he did not plan to tell Yin he had had been previously engaged was not only because of the above reason, but also because he did not want to give her any guilty feeling that she "stole" another's fiancé. He could not pick up the phone in front of Yin. He had to wait till she was not near him.

No one picked up, Judy left a message.

Richard did not try to take Yin to her bed or put her on another couch so that he could move. He knew a smaller action could wake her up and he did not like that.

At 8:30, a phone call came in Yin's phone. Richard took her phone from the table. It was Finn calling her. *Should I pick up? Finn was not her boyfriend; however, Michael Hernandez said Finn liked her. I'd rather dish his hopes now.* Richard picked up the phone.

"How are you, Yin? Sorry I went back home yesterday and did not tell you."

"It's me." Richard said in a low voice, not to wake Yin up.

A moment silence.

"…Why you picked up her phone? Where is Yin?"

"She is sleeping on me."

"She is what?" Finn paused, trying to calm down and rethink what Richard just said, "What did you do to her?"

Richard said, "I don't need to explain to you. Yin is not going to work today. Bye!" Then he hung up the phone and put it back on the table.

10 minutes later, Yin woke up. The first thing she asked was, "What time is it now?"

"It's 8:44." Richard said, smiling at her. *She looks so cute.*

"What?" Yin got up from his body in a fluster, angrily looking at Richard. She spoke very loud, "Why you didn't wake me up? I have work today. Why didn't the alarm clock work?"

Richard hugged her and said, "No worry. I already called up the station telling them you were not feeling well and wanted to take a day off."

Yin got even angrier. She wriggled free from him and argued, "Who are you? Who gave you the right to do that? This is my job and my life. How can you possibly do that? Just for sleeping with me longer? And you can't use my phone to call them or let them know you were the visitor and that you were in my home. Otherwise I will get fired easily. And I would dislike you to the end if you got me fired."

Richard stood there, listening carefully and fully understood how she felt now. *After all, her career was such important to her.*

Yin pointed at the door and yelled, "Get out of my apartment, now."

First, the purpose that Richard did not wake her up was because he wanted her to sleep longer due to her drink yesterday. And now she misunderstood it to be that he wanted to sleep with her longer. He did not like the idea that she misunderstood him and criticized what he did for her. Plus he hadn't had been criticized for giving someone care for almost thirty years.

He got annoyed also and left her apartment.

15

Richard, in an annoying mood, left Yin's apartment. He was not angry at her, but did not like to be misunderstood by the woman he loved. Richard couldn't deny that he did feel good when Yin's body pressed his. He was so comfortable with her sleeping on him. However, that is not his motive at all. He knew Yin loved her work, but he thought one day off was not a big deal. Maybe she was worried about their sleeping together would bring her trouble and was angry at him because he called up the station about her day off. Despite her worries, He had faith he could persuade her to go to New York City with him together. He would give her a wonderful life and caring love. He calmed himself down and forgot the annoying mood as long as he reminded himself of that they slept together yesterday night, even though nothing really happened. *That is the beginning.*

As he walked downstairs, he called up Michael Hernandez. Michael picked him up on the end of Moonlight Street, on which Yin's apartment building was located. There was not too much surprise on Michael's face. He was not very surprised that Richard went out from Yin's apartment, not the hotel, in the morning because yesterday he brought two dozens of wine to her apartment. Michael thought maybe they had intimate behavior even. He did ask Richard if he had a good sleep yesterday and Richard said yes. Richard asked Michael to keep it secret that he fell in love with Yin and was going to bring her to New York City. Michael told him it would be very hard to persuade her to leave the town and her work.

"Michael, where is the nearest jewelry store?" Richard asked. He wanted to buy an engagement ring for Yin. Even though there was nothing really happened between them and Yin did not promise anything to him and he knew she was not an easy one, he still wanted to give her an impression that he was very serious towards their relationship. He knew Yin was not going to work today. Not sure if she was going to stay at home all day, but definitely she would come back in the evening if she left home in the day.

Michael laughed out loud, "Richard, you want to buy a ring for her?"

"Yes, I am serious." Richard said, "So where is the jewelry store nearby? I want to go back to Yin's home in a couple of hours before she leaves."

"Ok, I know there is a jewelry store, not far, 5 minutes' drive. The jewelries including rings can't be as expensive as those in New York City, but I am sure they have some good stuff." Michael was still laughing. He knew it was going to be a piece of big news within the town if Yin Lin did agree to move to New York City with Richard.

Five minutes later, they arrived in front of a jewelry store. Michael explained to Richard that this was the best and most expensive jewelry store in the town. Michael went into the store with Richard. It was 9:30 in the morning and the store had just opened.

"Good morning." The staff said friendly, with a smile on her face, "Sir, how may I help you?"

"I need an engagement ring." Richard said demurely.

"We have some," the staff paused, pointing at one of the counters, "all are here."

Richard followed the direction of her pointing. In the counter, there are about 30 kinds of rings, by what she said, all for engagement. Among all the rings, there was one looked very special. In the middle of the ring, there was a big ornate circle made of diamonds, like a full moon. On the sides of the circle, two lines of diamonds were in order. The rest of the ring was made of 14K white gold.

Richard asked the staff, pointing at the ring, "Can you show me this?"

Michael stood besides Richard, "Richard, but you don't know her size, do you?"

Not letting Richard responded, the staff said excitedly, "Oh, this one is the most expensive ring in our store. A week ago, a young well known scientist came here looking for this ring, too. I guess you guys heard of her. Her name is Yin Lin. A gentleman was in company with her but she refused he was her boyfriend. She said she just passed by the store and wanted to have a look. Hehe!"

"Oh, that is wonderful. This gentleman wants to buy a ring for Yin Lin." Michael was startled that in this world there was such a coincidence. A minute ago, he was still worried that Richard did not know her size. Now maybe the staff had her size. Richard was not so happy with what Michael just told the staff because he needed to protect Yin from rumor, at least before he persuaded her to go to New York with him. However, he was happy to see that Yin had tried this ring before.

Richard said, trying to control his excitement, "Nice. Did she like this ring?"

"Actually, this ring is right for her size. This ring is named FOREVER LOVE. She liked this ring a lot. She said when she had a fiancé, she would ask him to buy this for her." The staff paused, smiling, "are you her fiancé?"

"He wants to be." Michael laughed out.

"I want this ring." Richard was very excited but pretended to be calm. In his life, he had learned how to keep calm no matter what kind of moods he had.

The staff put the ring into an ornate ring box. After Richard paid the bill, he took the ring out of the store, to Michael's car. Michael drove him to a nearby grocery's store to buy some food for Yin for her breakfast and then drove him to Yin's apartment.

Now it was 10:15 AM. Richard again stood in front of Yin's apartment building, with an excited mood. He pushed the ring.

"Who is that?" half a minute later, Yin spoke from the other end of the interphone.

Richard said in a calm but demanding voice, "It's me. Open the door."

"Why do you come back?" Yin asked nicely. She somehow forgave Richard after he left. She had been hoping his coming back since then. She was afraid that he would not come back. But now it seemed that she worried too much.

Yin immediately opened the door for him, afraid he would get angry and leave again. Half a minute later, Richard appeared in front of her again.

Yin pouted her bottom lip, looking at Richard. Richard could not control his like when he saw her expression like this. *I want to kiss her.* He moved a step further, grasped her hand, pulled her inside the room and closed the door after him.

"Today we will go out after your breakfast." He showed her the bag of the breakfast he just bought.

"But I don't usually eat breakfast." Yin gazed at the bag and then made discrete eye contacts with him, showing her shyness.

"Come and we eat together." When Richard showed his care, he sounded like a boss, "I will bring you out after that."

Yin somehow felt she had to obey him. She gave him a new toothbrush. They prepared themselves in the bathroom. Then they sat down on the soft couch and began to eat the breakfast.

They both looked content and forgot their earlier argument.

16

After sharing breakfast, Yin threw out the garbage. They both gargled. Yin asked Richard if he needed to take a shower. Richard told her he did have a shower yesterday afternoon. He was kidding saying that if she was willing to shower together, he would do it again. Yin gave him a teasing smile and then went into bathroom to take a quick shower. After that, she came back to the couch and sat down beside Richard.

Richard stared at Yin's face, smiling and asked, "You aren't angry anymore?"

"Not really, just don't do it again." Yin made eye contacts with Richard, thinking he was staring at her somehow, and pouted her bottom lip again, showing her shyness. She was very shy to express to him that she liked this kind of staring.

Richard kept smiling and said, "Should we go out today?"

"Where do you want to go and how to get there? But I just don't plan to go too far because I need to get back here in the evening." Yin paused, "How long have you lived here?"

"A week," Richard paused, "so I don't know here any better than you. Will you bring me somewhere you know?"

"Of course, it's my pleasure." Yin looked at Richard's muscular arms which were stretched from short sleeves of his white T-shirt, and then his eyes, finding that he was still staring at her. She did not feel any uncomfortable as she did usually when a man stared at her too long. She was just too shy to express herself to the man she liked. She could explain her like to her friends, but not directly to the man himself.

They left the apartment at 11:10 AM. Yin said she wanted to bring him to climb a small mountain. She told him that the residential area of the town was in between two small mountains; one was where the astronomical station located and the other, on another side of the town, was where she wanted to bring him to. She said the mountain was not high and there was a cliff on the top of it. From there, you can see the view of the whole town. Yin told Richard people in the town all believed that if you shouted out your wish on the cliff, the wish was going to come true. She said it was going to be a 30 minutes drive by car, but she did not have a car. Richard said he had a driver, a resident of Altimont, could take

62

them to the mountain. He asked her if she was worried that the driver knew that he was with her. She was not too worried because residents of the town were really nice people, unless it was a huge rumor known and broadcasted by more than dozens of people, usually that a couple of them knew about it was not a big deal, especially if they did business with Richard. She knew they would keep the secret. So Richard made a phone call asking Michael Hernandez to come and pick them up. Michael was very excited to hear that Richard was going to take Yin Lin to the mountain. He thought maybe Richard could give her the ring there, if he hadn't given it to her yet.

When Michael picked them up in front of Yin's apartment building, he greeted Yin first nicely, "Hi, Ms. Lin, really nice to meet you! I have heard of your name for a long time, today finally had a chance to talk to you in person." Yin smiled back and said she was very nice to meet him too. It was always her pleasure to know and talk to new people. Then Michael drove them towards the direction of the mountain.

On the way, Michael explained to Richard that only the residents here knew about the hill. It was not big, so people did not give it a formal name. Yet some residents called it Pine. It was not a tourist attraction, so most of the times, visitors would not know about it from the internet or tour agency.

About half an hour later, they arrived to the mountain. Michael said he would wait for them at the foot of the hill. He said he could wait for them the whole day and asked them to enjoy the trip. Then Richard and Yin waved to say goodbye to Michael, joined hands and walked together towards the cliff on the top of the hill.

It is almost noon time. The sun hung high in the sky, illuminating everything on the land, trees, grass, flowers, cars and people to shine a golden color. It was a little bit warm, but not hot. Winds came and cooled them down. The leaves of maples and oaks, under the affection of the winds, rustled, like playing light music. Yin loved light music the most out of all types of music.

Richard groped his jeans' pocket to feel the ring box. *I can give her the ring when we arrive on the cliff.* They walked through the small road and climbed on the marble steps. Now Yin walked in front of Richard, bringing him towards the direction of the top.

"What are we going to do after this?" Yin asked Richard, "Tomorrow I will definitely have to work."

"And then Friday night, we can stay together again." Richard's manner was so final and it seemed Yin had to follow where he led. Richard continued, "After this, we may go to eat lunch, then go for a walk and then I will bring you to my hotel room and we stay there until the morning of next day. I will send you to the astronomical station and pick you up in the afternoon after your work. Then we can spend weekend time together."

Hearing Richard's words, Yin blushed. She felt Richard already put her in the position of his woman, even though nothing really happened between them and they did not develop a relationship yet. She hadn't decided if she would accept him despite of strong feeling between them. Yesterday she wanted to reject him to the end, before they had the kiss in the evening. Yet now, she felt that there was something, probably a feeling, fresh and new, that she had never had before, echoing in her heart, making her heart beat fast. And yet she could not reject the desire for the development of it. She wanted more and more, out of her control.

17

When they climbed to the top of the mountain, it was the noon time. The winds got stronger on the top. Yin took Richard's hand and brought him to a platform on which they could have a bird's eye view of Altimont. There was a fence around the edge of the platform. Standing in front of the fence, looking down the direction, now Richard could see the cliff.

"Is it the cliff what you talked about earlier?" Richard asked.

"Yes, it is. Many lovers come here to tell each other about their love. Some young people come to make their wishes for their future love." Yin smiled to Richard. It looked like she was quite happy today.

"Are we lovers to tell each other about our love?" Richard was teasing her; yet in his heart, he was serious.

Yin thought he just made jokes. Yet due to her shyness towards love and feelings, she was somehow bushful and could not make constant eye contacts with him.

Richard held her hand tightly, using the other hand to reach his pocket. He stopped smiling, looked seriously, forced Yin to look into his eyes and said, like a boss demanding something, "Now close your eyes."

Hearing this, Yin first wanted to inquiry him the reason. Somehow she could sense that he wanted to give her a surprise, maybe a kiss again, maybe a gift. But she felt she had to listen to his order. She squinted, revealing an untrusting expression. Richard stared at her eyes seriously, without saying a word, until she tamely closed her eyes.

Richard took out the ring box from his pocket, still without smile, took out Yin's left hand, open it, turned the palm adown and said seriously, "Don't open your eyes now." He opened the ring box, took out the ring and placed the ring to her ring finger. She felt there was something brushed against her finger. She was startled and opened her eyes. Now she saw the beautiful diamond ring on her fourth finger of her left hand. She first thought maybe Richard wanted to hug her, kiss her or give her a cheaper gift. She had never thought it was a ring.

"I have seen it in the store." Yin paused, with shyness, looked at the ring and then his eyes, "But I had never thought someone would buy it for me without my knowledge."

"That means our hearts are together and so I know what you are thinking." Richard now had a smile on his face, "From now on, you are my fiancée."

"Fiancee?" Yin swallowed slobber and blushed her face. She felt there was a heat coming up from her body, to her brain. She staggered, almost losing her balance.

Richard instantly hugged her, held her and pushed her head to attach his chest. He said, "And you said lovers have to shout out their wishes to make it come true?" He then shouted, without hesitation, "I love Yin Lin. I want to be with her forever."

Yin's brain was filled without thoughts. She did not say anything, without any movement, letting it press all her weight on Richard. She felt so hot that she did not know what to think or what to do, like the feeling of having a fever.

Seeing no reaction from Yin, not even a word, Richard knew that she was too surprised and amazed and needed time to recover. He lifted her into his arms, brought her to the nearest bench, sat down, letting her sit on his legs. He used his left hand to embrace her back and the palm to catch her left arm, while putting his right hand on her legs, touching her silky skin. At the mean time, he smiled at her and enjoyed seeing her reaction due to the surprise.

Yin now lifted her left hand, stretched her fingers and concentrated her attention on the ring, observing it carefully. She had never had received such a beautiful gift in her life. It took her a while to recover her mind from the surprise. Finally words came out from her mouth, "It is beautiful, but we hadn't been in a relationship yet, how come we engaged the second day we met?"

Richard smiled, almost laughing out. He thought she was so naïve and cute. *Women want to marry me, Yin.*

"And, I haven't known anything about you, who are your family and what you do for a living." She asked.

"Trust me, you are the lucky girl." Richard said.

Yin said, "But the thing I am most worried about is how I am going to deal with the station if they know about this."

Richard fondled her legs and said, nicely, "I will find a solution for you, for both of us. You just need to give me the trust."

"Ok, I trust you." Yin pouted her bottom lip, looking at Richard. *I have no other ways.*

"As for your inquiries about my life and my family, so far I can tell you I make sufficient money for our life. I am single and don't have children." Richard smiled at her all the time. He looked extremely happy, even though he tried to pretend calm. *You are mine now.*

They sat there for a while. Then Yin stood up from Richard and said, "I am hungry. Can we go back and get some food to eat?"

"Ok." Richard stood up and grasped her hand. *Everything goes smoothly. It is time to go.*

They walked down hill.

Richard was so happy. He might had never had been so happy in his life. Despite successful career and large amount of money bringing him huge ego, he was never a lucky guy in love life. Either he pursued his first wife for utilizing her family's reputation to gain concrete benefit for himself, or later women scrambled to love him for his money and social status, he had never had such a strong feeling forcing him to love a woman from his heart and be willing to sacrifice for her.

Yin's thought was complicated. She was very surprised to receive such a gift which could lead to the change the trace of her life. At the mean time, she was worried about her career. Before she met up Richard, she contributed all her effort and attention to astronomy. She was so dedicated in making her dream come true. She questioned herself how much she was willing to sacrifice herself for this quick and uncertain love, especially when she was still not able to live freely without the impact of the bad memory she got from her early life experiences. But without knowing his actual identity, somehow she trusted this man to a point that she, first time in so many years, hesitated and stopped her footstep to question her heart.

18

All the way down hill, Richard held Yin's hand and used his thumb to fondle her palm. A few times, he stopped her and then hugged her, trying to kiss her lips. She was too bashful to be kissed. Each time Richard hugged her and tried to kiss her, she tried to disengage from his hold and walked down hill. She liked the feeling being kissed by the man she had strong feelings for, who was now her alleged fiancée. Yet she never had experience in dealing with a love relationship. This was the first time in her life that she actually had a serious relationship with a man; serious enough to a point of consideration of marriage. Actually, she never even had had a boyfriend, held a man's hands like that, kissed a man's lips or slept with him. These two days, everything changed. She had many new experiences that she had never had imagined would happen, as least not in such a pace or in this stage of her life. In her ideal imagination, she would be single until she made some progress in her research and became a renowned astronomer, maybe until she turned 35. She thought she could easily control herself avoiding a relationship at this young age, because she never had any love experience or paid attention to that. However, she found when love came, it was still out of control.

"Are you ok?" Richard asked nicely, smiling at her.

"I am fine, let's just go back first. I am hungry." Yin begged him.

"Yes, I think so too." Richard paused, walking with her, "What are we going to eat?"

Yin kept walking. Thinking for a while, she said, "Do you want to eat Chinese food? There is still some food in the refrigerator. I go to supermarket to buy food for a week on Sunday usually. There is still some food left."

"Oh, really? You know how to cook? I thought you were a lazy girl only." Richard teased her and grinned at her.

Yin glanced at Richard, strained her eyes, pouted her lips, showing her little anger, and then strode downhill. Richard followed her closely.

Soon, they arrived to Michael's car. Richard introduced his new fiancée to Michael. Michael asked Yin if she was happy. She just smiled and nodded, without a word. Michael drove them back to Yin's apartment. It was 3:30 in the afternoon. Richard told Michael later he would go back to the hotel with Yin and they could walk there after lunch, so no need for Michael coming to pick them up again today. Richard told Michael to come tomorrow morning at 8:00 to the hotel and send Yin to work. Michael agreed and left.

Yin Lin and Richard Meier walked upstairs to Yin's apartment. Yin turned on the air conditioner, brought iced Chai tea that she bought from the supermarket to Richard, poured a whole cup for him and asked him to drink. She liked iced drinks a lot – iced Caramel Macchiato, iced Latte, iced Chai and iced Chinese green tea. She drank iced drinks even in cold winter.

Richard began to sip the Chai tea, enjoying it a lot. He asked Yin what Chinese food she was going to cook. She opened the cooler and freezer and searched food. Not many options left for the week that indicated that she had to go shopping very soon. She brought the small pork steaks out from the freezer. They were for her two meals and now she could cook them in one meal for two people. She also brought out broccoli and four Korean cucumbers. She did not choose some very Chinese vegetables because she was worried that he would not adapt to eating those. She bought the pork steaks and broccoli in a Chinese supermarket. They really had some good and cheaper food there.

She put the pork steaks into the pressure cooker and then some Chinese sauces, oil, soy sauce, salt, sugar, hot pepper, black pepper, Chinese red pepper, Chinese ginger and star anise and started to cook them. Then she turned herself to the kitchen sink and started washing the broccoli.

Richard stood beside her, sipping the white Chai tea and watching her cooking the Chinese meal. When he was in NYC, sometimes he asked Victor Dupont to buy Chinese food for his lunch. But he somehow heard that it was way different between the food in a Chinese restaurant and the food cooked by a native Chinese from China. And he never really had had a chance to watch the process of cooking Chinese food, not even on the television. He was a busy person, after all. *I am so lucky that I can eat Chinese food and watch and even learn how to cook it all my life.*

When they were enjoying the cooking, Yin's phone rang. Her phone was put on the coffee table. She hurried to go there to answer it. It was from Finn. Yin swept the green button to pick up the phone.

"Hi, Finn, how are you doing today?" Yin said nicely.

Richard heard it was from Finn, knowing Finn was going to tell her what he said to Finn this morning. *But it does not matter anymore – she is now my fiancée.*

"Yin, are you ok?" Finn asked nervously.

"Yeah, pretty good. How about yourself?" Yin paused a little bit, "Why you are so nervous?" Yin laughed out to make the conversation easier. She cared about friends all her life and put them in a very important position.

"Did you sleep with the guy, Richard, yesterday night?" He questioned her.

"Ah? Yes, I mean, but who told you that?" She was embarrassed knowing that even her best friend knew what happened between Richard and her, even though she knew Finn was not going to gossip this in the station and would keep secret for her. And the only way he would know this was that Richard told him. But she could not figure out when and how he told him that.

"You don't need to care how I know this, but we really need to talk. Can you come out tonight? I mean is that guy still around you? I want to talk to you without him presented." Finn said, still sounded nervously.

Yin laughed out again, "Actually we did not do anything more than lying on the couch together. But there was something amazing happened this morning that I want to share with you. I will try to make time tonight to talk to you, maybe on the phone, maybe in person. May I call you after lunch. I am so hungry now."

Hearing that she did not have sex with Richard, Finn was now relaxed a little bit. He exhaled a bit but wondering what the amazing thing was that Yin wanted to tell him.

19

Yin finished cooking and brought the dishes to the coffee table, sat down beside Richard. They started to eat the meal. Richard said he liked everything she cooked. He told her his experience in Chinese food back in New York City and told her that her cooking made a big difference.

"Richard," Yin paused, "did you call or pick up my phone and tell Finn that we slept together last night?"

"Yes, I picked up your phone. Can't I tell him the truth?" Richard asked, "Or you are worried he may tell this to other people in Altimont Astronomical Station if he somehow knows that I was the visitor?"

"I know him. He would not do that. He is my friend and knows about the rules of the station. He knows the consequence of telling people about it." Yin said firmly. With her high intelligence, she could guess the reason why Richard would tell Finn the "truth", "You really didn't need to tell him because he was not interested in me. He is just a confidant, not a potential boyfriend. You couldn't make him jealous and there was no reason to do that."

"Look like you know everything when you know nothing."
Richard didn't like that Yin explained Finn's intention to him
when he knew better than her. *Innocent girl.* Richard used her
index finger to sweep the bridge of her nose and then continued,
"Then please tell him that we are engaged and are going to get
married. If he is your friend, he should share it."

"Richard," Yin paused, "Finn is my friend and if you want to
somehow be with me, you should also accept he is also your friend.
Why do you treat him as a rival in love. On phone, didn't I tell him
I had something amazing to share with him? Sure, I will tell him
that you gave me an engagement ring and I said I trusted you for
finding out a solution for me. But before that, I am not going to
accept your engagement, even though it is on my finger now." Yin
laughed out, pretending to keep a distance with Richard when she
really accepted him.

Richard was not worried about it. Even though Michael
Hernandez said it was really hard to persuade Yin from leaving the
station and the town, Richard believed the force of true love could
change her inflexible mind. He can help her to search for another
institute near New York City. Maybe she can teach in Columbia
University or New York University, or work in an astronomical
station in the state of New York. *Maybe I can set up an
astronomical station for her. As long as she was willing to stay in
the marriage with me, everything would be fine to me.*

Richard smiled and said, "Yes, my bride. I will talk to Finn with
you together." Every time Richard talked to Yin, it was like a boss
demanding things to his subordinate.

"But Finn said he wanted to talk to me without you presented. I think he did not like you in the first place because he thought you did too much to me out of my wishes, or say taking advantage of me. For example, you kissed me, stayed in my apartment overnight and told him you slept with me." Yin paused, thinking, "I need to explain to him a little bit. Can't you give me some freedom with my friends? I won't like a husband who is jealous about every male friend of mine." She pretended she did not like something when she really desired for it. In Yin's mind, she'd wish for this kind of husband, a very jealous one.

Hearing this, Richard wanted to be the ideal man in Yin's mind, he agreed not to go inside of Finn's home with her but demanded to stay outside of his house to wait for her. And Richard asked her to promise to stay with him tonight in the hotel.

Yin agreed with those conditions. After the lunch, it was 4:45 PM. Yin called up Finn and told him she would go to his house soon. After that, they left Yin's apartment, walking towards Finn's house.

Finn stayed at home after work. Initially, there was a party held tonight by one of the researchers of the station. The invitations were sent to both Yin and him. He first wanted to bring Yin there because Yin seldom had chance to attend a party. Sometimes after work, she went back home to continue her research papers or reading interesting astronomy magazines. She enjoyed staying alone. Also, she liked to know new friends but seldom spent too much time with people she was not familiar with. She liked to keep a distance with people. Even though she could easily trust people who she loved and who she believed loved her deeply, not necessary romance love, it was hard for her to change mind or listen to people who did not have a big affection to her.

Finn was always a studious student when he was younger. He got to the president's list when he graduated from college with a bunch of honors and awards. He could be considered a good looking man. He had a girlfriend when he pursued his phD in physics and astronomy. She was in phD student in Geophysics in the same campus. She was slim and petite. She loved him. They spent a wonderful three years together. They liked to stick together every minute – eating lunch and dinner together, sleeping together and going out together every weekend. So when they broke up their relationship, after their graduation, due to that they would go to different locations to work, Finn was so sad and he thought he would not forget her forever. Actually he did not forget her in the first few years he worked in Altimont, until the emergence of Yin Lin. Yin Lin was a special girl, to any man. With only limited experience in romance love and relationship, he was not as flirtatious and proactive as Richard Meier. He had waited for the response from Yin for four years. Because of the emergence of the guy Richard, now he thought he needed to express himself to Yin as soon as possible, before Richard took her away.

Finn was waiting at home nervously. After four years' waiting, now it was the time to speak out his feelings.

At this moment, the doorbell rang. Finn exhaled deeply, hurried going to the door and opened it.

He was startled to see not only Yin was standing in front of his door, but Richard was behinds her, smiling.

20

Finn was startled to see both of Yin and Richard stood in front of his door. Finn got a bit annoyed. He had told Yin that he wanted to talk to her alone. He needed a private time with Yin, to express his feelings to her. He definitely did not want to get into a quarrel or fight with Richard.

Seeing his unhappy expression, Yin immediately said nicely, "Finn, this is Richard. He wants to wait for me outside of your house. I know you want to talk and I can talk to you alone."

Finn held her hand and forwardly, pulled her over into the house and then closed the door vigorously. Richard was not shocked about this action. After all, there was no way to let Finn liked Richard as long as Yin's heart belonged to Richard.

Finn brought Yin to his living room and asked her to sit down. Now his attitude turned better. His anger disappeared.

"Yin, why do you stay with that guy that closely?" Finn said.

"Actually, I have some news to tell you." Yin said, laughing out.

"Ok, I have something to tell you too. Which of us should speak first?" Finn smiled back to Yin, handing a can of grape juice to her, "drink?"

Yin thanked him and said she did not want to drink anything now. She was more concentrating on the thing he wanted to tell her. She said, "I would like to hear from you first."

Finn swallowed slobber, lingered his eyes to hers and said, "Yin, I am anxious. I would like to tell you I like you, I mean kinds of romance like. Actually I began to like you four years ago, since we met. But I did not want it to bother you. I thought I needed to wait till you, yourself, had feelings for me. But the emergence of Richard disrupted my plan and my mood. So now I think I need to let you know that I like you very much, more than friendship."

Yin was bewildered for a moment, astonished to hear this from a trusted friend, who she always treated as no more than a confidant. She could not speak for a short while. *Richard was right. I knew nothing when I pretended to know everything.*

"Are you ok, Yin?" Finn looked at her with anxiously.

"Yes, I mean it is quite a shocking news from you." Yin paused, "But do you want to know what my news is?"

"Sure." He said.

Yin lifted her left hand in front of her face, stretched her fingers to let Finn see the ring and said, "Finn, I am engaged to Richard."

Now it was the turn of Finn that he was stunned. And then he abruptly laughed out loud, "Yin, are you serious?" He tried not to look like he was in a very low spirit, but still revealing his sadness, even though he was laughing.

Yin put her hand down, looking at Finn without any expression, and said, "Yes, I am."

"How long did you guys know each other that you plan to get married?" Finn still grinned at her.

"I mean," Yin paused, thinking if her answer would make Finn shocked, "I have known him for two days. I know it is not that long as what you expected, but in a short word, we fall in love so…"

"Falling in love in two days?" Finn now looked more seriously, with an unbelievable expression on his face, "But Yin, you can't test if a man truly loves you in just two days, especially he is too old for you. I don't know how old he is, but I guess over 45."

Yin now really did not know what to say to him and she did not care what he said. No matter what she said, he could find out oppositions to against it because she now knew he also wanted her. She kept silence, still looking at his eyes.

Seeing there was no response from her, he continued, "Yin, you are blinded by alleged attraction. But when you sit down and think, you will find out that that man may not worth your trust. Not only he is too old for you, but also there is no way for you to find out his history of love and relationship in such a short time. You are not his first love. What if he sends you an engagement ring to seduce you for a one night encounter, but with a wife and a family at home in New York City waiting for him coming back? Then what do you expect from him?"

Hearing what he said, Yin swallowed slobber. Yes, what Finn told her was reasonable. She had doubt too since she did not know Richard enough. What if Richard was a liar and only wanted sex from her? What if he already had a family? What if he only wanted her to be his mistress? But she told herself to listen to the instinct that she trusted this man. She believed there was no way to act out love when you did not have it. *Maybe I should sacrifice myself for love and try it once?*

Maybe she was right; maybe she was just too innocent to know the reality.

21

Richard Meier stood outside of Finn's home. He saw Finn's blue Toyota car parked in front of the house, near the steps of the front door. The weather of the late afternoon was good. A cool breeze washed against his face, making him vigorous. He needed to make some phone calls about his business and the cancellation of his wedding, when Yin was not with him. He did not want to make phone calls in front of Yin, to let her know how big his business was. He did not want his money and everything followed after it became a factor affecting Yin's determination towards their relationship. He wanted to tell her about his business after he brought her back to New York City.

He thought Yin was going to stay in Finn's home for a while, at least an hour, so he could begin to make phone calls. He looked at the screen of his phone, there were three voice messages. He listened to them one by one. The first one was left by Judy Kahn. Richard listened carefully. In the message, Judy sounded very upset. She said in a choked voice, sounded crying, "Richard, Victor Dupont told me something about the cancellation of our wedding. I think we need to talk. Please call me back. I love you, Richard." Then it was the second message from Victor Dupont. Victor told Richard that he had already canceled the wedding projection and told Judy what Richard wanted him to tell her. The other message was from a senior executive of RM Corps in New York City telling Richard she had represented the company to sign an important contract and she had sent an email attaching the details and the contract to Richard. He first dialed the number of Victor Dupont.

"Yes, Richard."

"There will be an important conference held on the address of the factory on Friday. There will be some reports announced that day. I want to hear the report about the effect of the environment. I think you already got the message that the factory will be set up in the mid of next month, on July 15th. Since now I don't need to go back to get married, I hope to be in Altimont that day to attend the construction ceremony. After that, I will bring my fiancée back to New York City. Oh, I forget to introduce my fiancée to you. Her name is Yin Lin, a Chinese young lady, a researcher in Altimont Astronomical Station. It would be very nice for you to meet her."

"Oh, how old is she?" Victor asked.

"I did not ask, but quite young, in her 20s." Richard answered.

"Oh, that is very young. I think she would be very beautiful. Since you already decided it, I would keep my comments. Congratulations! But may you spend a little bit time explaining to Judy? I talked to her earlier. She is not so well." Victor said.

"Ok, I know. I will call her in a while." Richard said.

Victor reported some issues within the company to Richard. Richard said he would check his email box tomorrow in the day time when Yin went to work.

After hanging up the phone call, He dialed another phone number to Ms. Maddalen Abendroth, his mother, who is 78 years old. Ms. Maddalen Abendroth bore Richard Meier when she was 24. She took care of him all along while her first husband, Richard's father, Paulos Meier, seldom came back home due to his busy work schedule in another state. Since so, their relationship was not as tight as before and when she divorced with Richard's father, she gained Richard's child custody. Richard loved and respected his mother a lot. After he became rich, he bought a multimillion-dollar mansion in upstate New York for her and her second husband, Richard's stepfather. He hired a few people to take care of their needs in the mansion and went there to see them once a month. Ms. Maddalen Abendroth knew about Judy Kahn because Richard brought Judy to the mansion a few times to live there and eat meals with his parents. Ms. Abendroth also knew Richard was engaged with Judy and was going to get married in a couple of month.

After a couple of phone beeps, Ms. Abendroth picked up the phone.

"Hi, Mom, how are things going?" Richard said with a smile on his face.

Ms. Abendroth heard it was from Richard, so she became extremely happy. She responded, "Hi, Richard, everything is very nice to us. When are you going to bring Judy to come to live here? We miss her too."

Richard suddenly did not know how to explain this to her. The purpose he made the phone call was mainly to tell his mother the cancellation of his wedding and the ending of the relationship between Judy and him.

"Mom," Richard paused a couple of seconds, "I have canceled the wedding with Judy. I broke up with her."

"Oh, really? What the hell are you thinking? Judy is such a good woman who matches you." Ms. Abendroth said, "Let me guess. You fall in love with another woman, a younger one. Is that right?"

A moment silence came. Richard abruptly laughed out and said, "You are smart, mom. Nothing could be concealed from you." He continued, "It is a young lady named Yin Lin. She is a researcher in Altimont Astronomical Station. She is quite intelligent and will become the next someone in science. I have faith you would like her better. I have engaged to her."

"Oh, engaged? how old is she?" Ms. Abendroth concerned.

"Why you guys always concerned about this? Victor asked me this question just now. I have to repeat that I have no idea how old she is other than that I can tell she is in her 20s." Richard said.

"Oh, so young. Do you think she is too young for you? I would think Judy is the right age for you. You know what I mean, right? You have to worry about the age difference and whether or not she truly loved you or your money. What if she does not like you in a few years and take your money away?" Ms. Abendroth truly concerned her son a lot.

"Yin truly loves me. She does not even know what my job is or how much money I have. And now she is engaged with me. She is a very innocent girl and she does not really care about money because she can make a lot of money by her own capability. You will notice that later. She will sacrifice herself for love. She will resign her favorite job and go back to New York City with me. She more than matches me." Richard changed his tone to a more serious voice.

Hearing what he said, Ms. Abendroth now could understand her son better. She hoped what he said was true and only time could prove it. However, it was not nice to cancel the wedding, at least to the woman he was previously engaged, who was Judy. Ms.

Abendroth supported his son's decision based on his own interests and his love. Yet all the way Richard grew up, she encouraged him not to be a coward. She thought he should definitely stand out to explain to Judy himself and make her feel better, if he hadn't done so yet. Ms. Abendroth said, "Richard, did you talk to Judy yet? How does she feel?"

"Not yet, mom. I asked Victor to tell her the news yesterday and he did so. Victor told me Judy is not feeling so well now." Richard responded, "I did not have a chance yet to explain to her myself, but I surely will call her up after I talk to you."

"Good, son. I like Judy a lot. Even though now she can't become my daughter-in-law, I still hope that you could tell this to her yourself and just give her a hand." Ms. Abendroth said, "No more words, please call her up now."

Ms. Abendroth hung up the phone and Richard then searched for Judy's phone number. Before he dialed her number, he thought for a few minutes about how he could explain this to her. It would not be a piece of good news to any woman who was previously engaged and the wedding had to be then canceled, especially when he was such a rich man. He could understand how Judy felt and nothing he said could console her really. He could try to make her feel a little better and help with her life by handing her a sum of money as restitution, which was the best solution he found out so far.

He dialed Judy's number. Judy picked up the phone immediately.

"Hello, Judy." Richard said.

Waiting for Richard's response for a whole day, now hearing his voice, Judy suddenly cried out.

22

Finn looked at Yin's reaction that she got shocked by what he told her, secretly felt happy in his mind, but pretended to be very serious.

After half a minute being in a shocking mood, Yin found words to defend Richard and their relationship, "Finn, Richard is single. He does not wear a ring. You know, if he lied to me, he will not have me in any way. So if he does not love me and truly wants to marry me, what will he get from all these? Would he spend that much money buying me a ring for a risk of getting nothing in return?"

"You are wrong," Finn said, "maybe the fee of buying a ring is not a concern to him. Maybe he makes sufficient money. Maybe he just wants to sleep with you and leaves and in order to make you go to bed with him, he uses the engagement as an excuse. There are many possibilities out there. But you just can't trust a man like this."

Yin did not want to listen to Finn and did not believe what he said, "No, if he wants to seduce me to bed, suppose he is married, what is the need for him to take off his marriage ring, and pretended to be single even before he even knew about me or met me up? Is it even a crime? I observed that he did not wear a ring when I first met him up yesterday. Oh, by the way, I forgot to tell you he was the visitor who you should have met yesterday. You couldn't come to work yesterday, so Ms. Frost changed me to be his introducer guide. So in this case, he never knew he was going to meet me before that and he was just the visitor to the station, why would he expect to meet a woman and be sure to want to sleep with her? It does not make sense. There was no need to act like that in such an important and professional situation. As for his age, I don't think it is a problem. He can teach me and take care of me more if he is older. Love does not depend on the age difference, does it? I think you worry too much."

"He was the visitor?" Finn was startled, "But you know, by the station's policy, you should not date him."

"Yes, I know. But you would not report it to the station, right? Plus Richard said he was going to think up a solution for me and I really trust him. Let me see what idea he will think up." Yin said.

Finn looked unhappy, but with no words to make Yin believe that she was at risk of making a bad decision. He said, "So you don't have any feelings for me? Or you think I am not handsome enough. I have loved you for four years, but you don't love me back; a guy emerged in your life for just two days, you want to marry him. Do you know how upset I would be?"

Yin sat down next to Finn, handed the can of grape juice to him and said nicely, "Finn, how come you never told me that you liked me? I always treat you as my best friend in Altimont. Thank you so much for your care in the past years! We can continue to be confidants in the future. But the amazing aspect about love, is that it always comes out of our expectation and control. Love does not make it from just one side."

A moment silence came. Finn took over the can, opened it and began to glug down the grape juice, swallowing down his despair. But he did not want to give up, "But you know, I would not give up my romance love for you. I will wait here till you get married. And if one day, you find out that Richard does not love you anymore, I will be here for you. Ok?"

Yin grinned at Finn. She said, "Thank you, Finn. You deserved to be called 'a best friend'."

Finn still looked unhappy, but somehow accepted the fact that Yin was engaged with Richard. Finn said the only way for Yin to marry Richard would be to resign from Altimont Astronomical Station and find another job. Yin barely agreed with it. Yin said she did not want to lose the job because that was a dream job for her, but she might have no choice, but to lose it.

After a while, Yin said she did not want Richard to wait for her for too long, so wanted to leave his home and talk to him another time. Finn sent Yin to his door.

From the other end of the phone, Judy's voice was so sad, "Richard, Victor Dupont told me you want to cancel the wedding. Tell me it is not true?"

Richard swallowed slobber, did not want to make her feel worse, but had no choice other than repeating what Victor told her earlier, "Judy, unfortunately, it is true. I am sorry but I canceled the wedding. Victor and my mom hoped I can tell you myself and I want to do it, too. I hope it all works out for you..."

Not letting him continue, she interrupted him, "Richard, no, it is not going to be true. I love you, Richard. I know you also love me. We were so happy together, weren't we? You must have something that you find it hard to disclose. Is there another woman and she is pregnant? Richard, let's think up a solution together."

At this moment, the door was open. Yin and Finn came out from inside, seeing Richard was making a phone call. Yin waved her hand to say goodbye to Finn, turned her body over towards Richard and went forward to him.

Seeing Yin coming out from Finn's home and walking towards him, even though he really wanted to say more to Judy Kahn and explain to her that he did not love her, he had no choice but to immediately hang up the phone.

Richard hung up the phone and smiled to Yin, "finished?"

"Yes, let's go. By the way, who were you talking to?" Yin asked him with curiosity.

23

"Oh, just now I had nothing to do so I called up Victor Dupont, a good friend, my mom and …hmm…someone who now can be considered a friend." Richard pretended not to care about the phone call, "Let's go for a walk. We still have wine at home. So let's buy some juice, pepsi and snacks. Then we bring them to my hotel room."

"Ok." Yin said.

Richard put the phone in the pocket of his jeans and secretly turned off the phone, worrying Judy might call him back. He held Yin's hand with their fingers crossed.

It was now 5:50 PM, late afternoon. It was at sunset. The sun was reluctantly dipping down from the horizon. Winds sprang up from the distance, growing heavier, blowing on their faces and cooling them down. They walked through the resident buildings and houses, along the small roads, to the direction of Yin's home. A few bicycles and cars passed them by and disappeared at the end of the roads.

"Richard, I think you were right that Finn liked me, as a woman. He expressed himself to me just now." Yin said.

"Not surprising." Richard relaxed the muscles on his face and then continued, "You didn't listen to me."

Yin gave a nice smile to him and said, "I didn't show interests to him, so somehow he accepted that. Yet he told me to be careful with our relationship because I have only known you for two days. He joked you might have wife and family in New York City and might only want sex from me. I was trying to explain to him that you are single."

Richard was a little uneasy hearing this because he did not tell Yin that he was not single before yesterday afternoon. *But I was single again then before I engaged to you and I am truthful to you.* He smiled at Yin, lingering his eyes to hers. He rather kept silent because he did not want to make a lie to her, not even a word.

Fifteen minutes later, they arrived at Yin's home. Richard told her, as she promised earlier, she had to stay in the hotel with him tonight. He asked her to pick up a change of clothes. He opened the cooler, helped pick up a few bottles of wine he bought yesterday and put them in a plastic bag. Soon they walked out again, towards the hotel.

On the way to the hotel, they first passed a candy and chocolate store. Yin said she wanted to shop here and brought Richard going into the store. It is not a big store, but with almost all types of candies, chocolates and cakes – Japanese marshmallows and jelly drops in different colors and shapes, German black and white chocolate, Italian fruit jam stuffed milk chocolate, stuffed chocolate cookies, different kinds of truffles and butterscotches, American jello, and tarts with lemon pudding and so on. Yin was not crazy about sweet cookies and tarts. She preferred candies. She chose some jelly drops, in shape of snakes with coke flavor and some others in strawberry, banana and hamburger shapes. She also chose some German milk chocolate stuffed with fragmentary crackers. She handed them to the staff and the staff helped to measure the weight of the candies and chocolate. When Yin was going to pay the bill, Richard picked up some romantic truffles, handed to the staff, took out his credit card and thrust upon her to pay the bill.

After they left the candy store, they went into a grocery store next by to buy some apple juice and diet Dr. Pepper. When they went out from the grocery store, their hands were fully occupied with bags.

After another twelve minutes' walk, they arrived in front of the hotel. They walked through the door and took the elevator to the top floor - 7th floor. This hotel was the tallest building in Altimont, even rarely to be seen in a typical small town in America. Other resident buildings and houses were generally two or three stories. They went into the hotel room, put things down on the floor. Yin sat on the only bed of the room and immediately got excited to see the scenery from the balcony.

"Oh, look, Altimont Astronomical Station, on the hill!" Yin shouted out, looking outside, pointing at the direction of the station. She continued in a lower voice, looking back at Richard with excitement, "I never stayed in this hotel before. It is wonderful!"

"You can live here every day." Richard said. He already took off his T-shirt, and now loosed his belt, unzipped and took off his jeans, standing in front of Yin with only black underpants on. He looked slim and pretty healthy with clothes on, but without clothes, he looked very strong and muscular, with muscles around his arms, legs and on stomach and belly. He looked very young and extremely attractive.

Yin stared at him when he took off his clothes. Richard went a step further which made Yin nervous. She covered her eyes with both hands, piping out. Richard walked another step further, sat on the bed next to her, put her hands down and hugged her tightly, looking at her seriously. He said, "You should get used to seeing me like this."

"What..." Yin made eye contact with Richard, swallowed slobber, not knowing what to think or what to do. She asked awkwardly, "What are we going to do?"

"What do you want to do? Hmm?" Richard kissed Yin's cheek and flirted with her. At the mean time, he put the other hand on her thigh, fondling her leg.

Suddenly, a heat came up to her brain from her body. She was flurried to be kissed and touched like that. For a short moment, her brain was empty without thoughts. She couldn't help but inhaled and exhaled a little heavily. She tried to conceal her uneasiness and said, "Ro... Richard, I... have to admit that... I had never seen a man wearing like… this in reality." There was a slight tremor in her voice.

She is a virgin.

"Yes," Richard kept kissing her face and then her earlobe, "but I am not 'a man'. I am your fiancé now."

24

Richard continued to warm Yin up till she lost her breathe. She thought Richard wanted to have sex with her when she had no experience, especially she was too nervous to try to make love to a man she barely knew, even though she had very strong feelings for him and now he was her so-called fiancé. Even though she had been living in the states for 11 years and was already an American citizen, got an American education and had learned enough about American culture, she indeed still kept her Chinese traditionally conservative way in her view point when dealing with a romance relationship. In traditional Chinese culture, as a fact back to the older days, a lady should only have sex after she got married. The traditional culture educated a woman to believe that love and sex came together, not separated from one another. In spite of her traditional way, she enjoyed reading and watching romance movies a lot, so she had seen a sufficient amount of plots talking about romance and descriptions about sex to guess what he was trying to do with her. But she just never did it in reality. For her, it was really a need to take time to know him more before too much intimacy.

It is so hot.

Richard did not stop his kiss and his stroke on her legs. Now he moved his lips to her neck, kissing it lightly. Then he slightly opened his mouth, pressed his tongue out and licked it while kissing it still.

Yin lifted her arms around his neck, hugged him, buried her face in his chest and said, "Richard, I am ... not ready."

Hearing this, Richard stopped kissing her. He laughed out in a nice way and said, "I am not forcing you to do anything. Sometimes things just would happen naturally." Still hugging her, he changed topic to cool her down, "What do you want to eat for dinner?"

"I am not hungry now, maybe we can eat later. Where to eat?" Yin asked and raised her head up, looking at Richard.

"So eat some chocolate and candies you bought first. Later when you are hungry, we will order food on the phone." Richard paused a second, buried her head in his chest again and said nicely, "Let's talk more, ok?" He definitely knew Yin had no experience in sex. No matter how much he desired sex with her, he did not want to rush it or push her to do something she was not ready yet. Despite of lack of knowledge about Chinese culture, based on his rich experience in dealing with people, Richard could sense what she was thinking and the way she thought. She told him earlier this afternoon that she hadn't accepted the engagement yet before they walked to Finn's home. He knew she had not felt secure about their relationship and that it is very likely that she might want more matured feelings to make love with him. And the best way to solve this problem was to communicate with her more, hear her stories and tell out his stories. Before he met Yin up, in his earlier life, he slept with many women, had two wives, yet not once did he feel a need to tell them about his past and his dream, how he straggled to his position, how he became rich, how many women he met and what his plan would be for the future.

Yin nodded and somehow adapted lying in his arms without his clothes on. She responded, "Ok, let's talk more." She paused to think for a second and then said, "Richard, I am still curious about what you do for a living and who your family members are, like parents and siblings, if you don't have children. I think I really need to know. And then can you just tell me a little bit about New York City? I come from a small city in south of China. I lived in Grand Rapids, Michigan for my college and then Berkeley, California for my phD. I have visited some states and cities in the Midwest and west, and also Florida. Didn't go to east coast that much. I know New York City is the biggest city in the US. Telling you the truth, I am not very crazy about big cities. I like quiet places and less people. Can you tell me a little bit more about it?"

Yes, you love Altimont, but you love me better. You will agree to go to NYC with me.

Richard smiled to her and said, "My parents divorced when I was only five. I lived with my mom most of the time since then. I had a step father and a half sister. As I told you earlier, I don't have children. But we surely can have one." Hearing this, Yin laughed out loud, attaching her body to Richard's tighter. Richard swallowed slobber and continued, "I actually have two ex-wives. As for my job, I do some business and make enough money for a good life." Yin smiled and said, "two ex-wives and yet no children?" Richard said no, ruffling her silky black hair affectionately. Yin laughed out again. Richard smiled and said

94

nicely, "What is it that funny?" Yin kept silent. A couple of seconds later, Richard continued, "As for New York City, it is a big city with a large population, but not the largest one in the world. London in area and population is both considered bigger than New York City. At the mean time, Hong Kong is somehow bigger than it, too. There are five boroughs within New York City – Manhattan, Brooklyn, where I grew up, The Bronx, Queens and Staten Island. I liked to explore New York when I was younger, always found out interesting places." Richard continued, "I can always tell you more about New York City later on." Yin nodded without a word. She was satisfied with his answers. Now she hugged him tighter and attached her nose to his chest that she could sniff his body fragrance.

Richard already could not control himself many times in front of Yin. He wanted to get into her pants. *I want you to be mine physically.* But it was clear that she was not ready and needed his effort to make her more open to him. *But I need to wait.*

As for the obligation he took over to help Yin forget about her past and get rid of that frightening dream, trying not to get her into the same position as yesterday night that she could not control her emotions, cried out and drank too much, Richard said, "Do you still remember what you told me last night about a dream that you still have? Tell me about your past. Just tell me what you know and how you feel, I am here to help you. Believe me, when you tell this out to your man, that dream will just go away."

25

Finn was now sitting inside a bar, drinking beer and talking to his friend Emily Lawless. After Yin and Richard left his home, he called up Emily to go out for a beer. Emily Lawless was also an immigrant from Europe, just the country next to Northern Ireland, The United Kingdom, where Finn Kane came from, which was Republic of Ireland. Many times, Lawless traveled to Northern Ireland and other parts of The United Kingdom, so she knew about The United Kingdom well. Her family owned some lands near Altimont. They planted corn all year around and flowers such as carnations and roses to be sold in local farmers' markets. Emily herself opened nails salons in both Altimont and Bellington, the bigger town 3 hours' driving from Altimont. She lived in Bellington Monday through Wednesday and Altimont from Thursday through the weekends. She just arrived to Altimont this morning. She helped her family to sell their products on weekends. She was a good friend of Finn Kane and knew Yin Lin. She liked Finn and had wanted to develop a relationship with him, yet knowing that in his eyes Yin was the woman he wanted the most. She expressed her feelings to him every time they had a chance to drink together. Today there was no exception.

"I am trying to explain myself again. I know it sounds very silly because I know you love Yin." Emily took a long sip of her large wheat beer, "Finn, I really like you. I began to like you 5 years ago, even before you knew Yin. At that time, I knew you could not forget your ex-girlfriend, so I chose to wait. But out of my control, you fell in love with Yin Lin later on. But you know Yin, I know her too, she is focus on her career and how she can succeed in astronomy and become famous. She does not care about your love. The reason I say that is because all people know you like her, but she keeps ignoring what people tell her and your feelings. I know her, and I am sure she would not be willing to have a relationship with any man, not just you. So why are you still waiting for something which is that far to get?"

Finn gazed at her, looked very unhappy. He kept silent for a few seconds, and finally said, "You are wrong. She is engaged to a man now. And what's more, she has known the man for only two days."

"Are you serious?" Emily was shocked to cover her mouth, "Wow! That would be a piece of big news within the town, I am sure. Who is the man?"

"I cannot give you the information of the man other than he is also from New York City. I am sure in a short days I will be able to tell you more about the man. Maybe you will hear from people too. But not now. Yin asked me not to tell this out right now, so you should keep it private, too." Finn answered.

Emily said, still had an unbelievable expression on her face, "I thought Yin would not want to mess up with any man. How come she is willing to engage to him in two days? Maybe that man is extremely rich. I mean that is all my guess. Or he is extremely handsome. Either one. Hehe!" Emily continued, "I am curious how she met that man up?"

"Again, that is so far a secret." Finn glugged down his beer, still looked sad, looking at the cup.

Emily saw he was not happy, understanding his feelings. She said, "Finn, did you have a chance to tell her about your feelings? I mean that you like her?"

Initially, Emily asked him that in order to console him a bit, because if he said no, then she could suggest him to express himself to Yin because Yin might not know about his like. But somehow she chuckled to herself that there might be a hope to be with Finn.

Finn slouched more hearing her question. He signed with his forehead in his hands. What made him really upset was not because Yin had engaged before he told her his feelings, but because she rejected him indirectly after he expressed himself to her and still chose the other man.

"Did I ask anything wrong?" Emily asked in a low voice nicely. She attached her palm to his hair, fondling it.

"No. I mean yes, I expressed myself to her 3 hours ago. Guess what? She rejected me and still wants to engage to that guy. Now she is with him, probably at her home. They slept together last night, the first day they met." Finn paused, signed again, and continued, "She even thought up every idea to defend that guy."

"I am sorry to hear that, Finn. I understand how you are feeling. I am here with you." Emily paused a couple of seconds, put her hand on his back and then said, "But that is crazy. It really does not look like something Yin Lin would do. It is unusual. I think that man must be extremely rich and handsome."

"He is quite old, at least 45 years old." Finn said, almost crying out, "Tall and handsome, yes, but he is sure too old for Yin."

Emily swallowed slobber and said, "Finn, I definitely understand how you feel. I mean Yin must have her own reason to love that man, maybe for money, maybe she is just attracted to older man.

But that is her choice and we should respect that. It is time to forget her and move on to next woman. I am here with you and hope you give me a chance." She moved forwardly and hugged Finn. Now Finn could no longer control his sorrow, he hugged Emily. Tears spread from his eyes.

I can't forget her, Emily. I love her even more than I loved my ex-girlfriend.

26

Yin loosed Richard's hug, looked a little bit serious. She said, "Richard, do you really want to know about it now?"

"Yes, here and now." Richard said, stared at her eyes with a serious smile, "Don't put too much emotion inside so you don't feel so sad, like you are telling a story about a third person. Just keep calm."

Yin looked at Richard's eyes. Initially, she was not that confident about her communication skills around strangers, but now she knew Richard for a while and they were engaged. She looked much more confident in front of him. She was not sure if she could keep herself staying cooled down without sudden emotion came up. She wanted to gain some encouragement and support from Richard's eyes. She responded, "I will try." Pausing for a few seconds, thinking how she should tell him about this, she continued, "Richard, if I tell you I had some mental disorders, or maybe still have some light symptoms of them… a few times, would it affect our relationship?" She asked carefully, worrying Richard might abandon her knowing she had mental disorders.

"Not at all. I love you no matter what kind of mental disorders you have." Richard gave her a big smile and said nicely, holding her hands. What he said set her at ease. She felt easier to tell him about her past now.

"Ok." Yin paused, "Can you guess what my IQ, intelligence quotient, is?"

"I can't guess it, but I guess you are very intelligent, and a genius." Richard grinned at her.

"How do you... know that?" Yin was started to hear that Richard said she was a genius. In her life, everyone who had a short contact with her would tell her that she was very intelligent, there was no exception, yet not a couple of them would know she was even a genius.

Richard said, "I just know it by my instinct, based on a lot of things such as your reactions to things, your personality and character, the way you speak and your ambition."

He is also very intelligent and probably another genius.

Yin said, "Amazed you know that. I moved to the states when I was 15. I lived in China before that. Actually, I had had not taken any IQ test before I was 15, when I was in China. I joined Mensa, the high IQ club after I moved to the states, at age 19. Then I took an IQ test. My score was 173. You know, score above 140 is considered a genius. I don't remember among how many people there is one who has IQ 173 or above, but I do remember there are only 3 or 4 people with IQ 140 or above among every 10000 people. So you can see that a person with IQ score 173 is highly genius."

"That is true." Richard still smiled at her, giving her the support she needed.

"My father told me, when I was three months' old, without my parents' teaching, one day I asked my dad to bring me to urinate in the dialect of Chinese, which was spoken in my city Shuiliang. That is to say, I could speak Chinese when I was only three months' old, without my parents' teaching. I actually began to read novels, the translation version into the modern Chinese of the four very famous books in Ming and Yin dynasties, when I was only 2 years old. One of the four books named Romance of The Three Kingdoms was my favorite. I read it for three times. I also read a dozen of books about Chinese history and the world history at that time. When I grew older, at age of 4, I began to read modern novels by younger Chinese novelists."

"Sounds like you are very talented in languages." Richard said, fondling her fingers and her ring.

"Yes, I am. Even now I still like reading novels. My parents did not expect or push me to study hard or attend school at a younger age at all, so I enrolled in elementary school at a normal age, which was seven at that time in China. When I began elementary school, I began to show highly talent in math instead. I did not pay attention to school that much. Sometimes I did not go to school for a consecutive week. Instead, I stayed at home watching TV and eating snacks, reading, doing some paintings and shopping in the supermarkets. I enjoyed those times a lot. In spite of absence of school, I was the top student in math among my classmates and I was selected to some programs, a couple of which I was the only girl joined in, among some boys. Students could see each other's grades and discuss grades with each other. They did that all the time. I skipped some grades and graduated from elementary school in three years, which normally would take a student 6 years to graduate, when I was 10 years old."

Richard wanted to say something, but Yin lifted her palm on his lips to stop him. She said, "Let me continue. Then I enrolled in one of the best middle school in my city the same year. You know, usually it would take a student to graduate from middle school in three years. In the second year, students would begin to learn physics and in the third year, chemistry. From middle school, it was legal and a common way to rank students' grades among the class in China. Beside the courses I took together with my classmates, I was so curious about science and languages. I secretly rent the books back and learned all the stuffs and knowledge a student should obtain about all the subjects such as physics, mathematics, chemistry, Chinese, English in the first year, not very hard working, but just the same effort as my classmates put in. After knowing that, my teachers recommended my parents to send me to a bigger city to get education. Under my constant request, at last, my parents agreed to send me to a big city Quanshang in another province to study. So I was sent to a boarding school in another city to get the second year education of my middle school. My new school agreed to let me to take the graduation test after I completed my second year of my middle school education. I took the test and was admitted by a top high school in Quanshang. I was very happy till then."

Richard was so curious. He felt there was a need to ask questions at this point. He fondled her hands more and asked, "So you didn't have mental disorders till then? So what happened in your high school that caused your mental disorders? Is that nightmare related to your high school experience, too? Too much stress in study? But I would guess more than that."

He is very intelligent and knows me. Yin nodded, looking at Richard's eyes seriously.

27

Richard worried that Yin might get nervous and depressed again, in order to keep her at ease, he walked to get the bag of candies and chocolate, sat back on the bed beside Yin, took out a truffle, opened the package bag and delivered the candy to Yin's mouth. Yin looked extremely calm did not like herself yesterday but she did not have the mood to eat. Maybe a bad memory could make her have extreme moods, either too much depression or too much calm. It seemed she already told him too much to a point that there was a need for her to tell him the rest before she could pay her attention to eating. She shook her head to express her rejection to eat the truffle and annoyingly glared at Richard.

Now Richard knew that she urged to tell out her experience of her high school education before anything else. He gazed at the candy bag, thinking if his action made her angry, but somehow realized that the reason she was urged to tell him the story was because she trusted him to a point that she was willing to give her heart to him, and then he stared at her eyes again and said, "Go on."

After Richard's sudden hanging up her phone, Judy Kahn was bewildered. She was angry at him hanging up the phone without even saying goodbye; but at the mean time, she knew Richard to some degree that she had reasons to believe he was not an impolite person. In the next hour, she called up his phone number a few times, but all the time the machine asked her to leave a message. *Maybe his phone does not have battery or there was no signal. I should wait till the next day.* She felt tired dialing his phone number without his picking up. It was still in the early evening. So instead, she dialed the cell phone number of Ms. Maddalen Abendroth.

The call went through. Ms. Abendroth did not want to answer the phone initially because she asked his son Richard Meier to contact Judy Kahn two hours ago and thought his son had contacted her himself. *Maybe that is the reason why she is calling me – she might not have a good talk with him.* She did not know what his son had told her, but somehow she liked this previous future daughter-in-law very much and wanted to console her a little bit. After all, she had no control of her son's marriage or who he loved.

With hesitation, Ms. Abendroth picked up the phone and greeted Judy Kahn, "Hello, Judy. How have you been? Had Richard talked to you?"

Hearing Ms. Abendroth's voice, Judy pretended crying out sadly. "Mom," she said in a choked voice, "Richard said he wanted to cancel our wedding."

"Judy, I asked Richard to give you a call a couple of hours ago. I want him to be brave and explain the situation to you himself. What isn't clear enough that you want to call me up? And please don't call me 'mom' in the public because you know Richard is a public figure, even though he never appeared in the news but his company does all the time." Ms. Abendroth said.

"Mom," Judy said, "I would call you Ms. Abendroth in front of others. Richard called me an hour ago. Yet while we were talking, he hung up the phone suddenly. You know I have many questions to ask him."

"Yes, I understand. You want to know why he changed his mind. I can tell you that." Ms. Abendroth said with sympathy.

Judy Kahn immediately asked what the reason was. Ms. Abendroth explained to her, "He falls in love with a Chinese young lady and is engaged to her. So now you need to move on and forget him."

Now Judy Kahn finally knew the reason why Richard wanted to cancel the wedding and break up with her, after a long day's waiting. She asked Ms. Abendroth how old the Chinese young lady was and told Ms. Abendroth that she was the right one to marry Richard. Although Ms. Abendroth asked her to move on and forget Richard all through the call, at last, before their hanging up the phone, Judy Kahn still insisted that Richard should still choose her.

Finn did not get drunk drinking down the whole cup of beer. He hugged Emily for a while with tears falling down. He couldn't calm himself down – it was the hardest night of his life. Six years ago, when he broke up with his first and ex-girlfriend, he thought he couldn't forget her. But now, he had to "break up" with Yin; not only did he think he couldn't forget Yin, but also he believed he would be fixated at Yin forever, very much. *She is such a special woman that you can't find another like that forever.*

They stayed in the bar till the midnight. Emily companied Finn talking about every detail memory he had with Yin. Emily, on the contrary, though giving Finn enough sympathy, was surprised by the pace Yin got engaged and happy that there was finally a chance for her to be with Finn, the man she liked for years.

28

Yin held Richard's hand, trying to keep herself from being depressed. She did not response Richard's stare, instead, she looked at their hands. She was thinking and tried to do what he asked her to do, that is trying to tell the story in the view point of a third party. She said, "At age 12, I was admitted to the top high school, in a highly competitive class. When I was in elementary school, I was not a very studious student – I loved knowledge and was curious to learn, but was not very hard working. As I told you earlier, when I was in middle school, I gradually developed some ambition, wanting to make a difference. I put great effort in middle school, at least not like when I was in elementary school that I did not go to school and not do homework often. You know in China, students normally study for 12 years, 6 years in elementary school, 3 years in middle school and another 3 years in high school, before they take a final test for the admission of colleges. And the final test for college admission is described as the only fair thing in China."

Without knowing too much Chinese culture, Richard nodded as Yin told him what she knew about. He believed her and thought what she told him might be the case. He didn't say anything to interrupt her, but listening carefully about what she said.

Yin continued, "There is a huge difference between Chinese culture and American culture so without spending a long-term in China, you would hardly understand what it really is about. Let me explain to you. There are a lot of unfair things in China – a person's success does not really depend on their intelligence or personality and character, and does not really depend on their social skills or their attitude towards work."

"So what does it depend on?" Richard was more curious and asked.

"It depends on mainly one thing," Yin paused and then continued, "relationship, which is to say, what the relationship is between your family members, let's say your parents, and government officers who have some authorities and how much benefit and influence your parents can give to them. For example, in many cases, in order to let their kid be admitted by a better class within the same school, some parents would visit the president of the school and other officers and send them gift cards or real money. Another example is, when there is a test followed by an interview held in the city to hire 10 government functionaries, the result is that the one with the second highest score does not get into interview process because he or she does not have a relationship; however, the one with the fiftieth score is given the final offer. Do you understand such "relationship" better now?"

Richard was a little bit surprised to hear those, but due to his strong belief in Yin, he accepted what she told him. He nodded and said, "I understand everything you said."

"In Chinese society, such relationship works in every aspect of life, like going to a school, finding a job and so on. Some students knew about this fact from their parents and teachers when they were young; a few others did not have too much knowledge about it and I was one of them. I grew up in a relatively fair study environment without being told by my parents before high school. When I was in elementary school and middle schools, teachers were too kind to us and treated everyone equally. I did not get into the way that Chinese society encouraged us to do. Then I was in high school, but everything changed." Yin paused for a couple of seconds, looked at Richard's supportive eyes and then their holding hands again. It seemed like Richard's method asking her to think like a third party worked well - she continued, very calmly, not showing any depressed mood, "When I was in high school, at least in my competitive class, everyone acted like what they would act encouraged by the society. Students liked giving flattering to class monitors and showing their friendlessness. On the other hand, teachers told students their admiration and showed more care towards students whose parents were government officers. They did not care how much talent you had towards your dream, but whether or not you got into the way they did things or whether you had the same view points as theirs; otherwise, you would be easily considered a strange and high-hearted person, who they would not care or like. From my previous education experience, I thought a school and a class should present their fairness and care to every student, so I disdained acting their ways. Of course, I was considered a strange person, who was repulsive. But could you imagine how they treated me?"

Richard held Yin's hands tighter with sympathy in his eyes. He actually could not know what exactly happened among her teachers, classmates and her. But he could sense, from what she had told him, that they actually repelled her and ignored her, maybe terribly to cause her get into mental disorders. He said, "They treated you not well and not fairly. Or more, they neglected your genius." Again, Richard knew what Yin really thought about and wanted to tell. *He is so talented and knows me well.*

"Yes." Yin paused for a second and loosed Richard's hands a little bit because he somehow was too worried about Yin to hold her hands too tightly. She looked extremely calm, totally different from what she reacted yesterday night. She said, "I can give you a few examples. Then you would understand better. My chemistry teacher, who was the teacher in charge of the class, when he taught in front of students in the classroom, he looked at other students supportively, the ones sitting in front of me, beside me, behind me, but never was able to look at me in his eyes, never. I felt I was totally despised and ignored. Another good example is, there was once we elected the class monitors for that year. Students wrote down the names of the candidates they chose in a piece of small paper, folded it and then handed the folded paper to the previous class monitors to count. I wrote down a few names who were not the ones the previous monitors would like to choose. When they opened my paper and read it out, they gave the paper a repulsive look and said, 'who is this boring person'. The other example is..."

"Speak slowly and relax yourself." Richard was worried and said, "I am listening."

Yin tried to do as what Richard demanded, and said, "The two examples I just told you was a couple among the many examples the way they treated me. Three years being treated in a wrong way, so you can imagine how I had felt during the whole duration of high school. The other example, which I had very deep impression about, we had a competition in the city in the last year of our high school education that the first five students with the highest first five scores would get an extra 20 points counted in the final test of college admission. Because the way I was treated among classmates and teachers, I had been very depressed and so could not concentrate on my study. I read psychology books myself and diagnosed myself with major depressive disorder. At that time, I was too depressed that I had bad sleeps during many nights, felt hopeless and helpless, and could only pay one third of my attention in study. I was crying all the time, more than 10 times crying out per day and it lasted for at least a year. Can you imagine how a person felt in such a situation? Yet I had to continue my study. I worked very hard and kept good grades even under such circumstances. I was very talented in math and sciences and should get to the first five scores in the competition. And I felt I did well in the competition. Yet the outcome was that a couple of the kids of government officers whose grades were not good at all got the awards and the extra 20 points. I was ranked the number 6."

When Yin was talking, Richard stared at her with sympathy and encouragement to support her to tell out the story. He again held her hands tightly. He was worried about her all the time, yet she showed more than easiness when she was talking, under the direction of Richard. Yin continued, "You know, too much unhappiness and sorrow about my high school education got me into huge depression. I took part in the final test for college admission and was offered to attend a good Chinese university at the age of 15. I did not enroll to that university. Within a few months, in the same year, I got a chance to move to the states to live so I chose to leave China and move to the states. After I moved to the states, I enrolled in a college in Michigan. I read a lot of psychology books and took a few courses about psychology in college and cured my depression myself. I did not feel depressed most of the time since then. But because of the stimulation I got from my such bad experience, it seemed I got into another mental disorder –OCD, obsessive compulsive disorder in the following years, till now, that I have been so obsessive to be successful that I have paid all my effort into study, research and work."

29

Finn Kane ordered another cup of wheat beer. He gulped the beer while Emily asked him to drink slowly and not to drink too much; otherwise he would get drunk. "I am not going home with you on my back. Haha!" Emily made fun of Finn, in hope that he could feel better. Finn finally listened to her and ordered a large cup of green tea lemonade and took a long sip. He said Yin liked green tea lemonade the best. He hadn't gone out from the bitterness of losing Yin. He started to tell Emily every small detail happened between Yin and him.

"My birthday was on August 1st. The second day four years ago, I began to know Yin. Her birthday is on December 21. That year, it was on a Thursday, a few days before the Christmas Day came. Do you still remember, that day, it started to snow heavily just after the noon and it snowed a whole afternoon?" Finn asked.

Emily shook her head.

Finn continued, surely thinking about Yin made him look a little better, "We were told when we were ready to go home that, because of the sudden huge snow, the snow scrapers would not finish shoveling the snow on the roads back home till late evening.

People were talking in the lobby near the front door of the station. I joined them. I stood for a while and finally found a seat to sit down. When I was resting myself and watching people talking, I saw Yin walking through the lobby and towards the front door from the other building behind it. She was new to the station and we had had known and talked to each other for times before that in the cafeteria, since my birthday. We had a good time talking to each other, but not once did we meet after work or know each other personally. When I saw her walking towards my direction, I stood up, walked towards her and forwardly greeted her. I began to like her already. She smiled to me and we started talking. I told her it was impossible to go home now due to the huge snow. She said it was a pity that it was her birthday and it seemed she could not buy herself a cake or a gift. We talked there for a couple of hours, exchanged phone number and addresses and added each other to social websites. We really started to know each other personally from that moment."

Emily nodded all the time, forcing herself to give smiles to him. *Maybe today he really needs to tell out all those to feel better.*

Finn continued, in a low voice, "At around 9:00 PM, there came the news that we could make our ways home. I asked to drive Yin home and she agreed. She climbed in my car and I drove her home. You know I like cooking. When I arrived my home, I used the rest of the evening, the time before bed time, to make her a home-made cake and brought to her office the second day. She became much more open to me since then and we really became good friends, often text chat, video chat, going to work together and hanging out together after work."

"Really nice," Emily said, forced a smile on her face, "But you should understand all the way, there is a huge difference between treating someone as a good friend, or a best friend and treating him as a lover, especially when she came from another culture. You know I want you to be my man all the time and I always let you have an idea about it. You loved her as a woman and you should have let her know earlier, not till she was taken away by another man who was more proactive. And now in her heart, there was only the other guy, no space for you."

Hearing what Emily told him and what seemed true, Finn now regretted a lot. Bitterness and sorrow came up to his mind. It was his fault not to let Yin know earlier and wait for four years foolishly. Now he had to taste the bitterness by his own mistakes. He did not want to remind himself of the fact that Yin walked away from him, but hoping to think about their past and how happy they were together. He said to Emily, "I rather talk about Yin more."

Richard listened to Yin carefully and now he had a better understanding about what she had experienced and why she still had such a scary dream, even 11 years later after her high school graduation. *The experience is not forgettable. The emotions followed by it can be controlled and she can be happy again. Yet there is no way to ask her to act like nothing bad had happened, especially when those emotions come back.* He did not want her to continue thinking about the astonishing experience, but he was careful not to act like he did not pay attention to what she told him. He said nicely, "Now you are going to be my wife that I will, as a husband, protect you from the bad memory forever. I would not allow it to attack you in any way. You just need to give me enough trust and belief in me. Now can you tell me what your name means?"

Yin was relieved to hear that Richard would try his best to protect her. In her own mind, not considering the situation about her job and the uncertain future or everything possible in reality needed her worry, she was more than willing to become his wife.

30

Yin smiled at Richard. It seemed she could, after a long straggle, under the guideline of Richard, beside her fiancé, finally handle her own emotions towards her past. Richard's hands loosed a little bit but still holding her hands, playing with her new ring. He was not as worried as a while ago. Yin said, showing her shyness again by avoiding straight eye contacts with him, "My name? I was offered an option when I became an American citizen to change my name. I thought about changing it to an American name. But at last, I decided to keep my Chinese name. I am very proud of my name. It is a 'mark' of me. It describes a lot about what I will do. As for what it means, I need to spend a little bit time to explain." Yin paused a second and then continued, "My name is Yin Lin, right? When it is pronounced in Chinese way, it is LinYin. Of course, there are many different words which have the same "Yin" pronunciation, but as for my name, Lin means a wood while Yin means the natural sound you would hear in the wood, especially in the early summer time. My parents gave me the name in a wish that I would find such a good place in such a good season, even if not existing in reality, that it would teach me something that I would cherish all my life. You know, the wood and its sound may symbolize something else, but I haven't gotten it yet. It's my destination to find the 'place' and the 'season'."

"I hope you will find them." Richard sort of laughed out, "And don't forget to tell me about it."

Yin, gazed at Richard's stare, again, pouted her bottom lip, acting like his little woman. She said, "Richard, I told you a lot about myself. People had told me that I paid too much attention on myself, acting in a kind of selfish way, not concerning others' lives and interests enough. That was not always true as for I helped many people in my life. I might just too focus on my own stuffs. I don't want to be described like that, not anymore. Especially, I don't want to be told that I don't even care about my future husband. Now can you share some stories of yours? It seems like you are really an interesting person."

"Glad you know I am interesting." Richard also pouted his lips, leaned forward his chin to Yin's face, acting like demanding a kiss. Yin attached her lips to his, moved back quickly and shyly smiled with an inner radiance. A heat came up to his face. Richard could not control his desire. He could feel the desire became stronger and stronger in an instant, taking control of his mind. He wanted to make love with her, here and now. However, by all his consciousness, he was telling himself to be more patient. He needed to wait till her totally opening herself to him. He said in a low and soft voice, trying his best to take charge of the uncontrollable desire, "You are my first love. I know it sounds unbelievable, but it is a truth to my best knowledge..."

Yin interrupted him, "But you got married twice. Didn't you have to love the two women in order to marry them?"

Richard looked very serious and stared at her, giving her an impression that he wanted both her body and soul, making her heart bumping faster and faster. He swallowed and said, "It is a long story. I married them for other purposes or I might just want to keep in marriage and did not understand what love was about. My first wife, she came from a rich family and I wanted to utilize her family's reputation to help to build up my career. As for the second marriage, I was single after the first divorce. At that time, many women threw themselves to me and wanted to marry me. I don't want to keep it as a secret that I slept with many other women besides my previous wives. But please trust me. I won't do it again in our marriage because I finally find my love – that is you. But you know, keeping in a marriage did help a lot to avoid the bothers by women who wanted a marriage with me. So I just found a suitable woman and got married the second time. Sorry to let you know those, but I want you to know my past, truly confess about it and still hope you can forgive what I did. Would you forgive me?"

"Forgive you?" Yin said. She hadn't had known Richard's past affairs a few minutes ago, but from what good looking he had and how fancy he was in dressing, she could imagine there were many women wanting to get closer to him. Now she had a better understanding about his past and she did forgive his behaviors due to his sincere confession. What's more, she believed in their love and their future. She turned around, rode on Richard's thighs and wrapped her arms around his neck, starting to kiss his lips. Richard was a little shocked by her action which was totally different than the impression he got about her that she was a very shy woman, but couldn't help hugging her waist and kissing her. Instantly, the same uncontrollable heat came up to him again; this time, even stronger.

I want it now.

31

Yin kissed Richard forwardly to express her forgiveness and her trust to their love. "Richard, I love you. I am willing to have sex with you." She mumbled. Richard interpreted it as a signal that she became open and wild to him. With Yin riding on him, he felt good. While they were vehemently kissing each other, Richard turned around, lifting Yin up, softly put her on the king size bed, started to pull up her flimsy dress, exposing her sexy slim legs, her rose beige panties and then her large breasts covered by a sexy same color bras and finally took off her dress. Richard then softly pulled down her panties, took it off from her legs and then loosed her bras. In just half a minute, she lied under him naked. Yin could not think anything other than the excitement and passion towards having sex with Richard. She felt very nervous that this was the first time she was without clothes on in front of a man. In a fast and vehement manner, he started to warm her up, kissing and licking her stomach to her private part, making her feel extremely hot. Her heart bumped extremely fast. Her breathe became heavier with unconscious chokes. Richard quickly took off his black underpants. He couldn't wait. He already had an erection. He penetrated inside her tight vagina and started to pump it. When his thing pressed inside her, she felt the huge pressure coming into her body and couldn't help sounding out. Richard continued pumping her vehemently; at the same time, he buried his face on her neck, kissing it, and used his hand playing with her breast. He had had never felt so good having sex with a woman before. Making love with a woman who he truly loved and who he was very excited about did make a difference. He enjoyed the huge comfort and tried to make her comfortable. After all, this was her first time and he needed to give her a good start. Richard didn't wear condom. He hadn't had wanted a child before because he did not meet the right woman who he wanted to be the mother of his child. And finally, in his mid fifty, he found his favorite woman and wanted to start a real family with her.

Yin dipped in a huge pleasure. She couldn't help enclasping his neck and head. She was passionate and enjoyed her first time.

After the excitement for a while, Richard ejaculated deep inside her. He took his thing out and lied next to her, gazing at her and caressing her breasts. She was still trembling. When she got her consciousness back, she took a glance at him, and then closed her eyes without a word, resting. Very soon, she fell asleep. After all, making love for the first time did cost all of her energy.

32

Richard gazed at her with full emotions. He stopped fondling her breasts and let her sleep. He knew she was exhausted. He somehow got hungry. He used the phone in the room to call up the front desk for a dish of jambalaya and then charged his cell phone without turning on the phone. He would have to get up at 7:00 AM tomorrow morning to wake Yin up and ask her to eat something before sending her to work because she fell asleep without eating dinner tonight. Also, tomorrow, after sending Yin to Altimont Astronomical Station, he would attend a conference on the location of the new factory. He would really need to listen to the reports from the managers. He was very concerned the promising future of his new factory and what could stand in the way of the development of it. He knew RM Corps was going to change the world once the factory was set up and run. As an experienced businessman, Richard knew how large the potential market was and where he wanted to get. So tonight, after having fun with his love, he needed to eat some food and go to bed.

It got dark and deserted on the streets, but dozens of people got together in this most popular bar where Finn and Emily were located in. People around them were happily exchanging their schedule for the coming weekends. A short guy with a moustache came closer to them, handed them a business card and asked them how they were doing. He immediately recognized Finn.

"Are you Mr. Finn Kane from Altimont Astronomical Station?" He said with a grin. Even though Finn was not as promising as Yin, because of her reputation within Altimont and their friendship or potential relationship, Finn somehow became as well known as Yin among residents of Altimont.

Finn didn't want to be recognized in such a situation because Emily was a big mouth and once people started to know that he "broke up" with Yin, they would start the gossip very soon and there would be a risk that people knew that Yin was "messed up" with a visitor of the station and finally this would be known by people worked in the station. Finn knew Richard was going to bring her back to New York City, but he did not want Yin to be fired from the station before that.

While Finn did not know what to do, Emily took a glance at him liked she was getting his permission to speak for him. She said, "Yes, he is Finn Kane, the one worked in Altimont Astronomical

Station. He is too sad to speak because he got rejected by the lady he loved." Emily wanted people to start the gossip that she was with Finn alone in the late evening in a bar and that she had taken the place of Yin.

"Oh, you mean he was rejected by Yin Lin? And he is with you now?" The man with a moustache laughed out loud.

Finn wanted to stop Emily but it was too late. She nodded and said yes. In an instant, the man turned around his body, facing other people, and announced in a high-pitched voice, "Listen to me, everyone. Big news! Big news! Our dear Yin Lin rejected Finn Kane."

Almost at the same moment, all people sitting in different places gathered around Finn and Emily. They were the "witnesses" to see Finn was with Emily in this late hour in a bar. Of course Finn would not lie about anything. Discussion started among people.

"Yin Lin broke up with Finn Kane? How come? I thought they matched each other."

"Why would she reject such a good man?"

"So soon being rejected, he is now with the other woman around?"

"Maybe she rejected him because he cheated on her, with this woman. Oh, I feel sorry about Yin."

One even asked loudly, "Are you his girlfriend now?"

It was not that people were not nice to Finn, but in their deep-seated perception, Finn Kane should be with Yin Lin. They started to blame Finn because they liked Yin Lin a lot and were proud of her. *She is the representative of Altimont. I am not. And people would all blame at me for it.* Being accused without a good reason and worrying about the coming rumors, Finn got angry and wanted to leave. He snaked through the people, paid the bill and left the bar without turning his head back. Emily knew Finn got angry but somehow felt good about it. *In a week, all residents in Altimont will know I am the new girlfriend of Finn.* She followed Finn leaving the bar with a smile on her face.

33

Richard woke up early the second day morning at 6. A nice sleep strengthened him. He gazed at Yin. She was still sleeping in his embrace naked, in deep sleep. She looked extremely serene. He guessed she was not dreaming the nightmare. He didn't move his hands away. Now he had time to observe her more. She looked so sexy and charming that he felt he could get excited and wanted sex with her at any time.

An hour later, she gradually woke up. Her eyes squinted, as a reaction to the morning sunlight coming through the balcony, half covered by the thick curtain. He hugged her more tightly and gave her a big smile when she took a half-conscious glance at him. Ten minutes later, she was finally awake.

"Good morning." She mumbled, still looked not recovering her full energy from yesterday's experience.

"Good morning." Richard paused a second and said, "It seems you did have a good sleep. How do you feel?"

Yin stretched and rubbed her eyes, "Tired. I need more sleep but have to go to work. What time is it? We didn't oversleep, right?"

"Right. It is 7:09 AM, still early, isn't it? Get up and eat some breakfast. I am ordering the food through phone. What would you like to eat?" Richard whispered near her ear.

"Anything. I mean, maybe milk and cheerios, a banana and mango banana smoothie?" Yin laughed out, loosed Richard's tight embrace, sat up and got off the bed. She walked to her backpack to get her clothes and then the bathroom to prepare herself for the morning. When she came back from the bathroom, her food was already sent to the room. Richard pointed his chin to the direction of the food to indicate the food to her, "Your food is there."

Yin walked to the food and started eating her breakfast. She took a look at her watch. *It is 7:20 AM.* She remembered yesterday Richard asked Michael Hernandez, the driver, to come at 8 o'clock. She would still have half an hour before getting off for work.

Richard got off the bed when she was eating her breakfast and went into the bathroom to prepare himself. He would send Yin to the station later on. And after he came back, he would eat breakfast and then get ready to attend the conference held on the new address of the factory. He needed to wear suit today. When he came out from the bathroom 15 minutes later, he dressed himself up with the most expensive cologne, a white cotton dress shirt, an expensive beige suit and, at last, a plain cobalt blue tie. Yin observed how he dressed up himself and realized that he looked extremely charming with suit on. *He is indeed a dude.* When Richard finished dressing, he gazed at Yin with a nice smile, sounded like asking her how she thought about his wearing today.

She grinned at him without any comments. He looked so handsome and charming that she could not think up a suitable comment in a short time. She was too shy to comment on him or give him a compliment. After all, she did not like flatter others at all.

Time passed fast. It was almost 8 now. Yin had finished her breakfast. Richard took her downstairs to meet their driver. Michael Hernandez waited downstairs and drove them to Altimont Astronomical Station. On the way, Richard finally turned on his phone with caution. He and Yin exchanged their phone numbers and made a deal that he would pick her up at 3:30 PM, when she got off work. When they arrived to the station, Michael Hernandez let Yin get off the car. Yin waved to say goodbye to them and walked inside the station. Then Michael drove Richard back to the hotel.

It was 8:45 A.M.

When Richard took the elevator back to his room again, he called up the driver of RM Corps to pick him up in half an hour, ordered a breakfast, ate it and then went downstairs again.

The driver drove him directly to the address of the new factory.

There are many rows of folding chairs on the open-air ground. In front, a temporary wood stage with a speech table stood in the breezes.

It was 9:43 AM.

Richard was not the first to arrive. Many construction workers, staffs, the new president of the factory, who was also the vice president of RM Corps, and a dozen of executive directors and managers already waited on their seats. Richard greeted and waved to people when he stepped out from the car. Everyone had seen their boss in the photos in internal books published within RM Corps. And everyone knew their boss' face would never appear in media because he did not like the idea to be reported in newspapers or on TV, in any way. But when they finally had a chance to see this richest CEO in person and found out that he looked even younger than he was in the photos, they started whispering to one another.

A receptionist guided Richard to sit down in the middle of the first row, among executive directors and managers, next to John Jacobs, the president of the new factory and the vice president of RM Corps. Some of them had seen and talked to Richard in person. John Jacobs was appointed by Richard himself. Jacobs had had worked in the New York City headquarter of RM Corp for 15 years, as one of the vice presidents of RM Corps for more than 3 years, and helped Richard a lot, before he was appointed as the president of the new factory and still kept the vice president title. Richard trusted him a lot so gave him an important work opportunity.

"Hi, Richard, nice to see you here! Welcome to our new factory." John Jacobs said, offering his hand.

Richard shook his hand and said, "Hi, John, I think we are not strangers to each other. Nice!"

"I have arranged this conference for weeks. We are all very excited about building up the factory. We have waited you to come. Everyone wishes to see you in person." John Jacobs paused, smiling to Richard, and said, "I will give a talk today about the importance of our Altimont factory, just after your beginning talk."

"Nice!" Richard nodded and smiled, "You know, the factory will begin to be built up in less than a month. I very much look forward to seeing the influence of the factory."

They were still waiting for a few late comers.

It was 9:55 AM now and the conference was going to start in just a few minutes.

Finn didn't sleep well for the second day. After saying goodbye to Emily, who made the situation more complicated and started the rumor, he got back home, lying on the bed, wanted to fall asleep, but again could only think about the fact that Yin now "abandoned" him. When he finally fell asleep and got up the second day, he felt exhausted and dizzy.

He drove to the station, parked the car, went through the arrival report machine and directly took the elevator up to Yin' office. He didn't want to call her up earlier when Richard was around her. He knew they slept together in the same room, either in Yin's apartment or elsewhere, yesterday night. But he didn't expect that Yin did have sex with Richard. He knew Yin was a very conservative Chinese young lady. He needed to let her know the rumor was started. Sorry, it was my mistake again.

It was almost 9:00 o'clock.

Yin's office door was open. Finn looked inside and saw Yin was standing near the window and looking at the scenery outside. Actually, that had become one of her daily activities. She enjoyed the breezes and the bird's eye view of Altimont from the window

125

of her office. Even in cold winters, she would have a look at the snow view of the whole town before she started work.

"Yin." Finn walked towards her and put his hand on her shoulder.

Yin was startled to turn herself back towards Finn. She lifted her palm on her heart and said, "You startled me."

"Sorry, again it was my mistake. I have made too many mistakes. Thank you that you still treat me as a friend. I have something to tell you. Yesterday evening, after you left, I went out with Emily drinking in a bar. I was too sad that I was not careful enough. Sorry I made a mistake. She spoke in front of dozens of people that you rejected me and that now she was with me. Don't get me wrong, people are really nice in Altimont, but still they would gossip about it soon, even in a nice way. You should be careful not to let them know Richard was the visitor of the station. I mean even though you may leave here, but I don't want you to lose job before that."

Yin thanked Finn and said she would be careful about it, sent him out and then started her work.

34

The second day morning after being in the bar witnessing Finn Kane was with another woman, who seemed also to be a resident of the town, Joseph Smith, 65, the man with moustache who broadcasted the first hand rumor to people in the bar, after getting up, told his wife what he saw yesterday night. After his retirement three years ago, he somehow developed a hobby to go to the bar in the evening to talk to people, sometimes alone, sometimes with wife and friends.

"Mary, do you know what I saw yesterday in the bar, the one we usually go to?" Joseph Smith said, "Out of your imagination, it is almost confirmed that Yin Lin rejected Finn Kane."

"Oh, really? You mean Yin Lin, the well known scientist of Altimont Astronomical Station? Yeah, the man I think she should be with is someone named Finn, yes, Finn Kane, her colleague, right? She should be with him. You mean she rejected him? What happened that made you think so?" his wife stopped the housework she was doing and looked at him with surprise. She couldn't believe her own ears.

"Mary, yesterday, very late in the bar, I saw Finn Kane was with another lady. She told me Finn was rejected by Yin Lin, in front of him, and that now she is with him. I called people in the bar to come and they all confirmed he was Finn. When they were questioning him, he left the bar without a word against the starting rumor." Joseph told his wife.

"Oh, that is weird. All people know Finn Kane loves Yin Lin very much. People believe they will marry to each other one day. I personally like Yin Lin a lot, as everybody does. And I like to see them together. They match each other. He would not be with another woman late in the bar alone and be a coward facing people's questions, unless Yin Lin did break up with him." Mary, Joseph's wife, paused and then said, "There must be something happened between them? Do you think the other woman was the reason?"

Joseph was ready to go out to buy food for weekends. His two daughters with their husbands would come by in the Friday afternoon, as usual. His wife and he would prepare dinner for his family. His two daughters and their husbands were also the residents of Altimont. Surely, the rumor would be a hot topic in the family get-together.

Before he went out of the door, he spoke loudly to his wife, who continued to do the housework, "That could be, Mary. Or she has a new love."

There are two main purposes of the conference. One is, of course and easily to see, let every construction worker and staff of RM Corps be encouraged by Richard Meier, the CEO of RM Corps who everyone wanted to see in person; the second purpose is to give some reports, especially to Richard Meier himself, about the importance, the market and the environment risk of building up the factory.

After a short prologue, the host came to the point - Richard was introduced to people. He was described as the CEO of RM Corps. He stood up amid deafening applause, stepped on the stage right at the speech table and paused to wait for the applause stopped. He looked extremely cool and calm in his expensive suit and tie. When the long-lasting applause gradually stopped echoing on the ground, he started speaking through the microphone, "It is a really nice summer morning, isn't it? Warm but chilly. Good to see you guys here!" He heard applause and whispers again. Then after the noise decreased, he continued, "I have waited to see the factory to begin the process of construction for 5 years. Five years ago, I got the idea that RM Corps needed a large developed factory to start advanced research and apply the most advanced genetic technology in producing transgenic plants and genetically modified food, in order to keep RM Corps the leading status in both technology and market. Finally the day to build up the factory is decided to be the 15th of July, the coming month. I appreciate everyone's determination and hard work to build up the most important factory in the history of RM Corps. After my talk, a few leaders of our company will give important reports on related topics. Now let's welcome John Jacobs, the president of our new factory and the vice president of RM Corps."

With the sound of clapping among people, Richard Meier walked down the stage leisurely and sat down on his seat. John Jacobs followed him, walking towards the speech table from the side of the stage. Not letting the applause stop, he grinned and started talking, "Good morning, everyone. My name is John Jacobs, the president of Altimont transgenic technology factory of RM Corps and the vice president of RM Corps. It is my honor to be selected as the president of our new factory and to speak in front of you. Thanks for Mr. Meier to give me the opportunity! Thanks for our hard working staffs and construction workers to help prepare the conference! Today, before we finally can start our journey of building up the factory, we need to know some more details to guide us in the whole process, as required by Mr. Meier. We have three leaders who will give us reports today. I am the first one and I would like to talk a little bit about the status of this factory within the whole RM Corps." Jacobs told people that this factory would become the most advanced and important factory in RM Corps' history and that 300 researchers and experts of transgenic technology from 43 countries would work in this factory. He said all the construction and decoration would be done in one and a half year and the factory would begin to operate very soon after it is built up, in two years. At last he repeated that the date to start the construction would be July, 15th.

After John Jacobs, an executive director gave a 15 minutes' talk about the potential market of transgenic technology. He described that the market and the need of transgenic food grew larger and larger each year. He gave some data statistics about the increase of RM Corps' market and the whole market. Before he ended his talk, he introduced the next and last reporter, the environment department director of RM Corp in France, Janell Williams.

Richard Meier had paid close attention on the environment risk of the new factory. He listened to some reports from a score of environment experts in secret meetings held in New York City before, but none of them gave an actual effect on the environment. 90% of the experts expressed their worries on the potential environment risk and their recommendations to close the factory if heavy pollution took place; a couple of them did not show their worries.

Janell Williams was from France and was appointed to give the speech by John Jacobs. By Jacobs' direction, Janell Williams was going to ask Richard Meier and everyone else not to worry about the environment risk and give full trust to Mr. Jacobs.

She walked to the speech table and started to talk.

35

On the way to the food supermarket, Joseph Smith talked to a score of residents of Altimont; while he was shopping, he talked to another dozen of people including cashiers; on the way back home, two dozens. They would say "hello" to each other in general, in any other day, but today there was a common topic that they might chat about. Joseph Smith knew every one of the residents who he told the rumor would then tell scores of other residents. Including the ones who witnessed the rumor in the bar, he was sure very soon, within a couple of days, half of the residents of the town would hear about the rumor and once another two days passed, most residents of Altimont would all find out that Yin Lin had abandoned her former love. When people heard about the rumor, they mostly were very shocked and then started to guess the reasons behind this unbelievable news. And when they heard that Finn was with another lady in the late evening in the bar, the first impression to them was, Yin Lin broke up with Finn Kane because there was a third woman getting into their relationship. And they all felt sorry for Yin Lin if that was the case.

In the afternoon when his daughters came to his house, he could then discuss the rumor with them. *Maybe they already heard about the rumor before that.*

Standing behind the speech table, Janell Williams looked confident about what she was going to tell. Although it was within her expertise and, personally, like most other environment experts, she was sort of worried about the potential environmental risk of this new factory, she was told to convince Richard Meier to fully trust John Jacobs and give Jacobs the most authority. She said, after people stopped applauding, "Good morning, everyone. My name is Janell Williams, the environment department director of RM Corp in France. I have represented the French RM Corps and worked here in Altimont for two more years. It is my great honor to represent the French RM Corps to talk today. My topic is the potential environmental risk of Altimont transgenic technology factory." She paused for a few seconds, opening up her notebook and said, "As the two leaders of our company just said, Altimont transgenic technology factory will become the most important factory in our company's history. It will open up the market and do a great contribution to RM Corps. We all hope the new factory will bring RM Corps a new future. What Mr. Richard Meier concerns the most, however, is the environmental effect or its potential risk. I was requested by Mr. Jacobs to give an overall summary here about the potential environment risk of the new factory and how we should prevent the possible genetic pollution and other environmental pollutions." Janell Williams paused, turned her notebook to the next page, and then continued, "First I would like to explain to you what is genetic pollution. Genetic pollution is defined by the Food and Agriculture Organization of the United Nations, or FAO, as 'uncontrolled spread of genetic information into the genomes of organisms in which such genes are not present in nature'. This term is frequently used in the field of transgene, in the application of transgenic technology in agriculture and animal husbandry. The simple fact is that, when we operate the factory, we will mainly do advanced transgenic research and produce transgenic products. Those research and products will then have a chance to associate with the environment of Altimont, such as its plants and animals, and may possibly cause their genes changed. And we don't want that. So we need to find out ways to prevent those things from happening."

Richard Meier listened carefully as if this matter was more important than the money he was going to make.

132

Janell Williams turned her notebook one more page and observed the reaction of Richard Meier. Knowing that he paid full attention to her speech, she continued with more confidence, "From what I know, Mr. Richard Meier has concerns on this issue a lot. Mr. John Jacobs, on the other hand, worked very hard with the environment experts to find out practical ways to prevent the issue. He spent days and nights discussing this issue with our experts and he has promised to take measures to solve any potential problems. Here, I ask Mr. Meier to trust Mr. Jacobs and us. We promise to take care of the environment of Altimont."

Richard Meier finally smiled, hearing Mr. Jacobs and the environment experts of RM Corps had paid full attention to the environment. He glanced at Mr. Jacobs and started to applaud. Others followed his lead, starting to clap their hands.

Finally, Janell Williams talked about the other aspects of environment risk, the general pollution, such as the pollution of the air, the water and the land. But she was very positive about it and thought those kinds of pollution were not going to take place.

36

Yin worked hard in the morning. She was working on an important research which might bring her renown. She forgot everything else while working, as always. Not even the "renown" itself could affect her attention to the work. She did not think about Richard or their unexpected encounter before lunch time came, although she kept some physical pain which might remind her of him when she stood up and walked.

When lunch time finally came, Yin started to miss Richard, apart from him for three four hours. She dissolved into helpless laughter on the way to the cafeteria. She took out her phone and dialed Richard's number.

Richard just finished listening to Janell Williams' talk when the phone call came in. A short beep, he picked up the phone. He started the conversation, in a tone of command with soft voice, "Hi, baby, how is your work? I miss you all the morning."

Yin laughed out and said, "It is quite strange that I didn't miss you while I was working. I forgot about you totally. But now I do."

"You are the person who can only think about one thing at a time, I don't blame you. But you should miss me any time after work, including in dream." Richard teased her, "I will be at Altimont Astronomical Station at 3:30 to pick you up. You just go out and will see me. What are we going to do after that?"

"I will figure out later, probably another talk like yesterday?" Yin said, "And it is your turn to cook for me. Let's go to the market to buy some food for the weekends and you prepare dinner for me."

"I see. You do enjoy talking to me." Richard said, "We will have a very nice weekend."

"Hope so." Yin took a short pause and said she was going to eat lunch and go back to work soon. Before she hung up the phone, she told Richard she did miss him a lot now.

When she moved to the cafeteria, bought food and started eating, Finn sat down in the same table, across her. He pretended to look ok to Yin, keeping the bitterness inside himself. He wanted to make her forget what he told her yesterday. He uttered a forced little laugh and said nicely, "Yin, how is your research going?"

Yin took a look at him, reminding herself of their conversation yesterday. She was still pretty shocked about that he said he loved her for years without her knowledge. She did not want to believe it or rejected it might indeed happen. She did not want to interpret it so she did not feel uncomfortable about his words. After all, he was her close friend.

"It is pretty good, thanks." Yin paused a second and said, "How are you doing today?"

"Good."

"Glad."

"Do you still remember what I told you this morning before work started?" Finn was still worried about the potential rumor.

"Umm… Yes, you said you were witnessed in the bar with Emily." Yin had a bite, chewed and swallowed down the food, "Will they start the rumor?"

"Of course," Finn nodded, looking at Yin seriously, "I am almost sure all residents are going to gossip it in a few days. And of course, they will stand on your side, as always. You know they are proud of you. They will talk about why you 'broke up' with me. I mean, even though you and I knew we did not have a relationship, but in the eyes of others, they already thought we were about to be together. And they would first speculate it was because of Emily. But I am worried soon they will find out you are with another guy and finally and soon administration of the station will know that he

135

was even the visitor. You know that can cause your job. I don't like it."

"Ok." Yin stopped eating and asked, "So your meaning is I should not let people see I am with Richard?"

"No, not before you choose to leave."

The time in the afternoon passed quickly. Richard spent another hour on the site of the new factory, talking to Janell Williams and John Jacobs to form an idea if they actually spent enough effort in protecting the environment. He hadn't had talked to the vice president in person for almost half a year. Since three years ago, John Jacobs spent most of his time in Altimont, not in New York City. Richard trusted them more now. He also talked to some construction workers after that. He was indeed a very popular boss. Workers thought it was a great honor to shake his hands and listened to his interesting small stories. He was kind of humorous when he started to tell them his own small stories.

Another hour later, he asked the driver of his company to send him back to the hotel. On the way back, he asked Michael Hernandez to pick him up from the hotel at 3:00 PM.

When he arrived to his hotel room, he took off his beige suit jacket and the blue tie, only wearing the white dress shirt and the pants. He rested for a while and ordered some iced caramel macchiato. He was thinking about how to ask Yin to resign her job and go to New York City with him. It would not be easy for her. He knew he needed to guarantee another good job for her which would also bring her same kind of renown. He needed to encourage her to try staying in a big city. He needed to make her confident to their relationship and her future in New York City. As a leader, he was good at persuading people and negotiation. He knew it would help. What's more, he believed love can make a difference.

Sipping the drink, thinking about Yin and their last night, he looked at Altimont Astronomical Station in the far distance from the balcony.

At 3:37 PM, Yin walked out from the front door of the station. She immediately saw the Mercedes-Benz car. Richard waved his hand from the back seat. He had turned off his phone on the way to pick Yin up, worrying to receive phone calls from Judy Kahn when Yin was with him. He eliminated the ring of the phone all day and did not have a look at the miss call list before getting into Hernandez's car. Judy Kahn called him twice today and left messages. He did not listen to the voice mail. He would find out a better chance to talk to her again.

Yin opened the car door and tucked herself into the car. Immediately after she closed the car door, Richard put her into his arms and gave her a sudden lasting kiss, making her hard to breathe.

Hernandez drove down hill and towards the residential area.

37

When Richard and Yin arrived to her apartment, they carried a lot of food, most chosen by Yin, for the weekends and next week. Richard chose some food which he was going to cook for Friday evening. Yin lied on her bed and fell asleep. She was weary after a long day's hard work. She did not get enough sleep last night.

When she woke up, it was 8:30. Richard already cooked a dish for her. He brought Yin to the coffee table and pressed her to sit down on the couch. He sat down and began to use to fork to feed her. It was a dish of Jagerschnitzel, made of pork steak, which coated with eggs and bread crumb. It was a typical German dish. He also made some French fries and German red cabbage. He cut the steak into small pieces so that one time she could swallow down one piece. He said he had eaten a dish an hour ago. He said He was too busy to learn how to cook, yet he had learned a few German dishes from his mother. Yin said she could eat the food herself, yet Richard persisted in feeding her.

"I ask you to go to New York City with me." Richard said, stopping delivering food to her mouth and looking at Yin seriously. But when she took a glance at him, he forced a smile. He was waiting for her answer.

She said, "New York City? I mean, people like New York City because it has prosperity. Surely you can make more if you live there. Can I tell you more?"

Richard nodded, still waiting for her agreement.

Yin said, "As I said earlier, even though I almost cured my depression, but I got into obsessive compulsive disorder. And in the first 6 years after I came to the states, I over thought the bad experience of my high school education and gave myself too much stress. It almost drove me crazy. I was not happy at all with too much sorrow, even though it seemed I stopped being depressed. When I finally moved here 4 years ago, things changed. People have been so nice here and treated me fairly. The scenery is harmonious and peaceful. I easily adapted living here. I walked more slowly and even my thought slowed down when I was free. I finally could stop pushing myself over thinking the past and paid all of my energy and time into my career and the promising future. I finally found the happiness I had wanted. Now you ask me to go to New York City with you, I am not quite sure I can give up the happiness I have gained and the emotions I have towards Altimont. And also, I am worried I might not adapt life there and get sick. I am worried I would lose myself again. Richard, I am worried."

Richard listened carefully and now he had a better understanding of what she was considering. He knew what exactly what he needed to say.

It was a happy Friday evening. It was an evening for family get-together. Joseph Smith's family was eating family meal together. Earlier in the afternoon, at around 5:00 PM, his elder daughter Susan came to his house, bringing some seafood. She prepared dinner together with her mother Mary. They cooked the seafood and made some delicious salad. An hour later, the other daughter Sandra came in and went directly to the kitchen to help her mother and her sister. Upstairs, Joseph talked to his sons-in-law. After a short discussion about the weather and how they were doing in the past week, Joseph told them what he saw in the bar yesterday evening that Finn Kane was with a third woman and he accepted the woman's words that Yin Lin broke up with him. His sons-in-law expressed their surprise. They talked about how promising Yin Lin was for a while and whether the rumor was believable.

At 7:30, Susan, Sandra and their mother brought the cooked food to the table and asked the men came downstairs to eat dinner. When they started to eat, the topic started among them was the rumor about Yin Lin and Finn Kane.

"Did dad tell you about Yin Lin's news, James?" Sandra asked her husband James.

"Yes, we talked about it just now." James stopped chewing the fried chicken wing in his dish and said, "Dad told me that he saw Finn Kane was with another woman late in the bar drinking beer, and when she admitted that she was Finn's new girlfriend, he had nothing to say but left the bar."

"So what do you think?" Susan followed James, "I mean, as we all know, Finn Kane loved Yin Lin very much. How come he did not say anything against what people had seen if it was indeed not the case?"

Joseph Smith said, "So that means they actually broke up. No doubt for that."

"Yes, but why?" Sandra asked curiously with great interests, "Why would they break up? Is it because of the other woman, the one who was with Finn in the bar?"

"I would say so." Mary and Susan's husband Patrick replied almost at the same time. Patrick was not a very talkative person.

Mary continued, "It must be that the third woman got into their way and that Finn had to choose one from them and that he chose the other woman. Is she very pretty?"

"The other woman?" Joseph paused and then continued, "I would say she is nice looking but Yin would be more attractive and beautiful to a man."

James stopped eating again and said, "Of course, I have seen Yin Lin many times. She is tall and skinny with a pretty face. I would say she is the most attractive woman in Altimont."

Sandra glared at him.

Joseph said, "So it looks very odd that Finn Kane would abandon Yin Lin and go for the other woman."

"Yes, it is very strange." Every one responded.

"I think it could be that Yin Lin first mentioned ending up their relationship. Maybe she had another man?" Joseph said.

"Oh, you think so?" Sandra asked.

"Yes, it could be that case." James grabbed the topic, "I know Finn Kane. He and I have a mutual friend. He is a handsome man with a good heart. Unless the other man is more attractive than Finn, I doubt Yin Lin would abandon Finn."

"Or very rich." Susan said, "But I doubt it because Yin Lin could make a lot of money herself. She is not a gold digger."

It got late, yet the family's interests in this topic did not descend. Just don't know how many other families were also discussing the same topic at this moment.

38

Richard stuck the fork into a piece of the pork steak and delivered it to Yin's mouth. Waiting until she chewed and swallowed it down, he began to talk again, "Sweetheart, you worry too much. First, you don't need to worry about the cost of living there because I make enough money to support it. And the next is, I am sure that you will find out great opportunities there, just like here. I am sure there will be some great astronomical stations in New York State or New Jersey. I guarantee that you will work in an astronomical station near New York City. Is it ok? And I know you are worried about your previous or current emotional state. As I told you, New York City is a great city. I guarantee that you will be very happy there. You will find out many interesting things there. I will bring you to movies and go shopping on the weekends. We can go for a walk after work or after dinner. The most important thing is, you can stay with the man you love, forever. How sweet is that? Love is about romance and love is also about sacrifice. My business needs to stay in a big city like New York and there is no way right now for me to get away from it. I will explain this to you later when we arrive to New York City, as a surprise, and I am sure you will support my idea after hearing about my business. But right now you just need to trust me that I will bring you happiness and go to New York with me. I am not asking you to sacrifice your dream to be with me, not at all. I am just asking you to consider switching to another employer which will be as good. So what do you think?"

Yin sighed and glanced at Richard. Richard looked very seriously, waiting to hear her response. Yet she could not give a response he wanted right away. It would be a tough decision to make. She sighed again and asked, "Richard, are you in a rush to go back to New York City?"

Richard shook his head and said, "No. I will be here until you decide to go with me."

"Ok," Yin paused and then said, "is it possible you can give me a couple of weeks? I need to think about it for days. You know it is not easy for me to make a decision right now. I love you and I trust you for whatever you told me. I will have my answer with me in two weeks. How is that?"

Richard knew he had to wait. Yet he was more than confident that Yin would decide to go with him. *The longer she stays with me, the more she will love me.* He smiled to her and delivered another piece of pork steak to her mouth.

Yin bit the piece, chewed it and swallowed it down. "Richard, I forgot to tell you something," She said, "Finn told me this morning that he was seen with Emily, his friend, in a bar yesterday night. She told people in the bar that she was his new girlfriend. People said that Finn had been my boyfriend all the time. I just didn't take it seriously. You know people here like me very much. That is one of the reasons I haven't decided to move to New York with you. They stand on my side. Finn told me they would start the gossip and very soon all residents will know about it. I didn't tell you that there is a policy of Altimont Astronomical Station that the introducer can't contact with or be contacted by any visitor. It would end up being a disciplinary action. If the administration of the station knows you, as a visitor, have a sexual relationship with me, I will be fired easily. Finn asked me not to be seen with you in front of others to protect me from being fired. We have to pay attention to this, before I hand in the letter of resign."

"Ok, so just not go out for a walk. If we need to spend time in the hotel, we can just depart your apartment at different times, for example, I will walk to the hotel first, and half an hour later, you may leave your apartment. If we want to go to the hotel room directly from Altimont Astronomical Station after your work, we may just leave Michael's car at different times with a 15 minutes in between. In that case, no one would easily find out the relationship between us."

Yin nodded and said she wanted to eat more. Richard fed her with food in the dish.

After Richard left the presentation of new factory, John Jacobs took over the charge. He arranged a buffet for all the construction workers, staffs and executives for lunch at 1:40 PM, right after Richard left. After the buffet, most of them left the presentation and drove back to the apartments rented for them in the residential area. Some construction workers stayed there to do some cleaning, fold the chairs and detach the stage. John Jacobs would be the last one to leave. He was always dedicated to work and supervised every details of the work. He was as ambitious as Richard. No wonder why he became a vice president of a world-wide company at such a young age. He had worked in Altimont since three years ago, from the day he was appointed as the president of the new factory. Three years ago, when he first came to Altimont, he and his work team negotiated with residents here to rent dozens of apartment buildings for construction workers and himself. Of course they kept every move secret, as required by Richard. Richard did not want anyone who did not work for RM Corps knew too much about the factory, including the residents of Altimont. Richard especially did not want his competitor companies to gain any information about the factory and its technology. John Jacobs wanted to become the next CEO of RM Corps, after the retirement of Richard. He knew he was 14 years younger than Richard and was the youngest vice president of RM

Corps. He knew as long as he did a fine job in Altimont, no one else would be able to compete with him for the title.

Workers were waiting for a party held in a bar, the same one Finn and Emily were witnessed together Thursday night, on Friday evening. Richard said he would not be able to come and he wished they had a great time. After the workers finished the cleaning job on the presentation of the factory, it was almost the time for the party. After all the workers drove their cars left, John Jacobs drove his car directly to the bar.

39

When John Jacobs arrived to the bar, everyone was there already. People gave him a glance and then continued whispering. Three to five of them sat in the same table with food on the table. It seemed there was a fresh common topic among them. Janell Williams waved to him. She sat there alone and left a seat for him. He moved to her side and sat down next to her.

"Hi, Janell, I finished my work today finally." John Jacobs said.

A waitress came. He ordered some Italian food and a cup of red wine and then turned to Janell Williams, "What are people talking about?"

Janell Williams took a long sip of her drink, shrugged and said, "Well, it is not a big deal. It is about Yin Lin again. They said Finn Kane was seen in this bar yesterday with another woman and that Yin Lin broke up with him. You know, many of our construction workers are new to Altimont. They would love to know who Yin Lin is. Now the ones who work here longer are telling them things about her. But it is a little bit surprising that she broke up with Finn Kane, isn't it?"

In the past three years, John Jacobs had heard enough about Yin Lin. Not like the residents of Altimont, he did not concern as much about Yin Lin's activities. But all the time, once there was a piece of news about her, even the smallest one, he would be told within days. He never met her in person or saw her photos, but heard that she was both extremely smart and beautiful. She was well known in Altimont. More or less, he wanted to meet her in person. *Something clear is that the more you integrated into Altimont, the more you would love to discuss the news about her.*

"Oh?" John Jacobs took a short pause and said, "I have heard that she was very beautiful. Is it true? I mean, how beautiful is she?"

Janell Williams said, "Once I went to a grocery store, last year, the owner of the store told me the young lady paid before me was Yin Lin. I did not have a chance to look at her face to see how beautiful she is, but her shape was very attractive to men and her long hair was very beautiful too. I have heard that she is the most beautiful lady in Altimont. I would say she is very pretty."

"Oh, yeah… Then how about Finn Kane? Is it also very handsome?"

"That I don't know. But I have heard that he is a very good man and people expected that Yin Lin would marry to him before." Janell Williams said.

"Then why would they break up? I am not stupid. She is such a beautiful young woman, as you described. He would not make her upset by getting closer to another lady." John Jacobs grinned at Janell Williams. Jacobs was a very smart man and was known for his keen insight within the company.

"You are so smart, John." Janell Williams smiled, "Yeah, I thought it was odd, too. Unlikely he would do that. So what do you think?"

The waitress brought his food to the table. People were still discussing.

Jacobs said, "It seems the reason is that he has another lady, but it is not the case. The fact would be that she has another man. And he was just sad and needed to talk to his friend in the bar."

"No wonder why Finn Kane did not say anything when the other lady said she was his new girlfriend. He must be very sad."

"Yeah… And I am sure soon people will find out who the other man is."

Jacobs started to eat his dinner. He somehow had great interests to know who would win her heart.

40

While Richard was feeding Yin, there was a sudden thought came up to her mind. It was just a thought, hadn't grown into a concern. She suddenly realized that Richard did not wear condom and ejaculated inside her yesterday. *Will I get pregnant?* She did not have too much knowledge in pregnancy, except knowing the fact that if a woman did not have her period over 10 days after the regular day she should have the period, then it was possible that she got pregnant. She remembered last month she began to have the period on the 20th, so she inferred that she should have the period no later than the 20th this month, which was next Monday. *Today is Friday and let me wait till next week to see if I will have the period.* She did not think too much about it, smiled to Richard and enjoyed the food.

In the next few days, Yin told Richard that her vagina was still in pain and refused to have sex with him. He understood it quite well so did not require more. They had a very nice weekend just talking to each other about their stories. Richard told Yin some interesting events he had and countries he traveled to. In return, Yin explained more Chinese culture to him and taught him some simple Chinese language.

From Monday through Wednesday, Richard sent Yin to work in the early morning and picked her up at 3:30 in the afternoon. He kept his phone turned off, not being bothered by anyone, and was seeking a good time in which he had the mood and Yin was not with him to call Judy Kahn to explain a little bit more and negotiate the restitution.

On Wednesday afternoon, Yin still did not have her period. After work, when she took the elevator downstairs and walked to the front door of the station, she began to worry and think about it more. However, she did not plan to tell Richard about her concern. She knew she needed to wait a few more days to decide if she needed to get a pregnancy test. At the mean time, she thought about going to New York City with Richard. She was still worried if she would adapt life there. *There are too many unknown factors.* She could not really decide to leave such a wonderful town. However, as long as she thought about that she could live with

Richard forever, she did not mind living there. She hesitated between these two strong emotions, the one she had towards the town and the one she had towards Richard, and the more she stayed with Richard, the more she thought she could make a decision.

On the way to the station to pick Yin up, Michael Hernandez told Richard that today he heard a rumor that Yin Lin broke up with Finn Kane. He said Finn Kane was seen in a bar with another woman; however, only a couple of the residents knew the reason they broke up was because Yin Lin was engaged to Richard. He told Richard he could have heard the rumor way earlier but recently the only client for his business was Richard and so he did not go out of his house as often as usual. Richard asked Michael to keep it secret that he was now Yin's fiancé. He told Michael he did not want people to know he was the visitor, or to know him at all because the policy of Altimont Astronomical Station did not allow employees to contact any visitor for any personal reason.

Yin got into the car. Again, Richard hugged her in his embrace and started to kiss her lips. Waiting till them stopped, Michael Hernandez greeted Yin, started to drive and told her about the rumor he heard.

He said, "Yin, I heard a rumor today. It was about Finn Kane and you. It seems many people have known this fact and gossip about it now. They told me Finn Kane was with another lady, in a bar, on Thursday evening. And when people questioned him, he left the bar without saying a word. You know Richard is my client, so I definitely would not tell people about him without his consent. However, no one seemed to believe the reason you left Finn Kane was because he got closer to another lady. You know what I mean, right? You are so smart, so pretty that they simply don't believe he would leave you for another lady."

Not knowing what exactly was said among people, Yin was not very surprised about it. Finn told her about it last Friday and she had told Richard. She glanced at Richard, turned to Michael and said, "So?"

"So…" Michael Hernandez paused for a second and said, "People now start to suspect that you have another man which caused you left Finn Kane. And they are curious about who the man is. As I said just now, I would not tell anyone else, except my wife, about Richard and I asked my wife not to tell anyone else, too. But people will eventually find out. I heard from Richard just now that the policy of Altimont Astronomical Station ruled that employees are not allowed to contact any visitor. Is it true?"

"Yes, indeed." Yin nodded, again looking at Richard to seek support.

"Ok, so…" Michael Hernandez said, "Are you planning to move to New York City with Richard?"

"Most likely, yes. I mean, if that is what Richard wants." Yin said and smiled to Richard.

Richard kissed Yin and said, "Of course, she will move to New York City with me."

"When will you hand in the letter of resign? People here are going to miss you." Michael Hernandez laughed out, continuing driving.

"Not sure yet, maybe in two weeks?" Yin said.

Soon, they arrived to Yin's apartment. Yin gave keys to Richard and asked him to go back home to cook dinner first. She asked Michael Hernandez to drive her to a nearby grocery store to buy a bottle of green tea lemonade. She suddenly wanted to drink green tea lemonade.

Yin was now in a grocery store choosing drinks. Minutes ago, he told Michael Hernandez that she wanted to go for a walk and that she could walk home herself. He asked her again if she wanted him to wait for her. She said no, so after letting her get off the car, he drove back to his home directly. She picked up four bottles of her favorite green tea lemonade, two for herself and two for Richard. *He will like it.* She first wanted to buy some more drinks because there were only Chai tea and pepsi at her home. However realizing Michael drove home and she had to walk to her apartment, she gave up the idea and moved to the counter. She took out her black Calvin Klein wallet. The staff of the store immediately recognized her and greeted her.

"Hi, Yin Lin, how are you doing today?" The staff grinned at her.

"It is really a nice day." Yin said, smiled back to him.

The staff already heard the rumor between Finn Kane and her and he was curious to know what exactly happened between them. As many others, he did not believe Finn Kane would break up with her for another woman. He wanted to know more from Yin's mouth so he asked, "May I ask what happened between Finn and you? Everyone knows that you break up with him."

Yin pretended not knowing the rumor. She still smiled to the staff and was ready to pay.

"Ok." The staff took the money from her and put it in the cash register. Picking the change for her, he said, "Is it because you chose another man? We heard that he was with another lady, but no one believes it. I think you have another man."

Knowing that anything she said might become the next rumor and might impact her job, she rather kept it as simple as possible. She said, the same as her always response to the topic about Finn and her, "Well, Finn and I are always good friends."

"Ok." The staff handed the change to her and said, "No matter what, we all hope you are happy."

She thanked the staff, wished he had a great day and then left the store.

Finn was right. Soon they will find out about Richard. I have to make a decision as soon as possible.

41

To Richard, time flies when he was with his true love. Soon it was Friday. Getting back to the hotel room after sending Yin to the station, Richard finally turned on his phone. After all, he was a CEO of a big company and needed to concern his business, even on vacation. There were 18 voice messages. As the founder of the business, he concerned the details of his company. Not everyone within the company knew his phone number. But surely, if a manager thought there was a need to mention something to him, he would love to have a listen. He listened to the voice messages one by one. Among them, there were a couple of messages by Judy Kahn. She still hoped Richard could walk back to her life. He was not ready yet to call her back. He moved to the computer in the room, sat down on the chair and turned on the computer. He spent the next hour reading and responding the emails.

An hour later, just about he was finishing the work with the emails, a phone call came in, from John Jacobs. John Jacobs did leave a message to Richard earlier asking Richard to go out for a meal. Richard picked up the phone.

"Good morning, Richard."

"Good morning."

"We hadn't had seen each other for half a year. I just would like to invite you for a lunch or dinner. We may talk about the new factory more if you wish. How is that?"

Richard first wanted to spend every moment of the weekends with Yin and he first thought, on weekdays when Yin was at work, he surely could go out to meet Jacobs. However, it would have to be in a day in which Jacobs was available, too. Richard knew Jacobs was quite busy preparing the construction ceremony and the construction itself on weekdays, so Jacobs might not have time on weekdays.

With a moment pause, Richard responded, "Good idea. When is that?"

"You know I need to worry a lot of things on workdays. How about the coming Sunday to eat dinner together? I know a good restaurant. Shall I come to pick you up?"

Richard said, "I hope so. You know which hotel I live in, right? Can you come at 4 o'clock in the afternoon?"

"Yes, I know where you live and no problem, see you at 4. I may need to get back to work now. Quite busy…"

Richard said goodbye to Jacobs and hung up the phone. It was almost 10:30 AM.

Richard then called up Victor Dupont to ask how things were going in the company and which the documents are handed in to his office. Then he ate lunch and took a nap. When he woke up, it was the time the pick Yin up.

After a long busy week, Finn at last had a chance to visit Yin's office on Friday after work at 3:23 PM, before Yin left her office. This week, except they had a couple of short talks in the cafeteria at noon, Finn did not call Yin up any other time. He knew she enjoyed the time with her fiancé and soon she would move to New York City and leave him. He needed to learn how to enjoy life without her, even though he thought it was unlikely that he would fall in love again. He knew he needed to start the learning from this week. *The sooner, the better.*

When Finn arrived to Yin's office, she was about to leave her office. Her door was open. He stood at the door quietly, looking at her. She just tidied up her desk and was now moving to the cabinet to reach her bag. Then she noticed him. A smile appeared on her face. Even though his eyes were full with sentiment, he responded by giving her a same type of smile.

For a few seconds, they both did not know what to say. Yin broke the silence, "Hi, Finn, what are you doing here?"

Finn shrugged his shoulder, paused for a second and asked, "Just would like to find out how you are doing."

154

"I am fine. Thank you, my friend..." Yin said, in a low voice, trying to understand how Finn was feeling, "I am doing great... How about yourself? Didn't have time to call you this week. Come and sit down."

Finn came a step further and sat down on the other chair near the door. Yin walked back to her desk and sat down on her leather chair.

Finn said, "I am ok... I am fine... Just..." Paused for a moment, he finally had the courage to ask out the question, "Would like to know when you will move?"

"Move? Move where?" She was puzzled and then realized what he was trying to ask. She said, "New York City?"

"Right." Finn asked again, "When will you move to New York City?"

"Well, it is a good question." Yin touched her forehead, thought for a second and said, "To be honest, most likely I have already decided to move to New York with Richard. You know I love Altimont and could not decide to move, but it is impossible for me to keep the job with Richard being my fiancé. And he needs to stay in New York for his business, too. You are right that love is how much you are willing to sacrifice for the other. I am going to write the letter of resign on the weekends and will hand it in next Monday. And then after that, we will just decide when to move."

Finn listened carefully and nodded. He looked at the watch and said, "Good... I know he is waiting for you. Let you go now. Don't forget me when you go to New York City... I will be always here for you."

Yin went to take her bag, turned off the light, closed her office door and walked with Finn to the elevator. After they took the elevator downstairs, Yin said goodbye to Finn and walked to the front door. Finn walked back to his office in another building.

Yin appreciated Finn's words a lot, even though she did not tell him that.

I will not forget our friendship, never ever.

42

Along the Friday night and the whole Saturday, Yin had been paying attention to the potential pregnancy. She was kind of paranoid. It was going to be the end of the week and she hadn't had her period which was supposed to come before the past Monday. She had not been crazy about the idea of having a child. Before she met Richard up, all she wanted was to be with good friends sometimes and to be alone the rest of the time. Actually, she enjoyed being alone. She had not had expected to have a fiancé, get married and have a child. Yet as long as thinking about to have a child whose father was the man she truly loved, she felt sweet.

Yin spent time with Richard in his hotel room all Saturday. She told him her decision to move to New York City with him and the plan to hand in the letter of resign next Monday and that she needed to spend time in writing the letter. She needed to think up good reasons why she wanted to resign, express herself well in the letter and wish Altimont Astronomical Station the best. In the past four years, she put too much emotion in this town and her job and now it was finally the time to say goodbye. As part of Chinese culture, she knew the fact that men are subject to the sudden changes of fortune as the moon is subject to the changes of being full and crescent, cloudy and clear. So as she was able to be with Richard forever, she shouldn't feel too sad to leave Altimont.

The whole morning, after the breakfast which Richard asked Yin to take for her health, they discussed how to write the letter of resign. Richard gave Yin good ideas. For example, he said she might just say it in a simple way that she wanted to move to a new location to start a new life and nothing more. She took this idea and started to write on the computer. While she was writing, Richard thought about how to explain to her that he needed to go out for a few hours tomorrow afternoon. An hour later, Yin finished the first draft. Richard asked her to take a rest for the protection of her eyesight.

And then he said nicely, "Will you allow me to have a dinner with an old friend who was also in Altimont for his work tomorrow afternoon? If you don't agree, I just won't go."

In the first place, Yin felt a little bit strange that Richard would have an old friend who lived in Altimont but she trusted Richard a lot to a point that she did not want to ask further about who that friend was.

"What time will you leave for dinner?" She asked.

"4 o'clock." He smiled to her, "I will be back in a few hours. I will call you immediately after dinner."

"No problem, you can just go." She said.

He kissed her and said, "Thank you, my wife. I will bring some food for you."

Richard left the hotel room at 3:45 PM on Sunday before he turned on his phone. Yin was writing her final draft of the letter of resign and asked him to take the door card in case she also wanted to go out later. He asked her where she wanted to stay tonight. She said it was ok to stay in the hotel. He persisted to leave the door card to her but she rejected. He said he would call her after dinner. Soon after he left the hotel room, John Jacobs called in and told Richard he would arrive in a few minutes.

Richard sat in the lobby for a couple of minutes before Jacobs arrived. Then Jacobs drove Richard to a restaurant Jacobs was familiar with. He asked Richard if he was hungry. Richard said he would have to leave in two hours so it was the best to order food now. They ordered their favorite food and waited on their seats. After talking about the weather for a little while, comparing the nice weather of Altimont and that of New York City, Jacobs suddenly remembered the rumor he heard recently about Yin Lin. He started this topic with Richard.

"There is an interesting rumor that all residents of Altimont are gossiping about it now. I guess you haven't heard about it yet." Jacobs said.

Richard raised his eyebrows. He knew it was about Yin and Finn Kane. He was surprised to know that even Jacobs heard about the rumor now. He pretended not to know about what Jacobs was going to tell and said, "Oh? What is it about?"

"There is an interesting woman. I have never seen her in person. But she is described to be both highly intelligent and extremely pretty. You know Altimont Astronomical Station, right?" Jacobs described with great interests, "She is very popular in Altimont, more than you can imagine. She works for Altimont Astronomical Station as a researcher. Three years living in this town, I heard enough about her. She was expected to marry a man named Finn Kane, also a young man, who is her colleague. The recent gossip is about that she broke up with him. They said Finn Kane was seen with another lady but I am sure it was because she had another man… I am a married man; otherwise I would want to meet her. You too, Richard. I know you are going to get married, so just forget about it."

Richard smiled to Jacobs, pretending that the gossip was somewhat interesting. He was not ready to tell Jacobs that he was indeed the man who Jacobs thought caused Yin Lin to break up with Finn Kane. *I can't tell him that before Yin is approved of leaving Altimont Astronomical Station.*

Soon after Richard left, Yin was done with the final draft of the letter of resign. Setting her mind out of the task, she again began to think about the potential pregnancy. Not knowing if Richard wanted to have a child, she told herself there was nothing to worry about. *If I get pregnant, he would be more than happy to become a father.* As for her reasonable "paranoia", which sometimes could be taken in the wrong way, she suspected that she did get pregnant based on the missed period. *I need to find out the truth as soon as possible.* Richard happened not to be with her. She thought it was a great time to get a pregnancy test now and give Richard a surprise later on when he came back. She smiled to herself and then dialed Finn's cell phone number.

"Finn, is that you?" Yin said.

Finn smiled and said, "Yes, it's me. What's going on? Are you with your fiancé?"

"No, he is away." She paused and said, "I have something to tell you."

"What's that? You are not going to tell me you broke up with him, right?" Finn laughed out.

"I think I get pregnant." Yin continued, "How can I get a pregnancy test?"

"Oh, really? That soon?" Finn was startled because he thought Yin would not have sex before she actually get married. *But nothing to complain, they were getting married anyway.* He continued, "Congratulations! But why do you think you get pregnant first?"

Yin said, "I haven't had my period for this month. I was supposed to have it last week. It would not be later than the past Monday. But today it is Sunday already."

"Ok, understand." Finn paused, thinking and then responded, "So let's go to a clinic now, ok? I know there is a walk-in clinic which can get you a pregnancy test."

"Ok, let's go there now."

43

It was 4:40 in the afternoon.

Finn arrived to the hotel to pick Yin up. He drove her to a walk-in clinic which she could get the pregnancy test right away without making an appointment. The clinic was not far, only 12 minutes' drive. On the way to the clinic, Finn did not ask her any questions regarding her concern. He told her the information about the urine test that she was going to get and how he got to know this clinic. It would take no more than 15 minutes to get the result and the accuracy was believable. She listened to his explanation carefully and kept silent.

Soon they arrived to the clinic. Finn parked his car on the side of the street and brought Yin into the clinic. She signed in and the receptionist asked for her ID and asked her a few questions. Then she was requested to sit in the waiting area. Finn sat down beside her. They did not talk too much. Finn asked her to relax. After 15 minutes, Yin was asked to go into a door. Then the door was closed after her.

It had been a long hour before Yin finally walked out from the door with the result held in her hand. Finn stood up, wondering what the result is.

"Finn, I am pregnant!" Yin walked to Finn, looked amazed, even though the result was not out of her expectation.

"Congratulations!" Finn smiled to her, "I am happy for you."

Yin smiled without a word.

Finn continued, "When are you going to tell your fiancé the news?"

"I don't know." Yin said. Not that she did not know the answer, but all she was thinking now was only the joy to be a mother.

They walked slowly to the outside, towards the car. Finn opened the car door to let Yin get into the car and then walked to the other side and tucked himself into the car. He asked Yin where to go. Yin said she was waiting for the phone call from Richard and before that, she had no idea where to go. Finn drove her to a small park near the hotel. They got out of the car and walked towards a long bench.

It was in the midsummer. The melodious chirp of birds awaked everything, making it looked full of vitality. The bench was one of the five benches located on the side of a winding road. On the mint green grass, every 20 feet, there is a tall tree which had developed dense green leaves.

Yin felt a sudden sense of contentment.

They sat there for a while before her phone rang. Finn asked her to take care of herself and her baby. He told her his knowledge about what a pregnant woman would pay attention to, such as the food and rest. She told Finn that she had already made the decision to move to New York City with Richard. She said she had already finished writing the letter of resign and was going to hand it in to Ms. Frost tomorrow.

Finally, her phone rang. She picked up the phone.

"Baby, I am done with the dinner. I miss you. Where are you?" From the other end of the phone, it came the familiar charming voice.

"Hi, Richard, I am in a park with Finn. Are you going back to the hotel now?" Yin smiled.

Hearing Yin was with Finn, Richard got very jealous to a point of anger. Yet he tried to make his voice sound very calm and nice, acting like he accepted it, "Baby, I am in the hotel room waiting for you. Come back now."

She first wanted to tell him that she was pregnant on the phone, but when the words almost came out from her mouth, she requested herself to wait till later when she could talk to him in person. She wanted to see his expression when he heard the news.

After the phone call, Finn drove Yin back to the hotel.

It was 7:53 PM.

Richard couldn't wait to see Yin. He thought about her all of the time. When he talked to John Jacobs about the other details of the factory and the future of the whole RM Corps, after the topic about Yin, he still had her in his mind. Not like Yin who could only concentrate on her research when she was working, Richard could think about her when he was at work or having a conversation. All the way Jacobs sent him back to hotel, he missed her. He couldn't wait to kiss her and touch her.

So when she rang the door bell, he immediately opened the door, hugged her inside the door, closed the door and started to kiss her lips. He lifted her by his two arms, walked to the bed and put her on the bed, continuing kissing her. She stopped him and turned her body to the other side.

"Still not comfortable, baby?" Richard asked in a nice tone.

"I... I am ok." Yin said, thinking, "Richard, I... I...I have a ..."

Richard already got off the bed and walked towards the bathroom. He said, "I am taking a shower first. I was sweat. Do you want to shower together with me?"

"I want to rest for a while first." Yin paused and said, "I am sweaty."

Richard went into the bathroom and closed the door behind him. Two minutes later, while Yin was still thinking how to tell Richard the news that he was becoming a father, Richard's phone rang. His phone was put on the nightstand. This afternoon when he went out of the hotel room, he turned on his phone and turned the volume up so that Jacobs could contact him for the dinner, but he forgot to turn off the phone later on. It was 15 minutes past 8 o'clock. Yin took Richard's phone from the nightstand. On the screen of the phone, it showed the caller's name is Judy Kahn. *A woman called Richard after 8 o'clock? Who would that be? His friend who he had dinner with?* Yin immediately became so curious to know who this woman is. Believing the woman was just Richard's friend, maybe an old and close friend, she felt kind of jealous. Like she also had male friends, not that she did not want Richard to have female friends, but she needed to let her know that Richard now had a fiancée and the space the friend needed to give to the couple. Her instinct told her to pick up the phone. So she did it.

44

Yin did not feel good to pick up Richard's phone even though her instinct told her to pick up the phone. It was not because she suspected anything, not trust Richard, not because of her paranoia, but because of her strong curiosity to know one of his friends and her dignity to let his friends know about their relationship. *If he could pick up my phone, why can't I pick up his phone?*

From the other end, a woman's voice came in, "Richard, I called you a few times this week. Last time we talked, you hung up the phone without letting me say more. I guess you have another woman beside you. You know I miss you so much."

"Miss you so much?" What is she talking about?

"Hello, may I ask who you are?" Yin finally spoke, with anxiousness, "Nice to meet you. I am Richard's fiancée."

From the other end, the woman started laughing out loud, "Fiancée?" Again, from the phone came a wild bray of laughter, making Yin kind of uncomfortable, "Finally catch the cheating. You are the other woman who tucks in between Richard and me. I am his wife, don't you understand? I don't know what kind of methods you use to seduce Richard so that he did not pick up my phone calls. Please leave Richard alone."

Judy Kahn sensed Richard was not with the woman. And of course she knew her lie would be given to the fallacy once Richard came back. It was clear to her that there was no hope for Richard to come back to her life again. Yet she felt good to make Richard's current fiancée, who she believed "stole" her fiancé, feel bad, even this could only last for a few moments.

There was a sudden vacuum inside Yin. She was too naïve to believe Judy Kahn's words. She suddenly felt dizzy and weak, fell down to the bed. The phone fell from her hand to the bed. She picked it up and put it back to the nightstand. She curled up herself to keep from feeling cold. Tears almost spread out from her eyes.

He is married. He lied to me.

10 minutes later, Richard came out from the bathroom. Seeing Yin lying on the bed still and facing the other side, he walked directly to the bed and sat beside her.

"My wife, you are not comfortable?" Richard asked nicely, in a low voice, with a smile.

Hearing he said "my wife", Yin's heart even more ached. She pretended falling asleep and did not answer him. Actually, she did not even know how to face this liar. Maybe she somehow still hoped the woman's words were not true, even though she believed what the woman told her. She doubted a woman would make such a lie for no reason. But as long as thinking about if she questioned Richard and if he had to admit that he had a wife, it was not just embarrassing, it would be the period to their relationship.

I don't want to hear his words. Finn was right. I have to leave.

Richard thought she fell asleep so he turned off the light and lied beside her. A long day's work got him fatigued. He moved closer to her and softly put his arm on her.

Baby, I love you. I couldn't live without you.

An hour passed, Yin did not fall asleep. She knew Richard fell asleep and it was the time for her to leave. She did not want to leave Richard. She felt extremely painful to leave him, especially now that she had his child. Yet she did not want to take the chances to hear his admission that he was indeed a married man and that she was not going to be his wife. She would rather leave.

Yin lifted his arm from her body, kissed it and put it on the bed. She took a last long gaze at Richard, trying to remember what he looked like. Maybe it was the last time that she could gaze at him like this. *He is the most handsome man I have ever seen. But he does not belong to me.*

She then went out of the room and left the hotel, going directly to her apartment.

Finn just lied on the bed when his phone rang. He was just back home from a long walk. He was tired. It was almost half past ten, too late for a phone call coming in. He impatiently picked up the phone without looking at who was calling.

"Hello?" He got a little bit annoyed.

"It is me, Finn."

"Yin? What happened?" Finn's voice immediately became patiently, yet mixed with anxiousness. He knew there was something happened, even though not sure what it was exactly. Something about Richard.

"Can you come to my apartment?" Yin sounded sad.

"Now?" Finn said, trying to figure out what was going on between her fiancé and her.

A moment silence.

"Ok, I know. I will be there in a moment. Just give me a few minutes.

45

When Yin opened the door of her apartment, she immediately swooped on to Finn. Finally, she couldn't help crying out. Finn hugged her waist, moved inside and closed the door behind him. He stood there, hugging her and kissing her forehead, as a way of consolation, until she stopped constant choking. He wiped her tears and then hugged her towards the couch and sat down.

"Yin, tell me what happened?" Finn asked anxiously, patting her back to calm her down.

"Richard lied to me. He is a married man! He has a wife." Yin said, not looking at Finn's eyes, avoiding the guilt of not listening to her best friend and his accusing look. Tears suddenly spread out again.

Finn took a couple of facial tissues and helped wipe Yin's falling tears. He was quite shocked about what she had just told him. He did not want her to feel guilty in any way. He knew how she felt at this moment. Even though Finn also believed Richard might be a liar, just as what he worried about a week and a half ago, he still doubted that Richard would be willing to abandon Yin, such a wonderful young woman, after they had sex and she was pregnant. Finn asked nicely, wanting to console Yin, "Are you sure about it? Did he ever tell you this himself?"

"No," Yin paused, exhaled and continued, "but his wife called him and I picked up the phone by accident. He had dinner with an old friend earlier. I guessed it might be his friend calling so I picked up the phone. But then the woman told me that she caught the cheating and she accused that I am the other woman."

"Unbelievable! You are not the other woman." Finn got a little bit annoyed about what the other woman accused Yin, "Did you question Richard about the truth? Did you tell him that you are pregnant?"

Yin thought for a little bit and said, "Finn, why would any woman make such a lie, especially when she knew Richard and Richard saved her name and her phone number in his phone? He is married. I am the other woman no matter whether I admit it or not. He lied to me. He has a wife and maybe children. He just wanted sex from me, nothing more."

Finn asked Yin again, "Did you ask him about what the woman said? Did you tell him that you are pregnant?"

"Why does it matter? The truth is that he lied to me. I am not that important to him." Yin tried to avoid the questions.

Finn kept arguing in a nice way, "I think you are trying to avoid the truth. You are worried about his own words because you love him so much. You don't want to hear that he tells you himself that he lied to you. I can understand you. But if you don't question him and hear his words, you may regret it later on. I don't think he would abandon you, such an attractive and intelligent young woman. If you tell him that you are pregnant, I am almost sure that he will leave his wife and marry you."

"Finn, I really don't know what to do." Yin cried out again, wiping her tearful eyes. She kept silent for a while, thinking and then said, "But I really can't face him. I don't want to marry a man who was not truthful to me, even if I love him very much."

Finn could understand Yin now. He asked, "Ok, I can understand you. But what are you planning to do? Leave him? Do you still plan to bear the child?"

"Of course, I love him and want his child." Yin said, "But I think I have to leave him. Finn, you are right about that love is about sacrifice. I could sacrifice to leave Altimont for him. I could sacrifice to leave my current job for him. I could sacrifice to try to adapt living in a big city. And I had made those decisions. Yet he lied to me. Does he love me? How much does he love me? How could he lie to me if he truly loves me? Even if he does love me, I would not forgive him for his lies. I have to leave him. Period."

They sat there for a while and kept silent, thinking about each other's words. Finn exhaled heavily for several times. Finally, he broke the ice, "Yin, I know how you feel about this. I am sorry about it. But if you did not talk to him, where was he when you picked up his wife's phone call? Where is he now?"

Yin said, with a pair of swollen and red eyes, "We were in the hotel. He was in the bathroom when I picked up the phone. I left him later when he fell asleep. I did not tell him about the phone call. He is now sleeping in the hotel."

Finn said, "Ok. Do you know when Richard will leave Altimont?"

Yin said, "Before he said he would wait till I agreed to move to New York City with him."

"Let me think. That is not a difficult situation… Let's pack your cloths and move to my home. Get some rest and then at around 4:30 AM, we will leave Altimont and go to anywhere else. Tomorrow morning, I will call up Altimont Astronomical Station to ask for two months off for both of us. And I will call up all people I know in Altimont and tell them that we are on a vacation. Very soon people will gossip about our 'reunion', as they are now discussing about our 'break up'. You know, once you give birth to the child, people will think I am the father of the child. We don't need to have any romantic relationship other than friendship if you wish. I am not asking you to tell your child that I am his father, but not letting residents know about the truth seems to be the best way to protect you and your baby from rumors. During the vacation, you will have time to get yourself together. As for Richard, I think he will go to your home, my home and the station to look for you. As long as he does so, he will find out easily that we left Altimont for a vacation together. He will be desperate and leave Altimont, especially he has a wife. He should have had nothing to do with you from the beginning. How does this idea sound?"

Yin knew Finn, as a good friend, tried to protect her from rumors. *It is the only way if I want to stay in Altimont.* She slightly nodded.

Based on the policy of Altimont Astronomical Station, there would be up to two months vacation time for a researcher annual. The time was flexible. You could either use it or skip it. Yet for most researchers in the station, they wanted to devote more time to work so they usually wouldn't take the whole two months off. There was another policy – a pregnant researcher might ask for a whole year off from work. So Finn recommended Yin to take the whole year off after they came back from the "vacation".

After 10 minutes during which Yin tried to calm herself down, they packed her cloths and locked the door. It was fifteen minutes to the midnight. Walking on the streets towards Finn's home, Yin felt cold. No cars passed the street. No bicycles. The lights were turned off in every neighbor's homes. It was dark on the streets even though with Some English lights scattering around the corners. The sky was shining with stars, as any other day during the summer time. Yin thought of a famous Chinese idiom "the things are still there but men are no more the same ones". *Yes, the sky is still as beautiful as yesterday, yet we cannot go back to the past. We changed or time changed us.*

Twelve minutes later, they arrived to Finn's home. Finn opened the door, turned on the light and invited Yin to come into the house. Yin felt weak and tired. Finn asked her if she was hungry. She shook her head and asked Finn where she could sleep tonight. Finn brought her upstairs directly to his room and told her she could sleep in his room and he would sleep in the other room. He told her he would wake her up tomorrow early morning at 4 o'clock and they would have to leave before 4:30.

After wishing her a good night, Finn closed the door of the room. Yin lied down on the bed, exhausted, and soon felt asleep.

A dark night.

46

Finn went into the other room, set up his alarm clock to 3:50 AM and lied on the bed, thinking about the earlier conversation with Yin. He couldn't count how many days within these one week and a half that he couldn't feel asleep. He felt tired earlier before Yin called him up. He thought he could finally have a good sleep tonight. But after the hours he spent with Yin, it seemed it was again another night which he couldn't fall asleep. Finn still loved Yin even though she "dumped" him in a nice way. But of course he realized Yin so far only loved Richard, even though he lied to her. As a man, Finn would not believe Richard only wanted sex from Yin, especially after they had sex. Yet he couldn't deny the fact that Richard did lie to her. It could be any reason: maybe Richard wanted to let Yin become his woman first, ask her to go to New York City with him and then get a divorce; maybe he just couldn't reject Yin from his life yet worried about his money; or the worst situation, with the slimmest chance, he only wanted sex from Yin or only wanted Yin to become his mistress, not his wife. *The point is that he lied to Yin and she did not like that. She has decided to leave him.* Finn knew Yin and he had to depart Altimont as early as possible, before Richard woke up and looked for her.

Half an hour later, Finn finally fell asleep.

A few hours later, Finn's alarm clock rang. He got up quickly, walked to his room in which Yin slept and knocked at the door gently, "Yin, it is me. It is time to get up?"

After a few knocks, Yin was awakened from the deep dream. She dreamed about Richard. She somehow had a headache and felt a little dizzy. She struggled to get up and opened the door for Finn.

"Yin, how are you today?"

"I am… ok. But a little bit headache. Maybe didn't get enough sleep. Feeling tired."

"Yeah… let me tell you more when we are on the way. Now let's take some breakfast quickly and get ready to depart. We will have to leave soon."

Yin followed Finn coming to the kitchen, sat down, lied prone on the table and turned her head towards Finn. She missed Richard so much that she wanted to see him every moment. However, she had her strong ego and determination that she would not go back and forgive a man who deceived her for sex. Finn prepared quick breakfast, peeled a couple of bananas, poured two cups of apple juice and two cups of milk, put them on a plate and carried the plate to the table. And then he walked to the refrigerator to get some croissants, brought them to the table and sat down across the table.

"Get up, Yin. We have to be quick." Finn shook Yin's hand, "Look, do you like the breakfast?"

Yin lifted her head and took a look at the breakfast. She picked a cup of apple juice and sipped a little and then lied prone on the table again.

"Hey, Yin, we have to be quick. Richard is waking up and coming. You should eat some food; otherwise, you will be hungry on the way." Finn explained to Yin nicely.

Yin raised her head and said, "Finn, I really don't want to eat. I want to throw out things. I don't have appetite. Let you eat and then let's get moving."

"I see. I think you have the signs of pregnancy. It is normal for a pregnant woman to not to have appetite." Finn said and began to tuck into the breakfast.

"What is that?" Yin was curious.

Finn swallowed down the food and said, "No time to explain now. I will explain later to you on the car."

Fifteen minutes later, Finn finished eating his breakfast. He brought Yin to his room, got her bag to her, closed the curtain, asked her to change cloths and then closed the door. Yin tried her best to change cloths as quickly as possible. Four minutes later, she opened the door, wearing a loose black Ralph Lauren Denim and Supply Jersey Maxidress and a pair of red Michael Kors leather flats, and walked to the bathroom to brush her teeth, wash her face and prepare herself for the trip. Another five minutes later, when she went out from the bathroom, Finn walked out from the other room, wearing a black Levi's T-shirt and a pair of navy blue cargos. He asked Yin to go downstairs to the living room to wait for him and then went into the bathroom. Yin went downstairs and sat in the living room near the front door. Another four minutes later, Finn went downstairs with a backpack on his back. He asked her to turn off her phone to avoid Richard's phone calls. She listened to his advice and turned off the phone. They were ready to leave Altimont for the next two months.

Soon they went out from the house and walked to Finn's blue Toyota car parked in front of the house. Finn opened the car door and helped Yin sit on the front seat, jumped in the driver side, closed the doors, started the car and drove towards the highway.

"Where to go, Yin?"

47

Richard woke up with a start at around 5:00 in the morning, much earlier than the time he usually woke up naturally. Yin was not beside him. He glanced quickly around the room and went into the bathroom to check. Yin was gone. Richard took his phone from the nightstand and dialed Yin's number. However, her phone was turned off. Suddenly, Richard couldn't help but start to feel fear.

His gut feelings told him Yin was not just going out for a walk; otherwise she would just tell him, not to let him worried. He thought she might leave him, for whatever unknown reasons. He went to the closet to take off a T-shirt and his jeans from the hangers and put them on as fast as he could. He tied the shoes up, took his phone and the door card and then went out the hotel room without morning bathroom preparation.

When he got out of the hotel, he strode fast towards the direction of Yin's home, almost like running. He didn't want to waste a second. He needed to change her mind before she walked too far if it was the case that she left him behind. He thought she might not want to leave Altimont and go to New York City with him. He needed to tell Yin his true identity that he was the CEO of RM Corps and indeed very rich and could build up an astronomical station for her near New York City. He knew he could persuade her because he believed she actually loved him very much. But he needed to find her first.

Not knowing why she left without giving him a notice, Richard was sure of one thing, that was that he couldn't live happily without her, not anymore. Since he met Yin up, he knew she was his dream woman, the thing he wanted the most, after all his experiences in relationships and business. He originally thought finally he could feel happy forever - a kind of happiness other than the one the ego of his successful business and money could bring to him. Now a sense of loss occupied his mind as he walked towards Yin's home. His heart ached.

Eight minutes later, he arrived to Yin's apartment building. He pressed the ring on the front door and waited for Yin's response. No responses. He then pressed it again and again, but still getting no responses. He stood in front of her apartment building for an hour and tried to call her many times, but her phone was still turned off. He left messages. The first couple of messages were to question her where she was and tell her that he missed her very much. However, he did not get any responses. An hour later, at last, he left messages begging her to pick up the phone and tell her that he needed her very much.

It was a little bit past 6:30. Richard thought it was not going to help for him to wait here longer. *She may not even be in her apartment. Maybe she is in Finn's home?* However, Richard was new to the town and only went to Finn's home once. He really couldn't remember how to get there for a second time. Not knowing why she left him in this early morning without telling him reasons, or if she wanted to break up with him, one thing Richard was sure about was that Yin would go to work today. It was a little bit too early to make phone call to Michael Hernandez, but Richard knew he had no choice. He could not wait; he felt otherwise he was going to lose her. Richard called up Michael Hernandez to ask Michael to come to Yin's apartment to pick him up and send him to Finn's home if Michael knew where it was. Michael sensed Richard's anxiousness and said he knew where Finn lived and was driving to Yin's apartment immediately. Richard told Michael if Yin was not at Finn's home, then he needed to go to Altimont Astronomical Station before Yin went to work. Richard knew he needed to wait there till she appeared in front of the station during 8 to 9 o'clock and question her for the reason she left the hotel room without telling him and the reason she turned off the phone.

Yin told Finn she wanted to go as far as she could for these two months. Finn then decided to drive to the south, as the opposite direction driving to Bellington, instead, to Orlando, Florida. They could have a look at the beaches and the ocean. Finn thought Yin would feel a little bit better seeing the ocean.

Very soon, their car was driving on the highway.

"I will call up Ms. Frost at 8 o'clock to tell her about our vacation. Then at noon, when we arrived some place, we will take a rest and eat some food. I will then call up all people I know in Altimont to tell them about our vacation. They will start the gossip right away. Then we will go on the trip. Does it sound good?" Finn said, concentrating on driving.

Yin did not answer him, gazing at the side of the highway. She was calm but feeling strange. She was thinking what had happened in the past week and a half, how she met Richard up, how she got pregnant and how she separated him. It was just like a drama.

A minute later, Finn continued, "Like you did not want to eat breakfast and had a headache in the morning, these are the early signs of pregnancy. From what I know, you will have some other early signs of pregnancy such as mood swings and nausea. I don't know too much about it but I will look them up online for you later today."

Yin nodded slightly but still kept silent.

Time passed fast as they sat inside the car. It was now 8:02, time to make the phone call to Ms. Frost.

Finn spoke to the earpiece and dialed Ms. Frost's cell phone from a handsfree mobile. The call was gotten through. Ms. Frost picked up the phone.

Finn immediately said, "Hi, Ms. Frost, this is Finn Kane, how are you today?"

"Pretty much good. What makes you call me at this early time?" Ms. Frost responded.

Finn said, "It is about a vacation. I am now driving to the south with Yin Lin. We would like to take two months off for this year. Is it possible?"

"Sure." Ms. Frost made an awkward pause and said, "Finn, I would like to ask you something. I heard that Lin was breaking up with you a few days ago. That was when I ate lunch in the cafeteria and some colleagues were discussing this with me. I felt it was strange but... now seems you two are still together. You two are still dating, right?"

"Yes, of course." Finn said with confidence, "We are going to have a vacation in Orlando, Florida, you know, around the beaches and the ocean. I am actually driving. Can we talk more later?"

Ms. Frost said, "Oh, wonderful! Please keep driving. I am going to put the two months off to the system for both you and Lin at 9 o'clock when we start to work. Have a nice vacation, Kane."

48

Ten minutes later, Michael Hernandez drove his Mercedes-Benz car to the front door of Yin's apartment building. Richard got into the car and asked Michael to drive him to Finn's home directly.

"What happened with you and Yin Lin? I thought you two were engaged." Michael asked while driving towards Finn's apartment.

"She was gone in the morning…" Richard swallowed. He could not conceal his anxiousness, lost the grace he usually kept as a successful businessman. He said, "I don't know the reasons behind it, and… there is no time to explain it. But I need to find her out immediately."

"She is not in her apartment? Then she is probably at Finn's home. If not, let's go to the station." Michael Hernandez said.

Soon, they arrived to Finn's house. Last time Richard stood outside of Finn's house waiting for Yin, he observed there was a blue Toyota car parked in front of Finn's house. But today the blue car was not there. *Finn was not at home.* Suddenly, a gut feeling came up to Richard's mind and it could be the worst case that he could think up, that was Yin dumped him to go with Finn and they drove away to avoid him. Richard suddenly had a feeling of being betrayed, by a woman he so deeply loved. Michael Hernandez got out of the car with Richard and walked to press Finn's front door bell, and then pressed it again. They waited there for five minutes but got no responses.

"I think they are gone." Richard said nervelessly.

"Go where? And why?" Michael asked, looking at Richard with huge confusion.

Richard said, "She dumped me without giving me a reason and now they were gone for another location to avoid me."

"Oh... Are you sure? I thought Yin Lin said she was going to move to New York with you. Why would she dump you without giving you a reason? I don' believe it." Michael Hernandez got even more bewildered.

"Maybe she thinks I am too old for her. Maybe she just does not want to leave Altimont..." Richard sighed.

Then they went back to the car and Michael drove him to the station, just hoping she would still appear before work. Michael simply did not believe Yin Lin would abandon Richard even without telling him herself under any circumstances, even if she really wanted to live in Altimont or she finally realized the man she loved was Finn.

Richard and Michael waited in front of the station till 9:30 AM. Yin and Finn both did not appear. Michael Hernandez then went inside the front door to ask. When he walked out from the station and again got into the car, he told Richard that both of Yin and Finn were on a vacation break.

It was almost 12 at noon. Finn and Yin drove from Altimont to Valdosta, Georgia. Finn planned to arrive to Orlando, Florida at 4 o'clock in the afternoon. Finn drove into the city of Valdosta. Valdosta was located in the middle of Lowndes County, which was on the border of Georgia and Florida. Valdosta was the 14th largest city in Georgia.

On the way driving to find a restaurant, Finn said he hoped Yin could eat something to have more energy for the drive in the afternoon; otherwise she would have low blood sugar and feel dizzy. Yin insisted that she did not feel hungry. Finn persuaded her to take some food not just for her, but also for her baby.

After fifteen minutes' looking for a restaurant, Finn finally stopped his car in front of a Chinese buffet restaurant. Yin walked into the restaurant, brought a dish and chose some Chinese food under Finn's assistance but she was very weak. Finn supported her to sit down, chose some food for himself and then sat down across Yin. Yin somehow could swallow some food down, as much as what Finn wanted her to eat, but soon she stopped eating. Twenty minutes later, Finn finished his meal. Finn took his phone out, looked for some number and then dialed someone's phone. When the call went through, Finn told Yin he was calling Emily Lawless. Finn explained to Emily that he was with Yin on the border of Georgia and Florida and they were heading for Orlando for a two months' vacation. He told Emily that the woman he loved and hoped to be with was only Yin. Then he said goodbye to Emily and hung up the phone.

Yin was curious, "What did Emily said?"

Finn raised his eyebrows, shrugged and said, "She was surprised that we were together. Do you still remember I told you that Emily and I were seen in a bar on a Thursday evening? That night I told her you were engaged to another man. I asked her to keep it secret. Now she was questioning me if it was true that I am with you. I did not want to talk more."

"She indeed likes you..." Yin said.

Finn then dialed at least another 11 numbers to tell them that Yin and he would take a vacation in Orlando for the next two months. Some of the people Finn called up were from the station; others were just friends who lived in Altimont. It seemed all of them had had heard the news that Yin broke up with Finn earlier.

Some of them had made phone calls to ask Finn if it was true. In most cases, Finn did not answer them directly. Now they were very surprised to find out that Yin and Finn were heading on a vacation instead. The earlier rumor was overturned.

An hour later, Finn decided to go on the trip. He looked at the contact list of the phone numbers on his phone; he had made one fifth of the phone calls. He said he would make more phone calls in the afternoon when they arrived to Orlando. Then he supported Yin to go out of the restaurant. They got into the car and headed for the south.

After coming back from the station, Richard lied on the bed in his hotel room with arms and legs completely limp. He did not cry as he never did. For a long time, since he became sensible, he never cried out, not even once, even when there were troubles in his business and when he was under huge stress. Yet feeling betrayed and dumped by his beloved woman, he was in a tearing rage and unspeakable bitterness. From the moment he woke up this morning and did not see Yin around, he had gut feeling that she fled away. Now the speculation was proved by the fact that both she and Finn were gone for a vacation. He couldn't figure out why Yin wanted to hurt his feelings and emotions like this – first by having sex with him and making him believe her and then by abandoning him and honeymooning with his rival in love.

Richard walked to get the bottles of wine which they brought to the hotel room from Yin's apartment a week and a half ago. He came back and sat down on the bed, gazed at the station from the balcony and started downing the wine. He wanted to question Yin clearly for the reasons behind her behaviors and to be told that she would be back to his life. Yet he knew this was his unreachable wish. *Yin is gone with another man. She cruelly dumped me without giving me a reason.* Only hatred and bitterness occupied his heart.

After a while, Richard was deeply drunk. For almost twenty years, this was the first time that Richard got drunk. He fell to the bed and began mumbling Yin's name again and again until, finally, he fell asleep.

49

The weather in Orlando, Florida, during June and July, was warm, humid and rainy. The average high was in the lower to mid 90s degree. During these months, strong afternoon thunderstorms frequently occurred, making the climate of the city different from that in other parts of the country.

After a whole day's driving, finally, at around 3:50 PM, Finn and Yin arrived to the city of Orlando. Finn drove directly to Downtown Orlando. He knew this city well because an uncle of his lived in the city of Orlando. He had some chances to visit the city when he was a kid, with his parents. They used to fly from New York City to Orlando, where his uncle picked them up and sent them to his house in Northeast Orlando. The second day, his uncle would drive them to Downtown Orlando to have fun. There were many places for arts and entertainment, dining and shopping in Downtown Orlando, but mainly only a few hotels, as far as Finn could remember. Finn told Yin that they could meet up his uncle if she wished. He said he was driving to a hotel to let Yin rest for a while first.

Fifteen minutes later, they stopped the car in the parking lot of a hotel in Downtown Orlando, walked into the five-star hotel, booked a standard room with two queen beds and went upstairs to their room.

When they got into the room, Yin chose the bed next to the window, put things down and lied down on the bed. Now Richard seemed far from her, in both distance and memory, even though she was still in too vile a mood.

Finn sat down on the next bed and took off his backpack. He asked her to take a rest or a nap. She agreed. She did get tired due to the long drive. She turned to the side of the window, closed her eyes and soon fell asleep.

Finn was not tired at all. Instead, driving all day gave him a good spirit. He looked at Yin for a while and then walked to the computer, sat down on the chair and started it. While Yin was in a deep sleep, Finn looked up information about the symptoms of pregnancy and the things a pregnant woman needed to pay attention to. He copied the useful information, sent it to the front desk and asked them to print it for him. Finn first wanted to call up people to tell them about the trip as he did at noon. But he did not want his voice to wake Yin up. He just gave up the idea. He would make the phone calls later.

One hour and 40 minutes later, Yin opened her eyes. Finn already brought the printed information back to the room, in his hands. He had read them again right before Yin woke up. He smiled at Yin and asked if she had a good sleep. She still looked tired so did not smile back.

"Look at what I find out for you, Yin." Finn moved from his bed to her bed and sat down next to her. He handed the papers to her and let her read them. She began to read the papers, but then he took the papers back and started to read for her.

He said that besides the symptoms she already had such as missed period, fatigue, morning sickness and lightheadedness, there were other early signs of pregnancy. He first read the explanation of the symptoms she already had and the things she needed to pay attention to related to those symptoms. Then he started to tell her about other signs of pregnancy. He said one sign she might have was tender breasts. She might feel her breasts become heavier. He read the explanation to her and told her that a licensed midwife suggested a pregnant woman to wear supportive bra. The other sign he read to her that she might be going to have was frequent urination. This would usually start to happen around the sixth or eighth week after conception. He then read the explanation to her.

After reading the printed information to her, Finn took his phone out and started to call the rest phone numbers recorded on his phone. It was 6:15 PM, still early for phone calls. He called those numbers one by one and told people about Yin's and his vacation. Till 8 o'clock, Finn had called two third of the phone numbers. He said he would call the rest of the phone numbers tomorrow. He was sure that no more than a week, new rumors would overturn the old one and everyone in Altimont was going to know Yin and he did not break up, instead, they went for a vacation in Orlando.

The next two hours passed quickly. Yin was prone to chat about Richard and guess what he was doing now. Yet Finn tried to avoid talking with her about Richard. He said he could understand how she felt but it was not healthy for her to talk about this man frequently in the future and she would eventually need to forget this man. However, Yin didn't consider Finn's advice and insisted to talk about Richard with Finn.

At 10:15 PM, both Yin and Finn got tired. They lied on their beds and turned off the light, continuing chatting about Richard and her pregnancy, till half an hour later, Yin fell asleep first.

50

In was at 3:02 AM, three hours earlier before dawn. Everyone in Altimont was still in their sweet dreams. Richard suddenly woke up with a light headache. A long deep sleep mitigated his pain the moment he opened his eyes. Yet he very soon realized what happened yesterday that Yin was no longer beside him. Panic came up to him. In a moment, he couldn't control the fear of living without her, following a strong emotion mixed with love and hatred. He might have to live an empty life in the coming future, or it was likely that such emptiness would last forever.

Richard struggled to sit up and lean on the headboard, thinking. Not knowing that Yin did not have the courage to face him to question him for the truth, he also did not have the courage to face the risk of hearing her words that she indeed did not love him and just wanted to play with his emotions. Gut feeling told him she had loved him, yet it was against the fact that she now tried to avoid him and go with the other man. He couldn't accept what she did no matter what happened in between or what made her worried.

With huge confusion, Richard rather escaped the problem. He was not a coward in his life, never ever, yet this time, he flinched. He would not forgive what she did to him, yet there was no way for him to take the risk to hear her own words that she was indeed playing with his emotions, especially now things went like this. Now He had decided to leave Altimont and go back to New York City.

He picked up his phone from the nightstand, dialed Victor Dupont's phone number. Victor would pick up his boss' phone call even in the late evenings or early hours, off the business time.

"Richard, is that you?" Victor picked up the phone and asked, worrying about Richard.

"Yes, it's me. Could you ask a business jet of our company to pick me up today in Bellington Airport? As soon as possible. I am leaving Altimont." Richard said.

Victor Dupont was shocked that Richard wanted to leave Altimont urgently, in such early hours. He asked, "Richard, may I ask what happened? You know, things go strange since you arrived to Altimont. A couple of weeks ago you wanted to cancel the wedding with Judy and now you wanted to leave it immediately. Will you bring your new fiancée back?"

"Victor, please." Richard paused, sighed and continued, "I don't want to be questioned, not now. I will tell you later when I arrived to New York."

Victor Dupont said he was going to contact a business jet for Richard. He asked Richard if there was a car for him to take from

Altimont to Bellington and said he would call back a bit later when he confirmed the time the business jet would arrive.

Victor Dupont sat on the back seat of the very expensive car of RM Corps. The car drove across George Washington Bridge from upper Manhattan, arrived to Teterboro Airport in New Jersey, which was just across the Hudson River from Manhattan. It was at 9:43 AM and Richard's business jet would arrive at 10:00 AM. Waiting for another half an hour, finally Victor saw Richard walking alone to the car slowly with a suitcase. His new fiancée was not with him.

Victor Dupont hurried to get out of the car, walk to greet Richard and pick his suitcase for him. When they again got in the car, the driver drove them back to Manhattan through the same route.

On the car, Victor Dupont began the conversation first. He tried not to ask him about his new fiancée directly. Victor said, "Richard, how was your trip?"

Richard knew Victor was curious about Yin and why he did not bring her back. He sighed and said, "I promised to tell you more about it. Yin, my fiancée, dumped me and went for another man."

"Oh, what did you say? Did I hear it wrong?" Victor cupped his opening mouth in his hand, put it down and said, "She dumped you? I think she was crazy... You are such a handsome and rich man. Or... Did you ever tell her that you are the CEO of RM Corps? I am sure she has heard of RM Corps."

"No, I never told her about it." Richard taunted himself silently and said, "She would dump me if the reason was that she did not

189

love me, not that she was worried about going to New York City, even if she knew about my business. And the fact that she is now traveling with the other man supported that the reason she chose to flee was that she did not love me, not that she was worried about going to New York with me."

"Why is that?" Victor was more curious, "I think she would be more than willing to marry you if she knew you have money. Plus you are such handsome. I don't understand why you did not tell her about your identity. And I don't understand her. I mean at least you look rich."

"You are wrong." Richard glanced at Victor and then looked at the scenery from the windshield, "She is a very special woman, and extremely intelligent. I mean a highly genius. She can make as much money as I made, but her ambition is to become a famous astronomer instead. She would not choose to love my money if she did not love me."

Victor nodded and said, "Got it."

Soon, their car arrived to Columbus Circle, 59th street, in front of Richard's Manhattan apartment. He got out of the car and went back home.

Today was June, 28th. The weather just warmed up in New York City this year. Richard went back to work the second day. He did not have too much energy for work. Sitting inside his huge CEO office, Richard thought about Yin all the time. Every few minutes, the moment he was with her came up in his mind. He hated her. He loved her.

RM Corps would have a few meetings about the new factory in the coming month. Since Richard was not going to stay in Altimont to have the construction ceremony on July, 15th, the day the factory began to be built up, he was requested to attend the meeting held in the headquarter in New York City. He had a meeting on July, 1st, about some specific issues about the new factory. When a manager tried to tell Richard something, he sat riveted on his seat – it was till the manager called his name the second time that he could give response. This was the first time throughout years that managers saw Richard did not pay attention to their words. Yet they were confused about what caught the hardworking CEO's attention. On the 15th of July, in the late afternoon, right before work ended that day, Victor Dupont brought the video of the construction ceremony held on the address of the factory in Altimont to Richard. Yet Richard said he did not wish to have a look. That confused Victor Dupont a little bit – before Richard had had been very interested in any small detail about the factory.

In the next two months, Richard did not eat enough and could not sleep well. He got drunk sometimes on workdays in order to fall asleep and was late to work the second day. He missed Yin so much to a point that he felt he could not continue to work without her. He did not talk to Judy Kahn since he came back to New York City, even though she still bugged him every two days. Two months later, one afternoon just going to end the work, suddenly he had an impulse. He took out his phone and sent Judy Kahn a text message, "Could you marry me?"

51

Five minutes later, Judy Kahn called Richard. Richard picked up the phone.

"Hi, Richard, I received your message!" Judy Kahn sounded very excited, "I am happy that you finally make up your mind and decide to go back to my life. Let's get married. Are you back to New York City?"

Richard paused for a couple of seconds and said, "Yes, I am in Manhattan actually. Is it convenient for you to come out for a dinner?"

"Yes, just give me the name of the restaurant. I will be there in a moment. I am in Manhattan too." Judy laughed out sweetly.

Richard gave her the name and address of the restaurant in upper west side of Manhattan and said that he would arrive in 30 minutes. He hung up the phone, took a quick look at the computer, walked out of his office and took the elevator down to parking lot.

Richard drove his white Ferrari FF car from downtown towards uptown direction. He bought the car almost a year ago. He had two other expensive cars, but he liked this one the best. On the way to uptown, he thought about the details he wanted to tell Judy Kahn. He initially did not have too much feeling towards Judy but booked the wedding just wanting to keep in a marriage. After he met Yin up, his whole world had changed. It was clear that there was no way for him to have feelings for another woman. The impulse he had was to marry Judy Kahn for the revenge so that if Yin came back to him one day she would have no way to get him back. He knew she would not break a family. That was the only way he could think up to get back at Yin and to mitigate his hatred, even though he understood that Yin might not even care about what he was going to do and she might not contact him again. Maybe he just did not think clearly to make the decision.

25 minutes later, Richard stopped his car in front of the restaurant, on the side of the street. It was hard to find a street parking space for a car in Manhattan but today thankful there was one. Then he walked into the restaurant. Judy Kahn waved her hand. Richard walked to their table, sat down and greeted Judy.

"I have ordered some food for you. I think you would love it." Judy gave a nice smile to Richard. She had had not seen Richard for a few months. It was like a big gift for her to see him again.

"Judy, I did send you a message earlier today." Richard paused for a second, assuring what he was going to say, and continued, "But one thing I have to say before I can apply for a marriage license is that I won't live with you after we get married. That is to say, we will live separately in two different locations. I will buy an apartment for you in Manhattan. And also, I won't buy you a marriage ring and there won't be a marriage ceremony. You may attend important gathering with me if there is one and tell people that you are my wife. However, I don't want our relationship to be reported on the news. I hope you can understand what I mean."

Judy Kahn was shocked about Richard's words. Back to a few months ago, she was his fiancée. They actually slept together and he was going to marry her. But things changed suddenly when Richard was in Altimont, which, to Judy Kahn, was a small unknown town that she would never travel to. Now that Richard agreed to go on with the marriage, yet he was no longer attracted to her. She knew it was because of the woman who talked to her on the phone two months ago. *Richard did fall in love with her and they were actually engaged.* Judy Kahn knew what she said to the woman and guessed it was probably the reason why Richard left that woman, or more likely, the woman left Richard, and get back to her life. *I can't let Richard know about what I told her; otherwise he is going to leave me again. I won't let this happen. I should accept his requirements first to keep in the marriage first. Anyway, it would be much better than getting nothing from him. As for getting back his heart, it will take time and effort.* "Richard," Judy said, still smiling, pretending that she did not mind what he just said, "It all depends on your decision. You know I love you so much that I would listen to you. So when are we going to get married?"

"Well, I will talk to a lawyer tomorrow about the contract that we are going to sign. And after that, we will sign the papers and apply for a marriage license and then get married. That's all." Richard shrugged and responded.

They had a quick dinner without talking too much. Richard finished his meal first, paid the bill and left the restaurant. The next day, Victor Dupont helped to contact a very good lawyer. In the afternoon, after work, Richard called up the lawyer. After he had a long conversation with the lawyer, the lawyer knew exactly what kind of contract he wanted. Richard told the lawyer he would email the lawyer the specific requirements that he wanted on the contract in the evening. A couple of days later, the protocol was sent back to Richard's email box. He read it, corrected it, added other details he wished and sent it back to the lawyer for a second look. Then he asked Judy Kahn to go to the same restaurant and sign the contract. Soon they applied for and got the marriage license and had a wedding ceremony.

52

The months before Yin gave birth were tranquil. The autumn came after summer. The weather became cool, but not chilly. The leaves were caught up by the curl of the winds. Still sunny in the sky. After coming back from the two months' vacation, she listened to Finn's advice to take the whole year off. Except that sometimes she went out to buy food and sometimes for a walk, she stayed at Finn's home most of the time. Time passed slowly without Richard's presence. Besides the loss of Richard made her think more, she felt a kind of peaceful that she had never felt before, a mixed feeling of the joy of becoming a mother, the calm of living in Altimont and the gains of both experiences and wisdom. Gradually she adapted the life without Richard. She did not need him as much as before, but still deeply loved him.

As Finn's effort to make the phone calls while they were still on "vacation", when they came back to Altimont from Orlando, the town had already known about their vacation together. People were happy to find out that the previous rumor was misleading and that they had never been apart. When the winter quietly came, people were even amazed to find out that Yin's belly grew bigger. Of course, they all thought that was Finn's baby. When they saw Finn on the street and greeted him, they would express their happiness for Finn to become a father. They would also ask him about Yin and the baby. Every time, Finn pretended to be happier than he was and patiently answered all their concerns.

Yin stayed at Finn's home, sometimes doing some reading, sometimes listening to music, sometimes watching TV. After a few months, she totally forgot about work. Since after her elementary school graduation, she could again forget about her huge ambition and struggle and enjoy a different kind of life. Finn went to work on the weekdays as usual. When he came back home, he would cook dinner and make tomorrow's lunch for Yin. When he cooked, he would ask Yin to go downstairs to the kitchen to talk to her. He knew she had no one to talk to all day. She did not talk about Richard as often as in July and August but liked to discuss the issue of her pregnancy. Finn was more than willing to talk about this topic. He felt she was doing fine as long as she was not obsessed with Richard.

Yin did not go back to her apartment often, after she left her apartment with Finn that midnight a few months ago after she left Richard. There were a couple of times she came back to her apartment to pick some clothes for the coming season. She did not stay in her apartment long. It could bring back her memory with Richard to cause her to become emotional. She knew she needed to stay calm.

The Christmas day was on the coming Sunday. On December 21st, Wednesday, Yin had a wonderful birthday with Finn. They held a small party which only themselves attended in the late afternoon, after Finn came back from work, and went out for a long walk after dinner. They talked a lot that evening. Finn said he was going to buy a Christmas gift for her. Yin suddenly remembered the mermaid doll Finn bought to her last year as Christmas gift. On Friday, Yin decided to go to her apartment to take that mermaid doll. In the morning, she went out of Finn's house at the same time as Finn went to work. Soon, she arrived to her apartment building. Since she left her apartment, she did not have a chance to open her mail box. Usually she would not received mails other than some advertisement papers and coupons. *Christmas is coming. Let me take a look at the advertisements. Maybe Finn and I can go shopping these two days. Nice!* Even though there were only a couple of malls in Altimont, but they were still places to go during the holidays. She opened the mail box and took out all the mails. She took a quick look at the mails; the first few were advertisements of Macy's. Then there came a letter. In the middle of the front, her name and her address were written down in printed form. On the left top corner, the sender's name and address were written down. *Richard Meier? New York City? It is from Richard!* Abruptly, Yin's mood became complicated. She couldn't wait to open the letter, even though she was worried about what indeed Richard still wanted to tell her. She carefully tore open the envelope and took out the paper. It was a single paper. Yin unfolded it. There was only one line. Yin read the words slowly and attentively.

Yin, this is Richard. Miss you and happy Christmas!

The new factory of RM Corps had been under compact construction since July, 15th. It was located on the east side of the town, across the river from the residential area. There was no bridge directly connected the residential area and the factory and no bridge nearby. The nearest bridge which one can reach the factory from the residential area was the one which Yin usually crossed when she went to work. That bridge was the largest and the oldest bridge in Altimont, across the southernmost part of the "U" shape river. No one lived on the east side of the river. Near the factory, it was an undeveloped land. Residents of Altimont hadn't been aware of the secret construction.

At the mean time, under John Jacobs' direction, RM Corps began to pay high salaries to look for more and more researchers of genetic field, especially transgenic field, from all over the world. All of them had a phD degree in either biology or chemistry and years of experience in genetic field. Most of them did an excellent job in their previous work and were experts in genetic and specifically transgenic field. They would come and work in Altimont when the construction, the decoration and the installation of the machinery and the apparatus were going to be completed, in a year and a half.

John Jacobs went to the building site daily on the weekdays. Sometimes he stayed for an hour or two, sometimes longer, talking to the construction foremen and workers. He encouraged them and appreciated their hard work. It was the same as to encourage himself for his own ambition, that was to do a great job in Altimont and to become the next CEO of RM Corps.

53

A long and warm winter had passed. In April, spring came as deciduous trees developed new spring green leaves. Winter, to Yin, was related to the color "grey" and always made her think about "life" more. As the due date of Yin's childbirth came near, this winter, not like the other winters she had in Altimont, brought her a joyful emotion that she was going to bring another life to this world. In the beginning of April, due to some signs of labor and her doctor's recommendation, Yin moved to the hospital. Finn took a couple of weeks off and companied with Yin in the hospital. The third day she lived in the hospital, in the evening just after dinner, her contractions became much stronger and more frequent. She was moved to delivery suite immediately. A nurse allowed Finn to stay outside of the delivery suite to wait for the delivery. Finn was too anxious to stand in one spot; he moved from one end of the hallway to the other end, moved back and then moved to the other end again. The process of delivery lasted for almost 3 hours. Every second to Finn was a long period of time. Finally, the door of the delivery suite opened and then Yin was moved out from the suite. She looked weak with a pale face but somehow comfort. She saw Finn waiting there and gave him a conscious glance. Finn could see tears still filled her eyes. Then she was moved through the hallway to her ward. Finn followed the gurney. When he walked into Yin's ward, nurses were helping her move from the gurney to her bed. Finn came near Yin and tried to help. Nurses looked happy. A nurse smiled to Finn and said, "We will bring your baby come in a short while." After putting Yin on her bed, nurses left. Finn, after a long waiting period, finally had chance to talk to Yin. He asked Yin how she felt and if the delivery went well.

20 minutes later, a nurse hugged the baby boy coming into the room and took him to his mother's embrace. "He is so cute." The nurse said, smiling to the baby and Yin. Yin kept smiling to her baby without words. She was too weak to talk. Finn expressed his appreciation to the nurse before she left.

"Yin, he looks very much like Richard." Finn did not want to mention the name of Richard, yet he was amazed to find that the baby did look like Richard, especially his big eyes. Finn held the baby's hand, smiling, and continued, "I know you are exhausted. Let me hug him for a little bit and let you rest for a while. Then we may think up a name for him." Finn hugged the baby over and gave him a big smile.

Yin looked at Finn hugging her baby with eyes half closed for a while before she finally closed her eyes and fell into a deep sweet dream.

Richard did not meet up with Judy Kahn often after their marriage. He bought an apartment in upper west side of Manhattan for Judy Kahn, 30 blocks from his apartment. Only two times which he met her up in the year which the new factory began to be built up were for the parties held for employees of RM Corps. Many employees who worked for RM Corps in New York City knew that Richard got married for the third time. The second party was held before Christmas Day, on a Saturday. Richard did not need to work that day. He slept till 11:00 AM, and then ate a little bit and watched a movie. That afternoon, around 4 o'clock, Richard drove his Ferrari FF car to pick up Judy Kahn. Judy knew about this party a couple of weeks ago from Victor Dupont. Since she did not have chance to meet Richard, for this opportunity, she wanted to show people that she, as the wife of the owner of an international company, had very good tastes in dressing, and, what's more, to attract Richard again. She bought some expensive make up, from shining lavender eyeliner to red lipstick and a designer's rose gown for the party. She spent the whole day to prepare herself for the party on Saturday before Richard came and then took Richard's car to the building of RM Corps in downtown. They took the elevator to the luxury cafeteria and started to greet people. Judy introduced herself as "Mrs. Meier". During the whole process of the dinner, Judy Kahn followed Richard everywhere, held his hand all the time, took the same food as Richard took and kept smiling to people, giving people the impression that Richard and her deeply loved each other. Richard, when observed by people, a few times, forced a smile and glanced at Judy, even though he was mainly thinking about one thing, that was if Yin had received the letter he sent out last week and if she would give a response such as calling him or writing a letter back to him. Even though the impulse caused him to marry to Judy Kahn with the intention to take revenge on Yin, but he was not sure, if Yin did come back to him one day, he would still be willing to keep in this marriage to let her suffer.

54

Yin gained a little bit strength when she woke up from the deep long sleep. The first scene came into her eyes was that Finn was still hugging her baby, sitting on the edge of her bed.

"Finn…" Yin mumbled, stretching her hand to the baby and smiling, bringing Finn back to earth.

"Yin, you wake up. Your baby is now sleeping." Finn moved further and bent to give the baby to Yin, "A while ago, he was crying loudly. Nurses came and they thought he wanted to be hugged by his mother."

Yin used both of her hands to take the baby over, hugged him in her warm embrace and gave him a slight kiss. "I have thought up a name for him." Yin said.

"Oh, in your dream?" Finn laughed out, "What should his name be?"

"Sgin." Yin spelled the name to Finn and continued, "Of course, last name is the same as mine."

Finn said, "Sgin Lin? Sounds nice, but what does the name mean? I don't think there is an English name called Sgin."

Yin took a look at Sgin and said, "Well, Sgin, even though does not look Chinese, but is indeed a Chinese name."

"Oh, really?"

Yin said, "Yes, it is a Chinese name. I can't find an English syllable which has the same pronunciation as Chinese pinyin 'si', which has similar pronunciation as 's'. You know pinyin is the way to tell how a Chinese word being pronounced."

"Yes, I know."

"And," Yin paused for a second, cleared her throat and said, "'si' in Chinese language has a meaning of 'look like'. As for 'gin', similar pronunciation as 'jun' in pinyin, is a respectful way to call a man, same as 'you'."

"Ah! Now I understand." Finn laughed out again and said, "A Chinese name."

Then they talked about how Sgin looked like his father for a while in the late afternoon. The next two days, Yin and Sgin stayed in the hospital. Finn brought Yin's favorite food every day and they had the meals in the ward. Two days later, on April 7th, in the morning Finn drove Yin and Sgin back to his house.

It was a lot happier with a child around. Time had passed very fast since Yin came back from the hospital. Another week later, Finn went back to work. At work, he would text her every two hours and call her during the lunch break. He would come back home immediately after work to cook for Yin and take care of Sgin. On weekends, they would go shopping with a stroller which Sgin lied inside. The year's work off was from June, 27, last year and was going to end on June, 26, this year. After a long period of rest, Yin was worried about if she was able to and how she could go back to work since now she needed to take care of her baby. There was one more thing becoming one of the most important things in her life, besides her dream to become a famous astronomer, Sgin was just as important. One evening, she discussed this issue with Finn, after Sgin fell asleep. The solution Finn found out for her was to ask Finn's parents to travel to and live in Altimont to take care of Sgin when both Yin and Finn were at work. Finn's father, Marvin Kane, was a retired electrical engineer from a big engineering company while his mother, Helen Kane, as a senior financial analyst in a bank, was retired a year ago. Even though never meeting Yin up, both of Finn's parents knew her very well through Finn, had a very good impression about her and heard of many stories between Finn and her including the one that she "stole" his lunch box. Finn always called up his parents every week and told them small details between Yin and him. As so, his parents had already heard about that Yin had another man's baby and that she left that man and now lived in Finn's house. Finn told his parents that residents in Altimont thought the child was his kid and he wanted to keep the secret to protect Yin from rumors. He also said he still deeply loved Yin and now there was still hope to make her fall for him.

The next day, after preparing dinner for Yin, Finn went upstairs and dialed his mother's phone number. Finn greeted his mother after she picked up the phone. He asked where his father was and how both his parents were doing. His mother said his father was out downtown and everything was fine and then asked about Yin and the baby, "Both Yin and Sgin are doing fine?"

"Yes, mom, both of them are fine. Thank you for asking. But there is a problem." Finn took a short pause and continued, "Yin's year-long break was going to expire. She wants to spend time with Sgin, but also hopes to go back to work. She is quite promising. You know, it is a hard choice for her. We can take Sgin to daycare, but if there is someone who we trust to take care of Sgin while we are at work, that is even better."

"Oh, your meaning is to ask your dad and me to live in your home with Sgin?" Helen Kane asked.

"Smart! You are so smart, mom." Finn spoke louder to express a compliment, "What do you think about it?"

"I don't know your father's opinion. I can't speak for him. But I like the idea." Helen said, "I would love to see Yin and spend time with the baby. Altimont is a good place to spend time after my retirement. I would love to help Yin and as a way, to help you to get her love."

Finn thanked her mother, chatted for a while on the phone and hung up the phone. He then went downstairs to company with Yin and told her about the good news.

The week before Yin went back to work, Finn's parents moved from New York City to Altimont and lived with them.

Altimont was shut off from the outside world by long-distance farmlands, so its quiet and beautiful scenery was also remained rarely known. If you look at the map of the town, between two large hills which were separately located in the south and the north of the town, there was a river coming from the northwest direction to the south and then smoothly going upward to the right hand corner. Altimont Astronomical Station was located on the top of the south hill while the unnamed cliff which was famous among local lovers was on the north hill named Pine. Residential Area were located north to the concave part of the river and south to the hill Pine. There were three bridges in total with the south one the largest. The other two bridges were across the west part of the river, connecting the residential area to the west, which were pieces of farmlands. East to the river was an undeveloped land, where the new factory was located. People went to the west daily to take care of their farmlands but no one would usually go to the east. The river brought needed humidity; Farmlands preserved fresh vegetables and fruits; large area of greens led to easier breaths - Altimont had been indeed a wonderful place to live. It kept its peace before the new factory began to operate.

55

As the new member and the captain of TTAM team 5, Zachary Zoller newly moved to Altimont and began his career in Altimont Transgenic Technology Factory of RM Corps. TTAM, standing for "Transgenic Technology in Application of Medicine", was one of four major research projects currently held in the new factory which just began to operate six months ago. The other three projects were TTAF, transgenic technology in application of food, TTAP, of plants, TA, transgenic animals. Under each project, several teams were involved. The numbers of the teams ranged from 4 to 8 and there were about 15 researchers in each team.

There were the most number of teams in TTAM, which was said to be the newest project and the biggest hope for RM Corps. Within RM Corps' history, it was famous for its transgenic food and plants. Not much information in medicine field was comprehensively grasped by the whole company. So the involvement of the research in medicine field was definitely a new exploration for all in RM Corps.

Zachary Zoller spent all his life in California before he moved to Altimont. Zachary was from a wealthy family whose parents were well known professors all over the country. His father published a dozen of biology text books which were widely used in many colleges. His mother taught painting and had held a couple of art exhibitions in the most famous museums already. Zachary himself was deemed as a highly genius in biology and chemistry when he was in school, took part in the International Olympic Competition in Biology and got a gold medal. Not only did he have an extremely talented brain, but also he gained great interpersonal skills. After his graduation from a top phD Biology program, when he was 24, out of his parents' expectation that he would become an excellent biology professor, he applied for a researcher job in one of the RM Corps factories located in California and, a couple of years later, was promoted to the position of the team captain. Under his guide, his team developed a new technology named GF, "Grow Fast", and used in improving the seeds of plants. The period from sowing the GF seeds to the harvest reduced one third of the time the regular seeds would cause and the quality of the GF crops was twice as the one of the regular crops, measured by the height of the plants and the variety of the nutrition.

Last year, soon after his 30th birthday, Zachary Zoller received an invitation to work in the new factory in Altimont as a team leader. It was a letter sent by John Jacobs, the vice president of RM Corps and the president of Altimont Transgenic Technology Factory. In the letter, Zachary was provided double amount of his current salary and the opportunity to cooperate with MDs and do research in medicine field which had had never been done within RM Corps before. Considering the invitation for a week, Zachary decided to leave his hometown California and move to Altimont. He contacted John Jacobs by phone and accepted the job opportunity. During the phone call, John Jacobs expressed his admiration and encouragement to this young researcher. Since then, Zachary received information about the new project continuously and spent his free time reading medical books which were used in medical schools to teach future doctors. He moved to Altimont four months ago, met John Jacobs in person and started his work in the new factory three months ago with many new colleagues.

56

In the first six months, the research within the factory had a new progress. It inspired the whole teams. The new progress was from TTAM team 5, the team of Zachary Zoller. The task for the team was to create a kind of medicine used to reduce the symptoms of schizophrenia and eventually cure it with minimum side-effects. As everyone knew, schizophrenia was a serious mental disorder with the symptoms of delusions, hallucinations, unclear and confused thinking and reduced emotional express. What people didn't know was that it was also a life-long disease and the most chronic major mental illness by the level of current medical treatment. This task was first approved by John Jacobs, and later by Richard Meier. John Jacobs knew that once the team created the kind of medicine and once the factory began to produce it, not only would it bring RM Corps great amount of profit, but also RM Corps would become a success in medicine field. It might also bring Zachary Zoller a Nobel Prize. Jacobs approved the task immediately. Since Richard came back from Altimont, he avoided talking about Altimont and the new factory which would remind him of his love and his hatred with Yin, unless there was indeed a need to discuss some issues that required his approbation. When the tasks of the teams were presented to Richard Meier, he took a quick look inadvertently. When he read the task of TTAM team 5, he gave an affirmative attention to it. As he knew Yin had some mental disorders now and before, he wanted to help more people with mental illnesses. However, he felt he was not able to manage the factory directly any more, he called up John Jacobs and told him that in the future Jacobs could decide the tasks himself.

The traditional medicines which were currently used to treat schizophrenia were antipsychotic medicines associated with antianxiety medicines and mood-stabilizing medicines. The antipsychotic medicines, on the one hand, helped patients with positive symptoms; but with large dose, the medicines would bring patients strong side-effects. The side-effects might include restlessness, drowsiness, muscle spasms, tremor, dry mouth, rash, dizziness and involuntary movements mostly with mouth, lips and tongue. The need to find a new medication which could both eventually cure the disease and reduce the side-effects in the process of the treatment was urged.

Encouraged by Zachary Zoller, the members of the whole TTAM team 5 got off work a couple of hours later than members of other teams. Sometimes they even worked on weekends and holidays. John Jacobs increased their salaries for their hard work. Yet their goal was not just for a higher salary. They wanted to complete the mission by creating and producing such a medication, which by their expectation, would bring RM Corps several billions.

By the newest technology of in vitro cell culture or tissue culture and advanced computer-modeling techniques, Dr. Leonard Morain from the same team discovered that the extractive of BH1314 crocus, an ancient lavender flower, contained an extremely tiny amount of a substance which could effectively restrain the secretion of dopamine in the brain cells, which was believed to be the reason causing schizophrenia. What's more, Dr. Morain also found out that the substance could stimulate the brain cells to refine its secretion process in some degree; with the help of the substance for a couple of months and then stopping using the substance, the brain cells still kept lower secretion of dopamine. That was to say, with the help of the substance for a period of time, which was much shorter than the period of the traditional treatment, the brain cells would voluntarily secrete less dopamine. It was amazing that the substance was extracted from a natural source and so the side-effects of the substance would be almost invisible compared with other traditional medicines. This substance was ignored in the studies of BH1314 crocus before due to its tiny content – it was impossible to find information about the substance in any text books or online. Zachary Zoller named this substance after Dr. Leonard Morain and called it LM-TTAM5, to praise the contribution of Dr. Morain in this research.

The discovery of LM-TTAM5 was indeed a significant phase in the whole creation process. However, soon, after their exciting mood had quieted, the team began to face the next difficulty, one that could stop their progress all in all. LM-TTAM5 was too little to be discovered in the previous studies – only 0.00001 mg LM-TTAM5 could be extracted in every 1000 flowers. Yet the flower BH1314 crocus was so expensive that the medicine they made from the flower would not be affordable. This problem might be solved by their transgenic technology, specifically, the application of Zachary Zoller's technology GF. They might need to improve the GF technology to fit the production better.

In the next month, Zachary Zoller and his team spent all their effort and time in applying the GF technology to BH1314 crocus seeds. According to their previous GF technology, the outcome of their hard work was that the content of LM-TTAM5 was increased 50 times in the plant. It was a good start, yet it was still not enough. In order to make the final medicine affordable and in the same level of other traditional medicines, the content of LM-TTAM5 had to be improved another 100 times in the BH1314 crocus plant. That required the team to make more changes to the gene, based on the current technology and result, of the crocus plant.

Zachary Zoller divided the whole team into three sub-teams, marked as sub-team 1, sub-team 2 and sub-team 3, with each team five researchers and doctors. Each team was responsible for different tasks. The responsibility of Sub-team 1, which Zachary Zoller himself was in, was to change the different parts of the gene of BH1314 crocus to create new plant seeds; sub-team 2 was asked to extract LM-TTAM5 from the plants and observe the content of the substance; the assignment of sub-team 3 was of the analysis of the data and the advice for the next changes to the gene. Since then, the next phase of the research started to fall into place.

With another 9 months' restless hard work, finally, the team created the transgenic BH1314 crocus they desired, which could produce 180 times LM-TTAM5 of the previous GF plant. The new transgenic plant had larger lavender flowers with a yellow spot on each of their petals. So now every 1000 flowers of the transgenic BH1314 crocus could produce around 0.09 mg LM-TTAM5. According to Dr. Leonard Morain's previous research, a 1 mg tablet of the new medicine should contain 0.01 mg LM-TTAM5, which required the contribution of around 111 flowers. On the one hand, the upgraded GF technology produced the transgenic BH1314 crocus needed; on the other hand, it also led to the fast growth of the new plant, which significantly reduced the price of the plants. Soon, the first batch of the new experimental medicine was produced.

57

Since the samples of the medicine were produced, they were tested in many practical ways to prove the drug quality, safety and effectiveness. Getting approved by FDA, the last phase of the testing was clinical trials. It took the team and the factory two years to collect data and evidences and submitted them to FDA's Center for Drug Evaluation and Research. The new medicine was named Cure 5. During the clinical trials, 99.35% of all schizophrenia patients who took part in the research had more or less improvement of their brain functions, positive symptoms and negative symptoms after three to four months' taking Cure 5, even if they stopped taking the medicine after the period. Among them, around 63% had obvious improvement and stopped relapses.

Soon, with a lot of data and strong evidences, the new medicine Cure 5 was approved by FDA for wider use in the general population and it was labeled as a prescription drug. The day the new medicine was approved to be prescribed nationwide, TTAM team 5 had a short meeting with John Jacobs, in the afternoon, inside his office, to discuss the process of marketing the medicine.

John Jacobs first expressed his congratulations and his appreciation of the team's hard work in the past three and a half year, "Congratulations, everyone! I just got the message that our new medication was approved for the market by FDA. Thanks for your hard work."

Everyone else nodded and smiled. They thanked for John Jacobs' support.

John Jacobs said, "So the next and the last step for us before putting Cure 5 into the market is to produce it. Of course, the work of marketing will be done by the marketing department of RM Corps. Our work is to produce the medicine, as much as we can. I have decided to divide the rest of the 183 acres of land owned by our factory into two fields of 150 acres and 33 acres. The 150 acre field is used to plant the transgenic BH1314 crocus to produce Cure 5 and the other 33 acres is for other research topics. I have also made the decision that TTAM team 5, your team, Mr. Zoller, is responsible for planting and extracting the transgenic crocus and producing the medicine."

"Yes, that is wonderful. That is the honor of my team."
Zachary Zoller paused, grinned at Jacobs and continued, "My
question is, when will the factory begin the process of planting the
crocus and producing the medication?"

"Let me think. What do you think?" Jacobs asked, looking at
the team members.

"I think as soon as possible. The sooner Cure 5 goes to the
market, the sooner RM Corps would make much profit." One of
the team members said.

Dr. Leonard Morain followed, "I agree. When is the earliest
date that we can begin the process?"

Jacobs thought for a short while and said, "As soon as
tomorrow. But tomorrow is a Friday so I would suggest we start
the process next Monday. I would like to give you guys a day off
tomorrow. But if you want to come to the office and discuss with
me further, that is fine too."

Zachary Zoller first agreed to come for further discussion
tomorrow; others followed his decision and agreed to work. Then
the meeting ended and the team members went back to their
offices. Before they left, Jacobs again expressed his joy for their
creation.

Richard still looked as handsome and young as five years ago.
With his looking, nobody would guess he was going to turn 60
years old this year. He looked like someone who just turned his 40.
His birthday would be in the coming month, the first day of
February. He spent time alone for the past three birthdays. No
friends companied with. No lovers. Actually he did not touch any

woman in the past five years, keeping in a marriage in name only. Judy Kahn tried to ask Richard to go out for meals for times, but failed every time. He rejected her invites without giving her much explanation, just asking her to remember the deal they made before registering the marriage license. During the week, every other moment he worked, a name came unbidden to his mind – Yin, who the only woman he wanted to be with and who no longer wanted him years ago. Sometimes he spent the whole night thinking of Yin and had a hard time falling asleep. His passion and love and even his hatred for Yin's leave didn't decrease, not even a little bit. He still could clearly remember how she looked like, her pretty smile and her unspeakable shyness. She looked even more beautiful in his mind than she actually was.

Since the first letter for Christmas Day three years ago, Richard had sent at least 20 letters to Yin already, even though none of them she had responded. Every letter was short and not too much emotion was exposed, only asking if she was doing fine or wishing for a happy holiday. He didn't know Yin's birthday – she never told him, so he assumed the date they met, the 15th of June, to be her birthday. Every year when this date came, he would send her a gift wishing her a happy birthday. With his coming birthday, he wanted to write another letter to Yin. With too much emotion towards Yin, he didn't know how to express it out in the letter nor was he willing to beg her for another chance because of the hatred he kept.

The week he was thinking about writing the letter, he received a phone call from John Jacobs. Jacobs left a message and asked Richard to call back. Richard knew it was about the factory and their products. Richard had received a few emails earlier telling him about the progress of one of the research topics in the factory – they were trying to test a medicine which they believed could cure schizophrenia. Richard took a quick look at those emails without too much interest, even though he agreed with the promising research. Anything about Altimont and the factory would not raise his concern. Richard himself couldn't explain the ambivalence – on the one hand, he missed Yin every single moment; on the other hand, he did not want to step in Altimont anymore or knew about anything from the factory. Every time, Richard forwarded the email to Victor Dupont to ask him to give responses.

Richard reluctantly called up John Jacobs and they had a "long" conversation. Called it "long" because it was longer than any other conversation they had in the past three and a half years since the factory began to operate. Jacobs sounded very happy. They exchanged the weathers and asked how each other was doing. Jacobs asked about Judy Kahn. Richard murmured a little bit. Then Jacobs started to tell Richard about the approval for marketing of their new medicine, Cure 5, and the plan of producing it. Richard expressed his trust and appreciation to Jacobs and said it was wonderful to hear the news.

After hanging up the phone, Richard continued to consider the letter he was going to write to Yin without thinking about the conversation with Jacobs again. He went off work early to Midtown and bought a post card which printed the picture of Empire State Building, the landmark of New York City, on the back. Richard still remembered Yin wanted to know more about New York City. *She must like this post card.* When Richard arrived home and put the post card on his desk, he started to think about what to write on the card. He first filled out the addresses and then went to eat the food he bought earlier from a restaurant near the store where he bought the post card. When he came back to the desk, he spent the whole evening in thinking up what to write but, at last, only wrote two words.

"Miss you!"

This was the first mail in these 20 more mails which Richard sent to Yin in the past five years that Richard first expressed his emotion on it.

58

Sgin was 4 years old now and was going to turn 5 in April. New Year just passed. Chinese New Year, also described as the spring festival by the Occident, would stride over the late January and the beginning of February this year. Known as the lunar New Year by Chinese people, the spring festival would begin on the second new moon after the winter solstice and end on the full moon fifteen days later. Yet the day before the first day of the New Year, which was called Chu Xi, played a very important role in the whole festival. Growing up in China, Yin took part in the celebrations of the festival with her family for many years. She helped do some housework and prepare dinners for the family and watched the celebration TV shows during the festivals, so she had a lot of experiences in how Chinese people celebrated the festival.

She remembered every year her parents bought her new winter coat a week before the spring festival came. Yet she would wait a week and wear the new coat on the first day of the New

Year. A day or two before Chu Xi, her family usually would clean up the apartment and post the New Year's scrolls on the doors, usually written down some Chinese characters on a red paper, hoping to get some luck in the coming year. On Chu Xi, her parents would bring her to her grandparents' home in the early afternoon to help relatives prepare the dinner for the evening. A lot of dishes would be cooked before dinner time such as dumplings, water cooked shrimps, steamed chicken, shredded spiced fried beef, spiced pork and taro, fried eggplants and other Chinese vegetables. During the dinner, at 8 o'clock, family would turn on the TV and watch the New York celebration show until the midnight, the beginning of the second year. The second day, which was the first day of the New Year, in the morning, when Yin woke up, she greeted the family and wished them good luck in the whole year. Then her parents and relatives would give her small amount of money, usually 100 or 200 Chinese RMB, in red packets, as a New Year gift, and give her wishes.

Since Yin moved to the states, she seldom had chances to celebrate the spring festival. Part of the reason was due to her busy schedule; the other part was because she gradually adapted the life in the states - the importance of the spring festival was faded from her memory. She had lived in Finn's home for five years. Finn's parents moved here since four years ago. She got along well with his parents. Living in the same house with Finn's happy family, sometimes Yin was reminded of her parents and the life she should have had with Richard. This year, Yin suddenly missed her childhood and the warm feeling she gained during the spring festival, the one which she would only have surrounded by families and relatives. She wanted to hold a small celebration at Finn's home for the coming spring festival and tell Sgin some

Chinese culture. She told Finn and his parents the idea and they agreed on it. They wanted to learn some Chinese culture from Yin during this spring festival.

Two days before the festival, on the weekend, Yin took Sgin to go shopping, together with Finn's family. On the way back, she passed her apartment building. When they walked 30 feet away from her apartment building, she remembered that she forgot to open the mail box. She told them to wait there and walked back to her apartment building to get the mails. She opened the mail box and took the mails out. Among the mails, She received a post card from Richard with two words "Miss you!" on the front and a picture with a short introduction of "Empire State Building" on the back. Yin stood there, read the introduction and stared at the two words. Suddenly a remote memory and an endless emotion came up to her, making her heart bump fast. Warm tears filled her eyes. She wanted to cry due to an impulse. For a long time, years, never once did Richard ever tell her how he felt in the mails. He never again made phone calls to her. Every time in the letters he sent to her, he only asked how she was doing in short or just wished her a wonderful holiday. She hadn't had known how he felt about her and their relationship or if he still loved her. Now it was clear that he still had feeling for her years after.

Yin stood there for a while with back to the direction of Finn's family and Sgin. Not knowing why it took her so long to get the mails, Finn walked back towards Yin and called, "Yin, what are you doing?"

Yin was startled to wipe her tears and quickly put the post card into her bag. She turned back and forced a smile, "I am done. Let's go."

The post card stayed in Yin's bag for a few days. In the next few days, the beginning of the spring festival, after work, she taught Finn's family how to make Chinese New Year dishes. She mainly told them how to cook the dish spiced pork and taro, which was a very popular dish for the spring festival. They were all happy to know a different cooking way and taste delicious Chinese food. In the evenings, she explained to Sgin and Finn's family the traditions of Chinese New Year and taught them to read Chinese ancient poems. During these few days, she again felt the warmth that Chinese New Year brought to her in her early life. As now she had published many important research papers, gave talks in many places and was known by many in the field of astronomy, and, after all the years she studied and worked, after she experienced love with Richard, after she gave birth to Sgin and looked at him growing up, at the age of 32, she finally could understood that not only did she need to know how to work and struggle for her dream, life would also have other aspects that she needed to learn from, and as important; how to love and take care of Sgin was one of them.

A few days later, Yin recalled the post card in her bag. She took it out from her bag and again read the words by Richard and the introduction of Empire State Building. She still remembered the night in which she asked Richard to introduce New York City to her. She slightly lifted her left hand and straightened her fingers, gazing at the engagement ring which Richard gave to her and which she still wanted to wear after years and recalling the words Richard shouted out near the cliff, that he wanted to be with her forever. Thinking for a while, she took a paper, quickly wrote down "My son Sgin and I are happy" and put the paper into an envelope. She copied Richard's address and planned to mail this letter out the second day. Of course, in order not to affect Richard's family life, Yin did not plan to tell him that Sgin was his child.

59

From the next Monday of the approval of marketing of Cure 5, under TTAM team 5's guide, workers of the factory began to dig up the 150 acre field and carefully sow the seeds of the transgenic BH1314 crocus. The team had had planted this transgenic crocus in a small field before in order to collect samples used for the test and the seeds for the mass production and they had already figured out the regularities of cultivating this plant – the plant needed sufficient sunshine with less water and plenty of land was required for the growth of just one plant. One of the many advantages of this transgenic crocus was that all year around was the growing season for it – it would not slow down its growth even in cold winter. The period of the harvest was normally two months and then the next batch of sowing seeds could follow.

Since the seeds were sowed, Zachary Zoller and his team members went to the field daily and stayed in the field for the whole mornings. They walked around the field, observed the process and made sure every step from watering to weeding was consistent with the regularities they found out earlier. With the plants breaking through the soil and fast growing, soon the lavender flowers grew out. They collected sample plants, leaves and flowers from time to time and sent them to their laboratory. There they checked the content of LM-TTAM5 and wrote down every detail of the increase. In the afternoon, after spending time in the laboratory, they had small meetings discussing the growth of the plant and, a few times, reported the data to John Jacobs.

Two months later, one morning, when Zachary Zoller arrived to the field, a boundless blossom sea was presented in front of him. *It is amazing!* Along the straight footpath, Zachary Zoller walked into the field. A thick fragrance came. Squatting down and touching the two-color flowers brought him not only just the happiness of appreciating the nature, but also an awesome feeling that he was becoming successful. He enjoyed himself in the field and forgot the time. An hour later, he slowly walked out of the field and saw other team members. They were waiting for him. After a short observation and collection in the field, they went back to the laboratory, checked the content of LM-TTAM5 from the flowers they just collected and then decided that LM-TTAM5 was dense enough that the flowers could be cropped. They asked the workers to crop the flowers and then went back to the field to help the harvest.

---

50 days later, Cure 5, in 1, 2, or 3 mg tablets, was prescribed to patients by doctors around the country. The marketing department of RM Corps kept in touch with John Jacobs and, by his request, tried to get the medicine sold abroad as soon as possible. It would be a long process to make it used internationally, normally taking a couple of years at least. John Jacobs was not worried about their technology being copied by other medicine companies. Even if other medicine companies found out the usage of LM-TTAM5, they would have no way to produce as much the substance. One of the reasons was because it was almost impossible that they would know where to find this substance – they would not know it was from BH1314 crocus because LM-

TTAM 5 was not known by the outside world yet and the content of LM-TTAM5 in a regular BH1314 crocus was too little to be perceived. The other reason was that it was impossible for other medicine companies to copy the transgenic technology in making BH1314 crocus produce as much LM-TTAM5; even for Zachary Zoller, this highly genius himself, in succeeding the final gene change, half was due to his good luck.

John Jacobs received a report about the market analysis of Cure 5 from their marketing department a year later. He shared the information with TTAM team 5. The report showed that the selling of Cure 5 had been ranking number 1 since the third month, gave some specific examples of how this medicine worked and predicted the future market. In the report, a patient named Brian was diagnosed with schizophrenia 8 years ago and had had never stopped a traditional medicine since then. He had had a few relapses during the years. When Cure 5 went to market, he immediately changed his medicine to it. From what he described, after taking the medicine for three months, he felt much better from the negative symptoms such as laziness, lack of interest in everyday activities and inability to feel pleasure and was able to stop taking Cure 5. His families said that, in the next half a year, he became more diligent and regained interests without any more relapses. Another patient, Diane, had had lived under relapses for 20 years. She changed her medicine to Cure 5 a couple of months later after the medicine went to market. She had no relapse since then. Now she was able to manage her negative symptoms and was considering reducing the medicine and eventually stopping taking it. There were some more examples in the report.

After reading the report, John Jacobs and TTAM team 5 members went back to their duties with delight. The team members were busy preparing the harvest of the 10th batch of the crocus flowers.

60

It was again a Saturday morning in autumn. After saying goodbye to Finn's parents who wanted to spend the weekend themselves in Bellington, Yin and Finn brought Sgin to a nearby park. They stopped their car near the park and walked into the park along the footpath. The leaves of most deciduous trees turned into yellow, red and orange, decorating the autumn with colors. Yin and Sgin walked in front of Finn. The mother held her son's hand. She did not pay too much attention to the sides of the road. Suddenly, Sgin shook her hand and called, "Mom, the purple flowers are beautiful!" She took a quick look at the sides of the road. Each side was full of flowers, in the color of lavender with bright yellow spots. "Finn," Yin jerked her head in Finn's direction, "Can you walk a step forward?"

Finn walked to Yin's side, "Yes."

"Sgin just reminded me of these flowers." Yin knitted her brows and continued, "Do you think it is a little bit rare that in such an autumn day these plants are blooming?"

Finn took a quick look at the flowers and seemed attracted to them. He said, "I had never seen so many plants like that in this park before. To tell the truth, I had never even seen them in Altimont. Maybe they newly grew it. Do you know what the name of these plants is? I learned biology a lot time ago... Almost forget."

"Um, I didn't pay attention to it... Let me see." Yin took a pause, brought Sgin walking closer to the flowers, squatted down, carefully observing the flowers, "Ah, they look like crocus... No wonder... But they do not like the types I have seen in books. The ones I have seen in books do not have the yellow spots."

Finn followed Yin squatting down and said, "Crocus? Never heard of it, but they look really nice."

"Mom, what is crocus?" Sgin was curious.

Yin turned her face to Sgin, smiled and said, "Crocus is a flowering plant which usually has its flowers during the cooler seasons like autumn, winter or spring. So it is nothing strange for them to bloom in this season. Just my common sense told me that the season for most flowers was spring."

Finn stood up and assisted Yin to stand up. They three walked around the park and found that these crocuses were scattered almost everywhere disorderly. They simply did not believe these plants were carefully cultivated.

On Sunday night, Finn's parents arrived back to Finn's home. The second day, Yin and Finn rode bicycles to the station. When they just crossed the bridge, they saw the same type of crocus distributed under the trees, boundless, spreading all over the wood.

"I didn't see them last week." Finn was surprised and stopped riding.

"Me, too." Yin stopped her bicycle, looking at the farthest distance in the wood where she still could see the purple color. She said, "We might not pay attention to the plants without flowers. I think they started blooming on the weekend."

"Agree."

They did not know what exactly happened that there would be so many crocuses. They were not experts in biology and did not know where this crocus came from. But with limited knowledge in biology, they sensed that nothing could be worse than a species invasion which would cause them begin to worry.

By noon, the topic within colleagues in the cafeteria was only the crocus. When Yin arrived to the cafeteria, she was invited by Finn to sit around the same table with another researcher Peter Davis.

"Listen to what Peter found." Finn brought Yin to the table to sit down and then sat down himself.

Yin greeted Peter and asked him urgently, "So what did you find out about the crocus?"

"There is a new factory, on the riverbank of the east side, across the river." Peter said, "I happened to be in the east of the residential area on the weekend and saw the large factory across the river. They are planting acres of this crocus. The seeds of the crocus may spread from the air and the discharge and you know, the crocus itself may be very easily to grow."

"I was wondering where it came from. And now I know. A new factory?" Yin was surprised to know that there was a factory on the east side. She had had not been aware of it till now.

"Yes, a new factory." Peter said, "I think they use the crocus as an ingredient of their products."

"So what do you think they are producing?" Finn was curious, looking at both Peter and Yin.

"I have no idea." Peter shrugged and said, "Perhaps food."

"I would say so." Yin responded.

Since Cure 5 came into the market, it immediately became the center of attention, especially after many successful cases proved the effectiveness of the medicine. Cure 5 had hit the headlines in different newspapers and front-paged many magazines in consecutive months. All of the media gave Cure 5 highly acclaims. One of the newspapers which influenced the northeast even called it "The Medicine of The Century".

A few times journalists who worked for TV stations and newspapers wanted to interview Richard Meier himself but instead, Richard asked Victor Dupont to speak to them. As always, Richard did not want his face to be recognized by the general public even though his name had already made him a public figure. During the interviews, besides the amazing efficacy in the treatment of schizophrenia and relevant psychotic disorders, what the journalists concerned the most were the major ingredients which contributed to the efficacy. Of course, every time being asked by the same types of questions, Victor Dupont could only say that the ingredients were a secret of the company. Once, Victor was asked the reason why Mr. Meier did not want to accept interviews. Victor actually prepared the answer for this question a long time ago. He knew the question would be raised in the near future - it might be quite strange that, as the CEO of such a huge international company, Mr. Meier did not want the public to know what he looked like. Victor knew that it could easily be misunderstood to be the case that Mr. Meier wanted to create some mystique of himself. Victor answered the question by the answer that Mr. Meier was a low-key and private person.

Yin received letters often from Richard asking how she and her son Sgin were doing after the letter "My son Sgin and I are happy". Richard naturally thought Sgin was Finn's child and so he didn't question Yin in the letters. Richard sent Yin gifts every time and asked her to forward them to Sgin. Richard himself didn't know the reason why he cared for Sgin that much. Maybe it was because Sgin was Yin's child. Finn's family gradually knew that Yin kept in contact with Richard by mail and received his gifts. To the residents in Altimont, Finn was the father of Sgin. Yet to Finn himself, he understood that Yin always treated him as a best friend and that she was not interested in him romantically. For several times, He asked Yin to tell Richard the truth or to get Richard back to her life. Yet Yin politely rejected the ideas.

In this autumn day, Yin received Richard's letter and his package. Yin went upstairs to her apartment. She first read the letter; again it asked about how she and Sgin were doing. "Good." She mumbled, put the letter inside her bag and then opened the package. There were two things in the box. One was a CD recording some piano songs; the other was a winter jacket for Sgin. It was a khaki color down jacket with a hood. When Yin arrived to Finn's home an hour later, she asked Sgin to come and try the jacket on. Amazingly it fitted perfectly.

"Mom, you bought me this?" Sgin looked happy.

Yin brought Sgin to the couch to sit down, smiling, and said, "You daddy sent it to you."

"My daddy?" Sgin asked, putting his hands inside the pockets of the jacket, "Where is he?"

Yin took an awkward pause, looking at Sgin, and said, "You daddy, he lives in New York City."

"New York City? I have heard of it on the TV." Sgin said, "Mom, could you bring me to New York City to meet my daddy?"

Again, a long pause. Yin really wanted to bring Sgin to meet his father, but she also realized Richard was a married man. She responded, "I will try."

61

It just rained. The weather was chilly in this November Friday afternoon. In the morning, when Yin and Finn went to work, the weather was nice, so they rode bicycles to the station. Just passed the noon, the weather changed. Yin and Finn had a meeting in the station earlier. When they got off work at 5 o'clock, it started to rain again. They planned to wait till the rain stopped and then walk down the hill with the bikes. They came to the lobby and sat on the couch, waiting for the rain to get lighter. Outside, the sky was dark, probably due to the heavy rain. Sitting inside the building, they could feel cold winds flapped the glass of the front door and start to shiver. An older man with a cough walked passing them towards the front door, seeing the heavy rain, and then walked back, standing next to them. Yin took out her phone and dialed Finn's home phone number.

"Hi, Yin? How was your day? It is raining outside. Do you need us to pick you and Finn up?" Finn's mother, Helen picked up the phone.

"Finn and I are waiting for the rain to stop. We had a meeting earlier. How are you and how is Sgin today?" Yin asked.

The older man did not stop coughing. His hands covered his mouth but could not stop the noise caused by the cough.

Helen said, "I made Chai Latte for Sgin just now and he is now drinking the tea. Do you want him to pick up the phone?"

"It is ok. Let him drink the tea." Yin said.

At this moment, the older man sat down on the couch, next to Yin, still coughing badly.

"Is that Finn coughing?" Helen concerned.

"No." Yin said, and then covered the phone and jerked her head towards the older man, "Are you ok?"

The man coughed, looking at the floor, and then nodded. It seemed he had a really bad cough that it was hard for him to speak.

Yin turned her head back and spoke to the phone, "Helen, there is no need to pick us up. Please take care of Sgin. We will be back later." Yin hung up the phone and looked at the older man. Finn now walked to the front of the older man from Yin's other side.

The man was still coughing.

"Are you ok?" Finn asked.

The man temporarily stopped coughing, looking at Finn, and finally spoke, "have a bad cough. It started days ago."

"Do you work here?" Finn said.

"No, but my son works here. He also has a cough. He took a few days off but still wanted to attend the meeting in the afternoon. He asked me to company with him on the way. That is the reason why I am allowed to stay in the lobby to wait for him. You know usually they don't allow visitors to go inside the building." The man coughed and tried to balance his breath. Then he continued, "Actually, many people in my family have a cough – my wife, my son and my nephew."

"Ah. No wonder that I always heard the noise of coughing during the meeting." Finn mumbled.

"You two work here, right?" The man asked. He took a quick glance at Yin and said, "Oh, are you Yin Lin?"

"…Yes." Yin said, glanced at Finn and then looked at the older man again, "We just attended the meeting. May I ask what your son's name is?"

"Glad to meet you, Yin Lin. My son's name is Edwin, Edwin Luptak." The man said.

At this moment, Edwin Luptak walked towards them. "Dad." He called from a distance. The old man waved his hand, "Here", and then started coughing again. Yin and Finn greeted Edwin Luptak. They four talked in the lobby for almost an hour till it stopped raining. Edwin told them not only his families started to cough, a few friends of his were coughing too. Yin asked if there were other symptoms other than the coughing. Edwin said one of his friends and his cousin also companied with a fever which he did not know if is related to the cough. He said he had made an appointment for his families to see a doctor the day after tomorrow.

Maybe it is a flu?

After the rain stopped, Edwin and his father said goodbye to Yin and Finn and went back home first. Yin and Finn went to take their bikes and then walked down the hill. The weather became nice again. The sun came out from the clouds, hanged near the horizon.

Yin and Finn had a nice Friday evening with families. Maybe due to a long week's work, the second day morning, Yin woke up late at around 10 o'clock. Finn's parents Helen and Marvin were watching TV in the living room. Sgin and Finn were preparing food in the kitchen. She went downstairs and joined them.

"Yin, Sgin is a little bit coughing this morning." Finn reported to Yin.

"Coughing?" Yin paused and remembered Edwin and his father's cough. *The flu?* She began to worry. She turned to Sgin who was sitting at the table and stirring some eggs, "Is it serious, Sgin?"

"Mom, don't worry. I am ok." Sgin didn't stop his work and slightly coughed again.

Yin turned back towards Finn. She said, "Finn, do we need to bring him to the doctor?"

"Mom, I don't want to go to the doctor. Let's have brunch and then go out to the park, or the hill Pine, or go shopping. I don't want to stay at home all day." Sgin said.

"Finn, what do you think?" Yin persisted to hear Finn's opinion.

"Let's wait a bit and observe the symptoms?" Finn stopped dicing up the peppers, looked at Yin and said, "You are Sgin's mother. You need to make the choice."

"Do you think it is the flu which Edwin and his father talked about yesterday?" Yin asked.

"Maybe, um… maybe not. There is no way to know unless you bring him to the doctor." Finn said.

"Mom, I really don't want to go to the doctor."

"Ok, let's wait and observe a little bit." Yin said.

After the brunch, Yin and Finn brought Sgin to go shopping in the mall. Sgin wore the down jacket which his father sent to him. He looked very happy and was talking all the time. However, his cough turned into a bad cough gradually. For a few temporary short moments, he did not cough. Yin thought it stopped. But other moments, he was coughing. In the late afternoon that day, the cough became loud, noisy and very frequent. Sgin told Yin that he had chest tightness. On the way back home, on the car, Sgin fell asleep. When he again woke up, he was lying on his bed and covered a quilt. A small bag of ice was on his forehead. Yin sat on a chair next to the bed.

It was 11:28 PM.

"Mom…" Sgin mumbled.

"Sgin, you wake up?" Yin took the bag of ice up and put her palm on Sgin's forehead, "Temperature is still high. Let's go to the doctor tomorrow morning. I have made an appointment with a doctor."

Sgin asked, "Am I running a fever?"

"Yes, you are." Yin said, lifted a cup of water from the nightstand and delivered it to Sgin, "Drink much water."

After Sgin drank down some water, Yin said, "Let's go to the kitchen. Mom will cook dinner for you. What do you want to eat?"

"Chinese porridge."

Sgin still coughed a lot. The cough and the fever worried Yin. She was not going to sleep tonight. She would observe the symptoms of the cough and the fever till Sgin was seen by the doctor tomorrow morning.

Hopefully, everything will be ok.

62

Sitting outside of the doctor's office and waiting for the doctor, Yin again asked how Sgin felt. Sgin said his chest felt tight that he couldn't breathe easily. Yin touched Sgin's forehead to feel if Sgin's fever was gone; as her wish, his fever had remitted. Soon, they were asked by the doctor to come into his office. They went into his office and he closed the door behind. Sitting down, Dr. Karson said it was rare for him to work on Sunday but the symptoms worried him. He said it was very nice to meet Yin and that he listened to her speeches from time to time. Yin thanked Dr. Karson. Then they started to talk about Sgin's symptoms.

"First, let Sgin himself tell me what symptoms he has." Dr. Karson faced Sgin and asked, "So Sgin, tell me what symptoms do you have?"

"chest feels tight, harder to breathe…" Sgin paused, thinking and continued, "Coughing all the time."

"Do you have a fever?" Dr. Karson asked.

"Yes, a fever." Sgin answered.

"Do you feel dizzy?"

"A little bit, but not too much." Sgin said.

"It could be from the fever." Dr. Karson continued to ask, "Any problem with sleep, mom?"

"No, actually he sleeps well." Yin answered.

Dr. Karson kept asking some more questions. Yin and Sgin answered the questions as close as to the facts. Then Dr. Karson brought Sgin to do a blood test and when they were waiting for the result, Dr. Karson told them that the symptoms which Sgin had prevailed in Altimont recently. Dr. Karson said, "After seeing a few patients myself with the symptoms, the symptoms caught my attention. I know a couple of doctors in Altimont. Both of them had patients who have these symptoms, coughing, chest tightness, fever…"

"So Dr. Karson, what would be the diagnosis? Is it a flu?" That was what Yin concerned the most.

Dr. Karson said, "I didn't finish what I wanted to say. I discussed the symptoms with the other two doctors. You know these are common symptoms which can be easily misdiagnosed. One of the doctors thought it was a flu so she prescribed medicines dealing with cold and fever; the other doctor thought it was a chronic asthma. I had tried to figure out what was the cause, but had a hard time finding it out until I did a blood test with a patient on Friday. Let's wait for the result of the blood test and then I will explain to you further."

20 minutes later, the result came out. Dr. Karson received the result from his assistant and brought it to Yin. He said, "That's it."

"What?" Yin asked urgently.

Dr. Karson said, "We worked on Sgin's blood sample and found out that there is a chemical substance, HW9870 in his blood. The content is not high, yet it exists. With comparison to the blood test result in the other case on Friday in which the patient has similar symptoms, the common fact is that there is HW9870 in the blood samples. My suspicion is correct."

"What is HW9870? What suspicion?" Yin kept asking.

Dr. Karson explained, "It is a common chemical substance used in transgenic field to stimulate plants to mutate the genes. And this substance is probably from the factory. On Friday, after the patient left my office, I started to suspect the symptoms are caused by a substance which is discharged from the factory. That was the reason why I suddenly checked the content of HW9870 and a few other commonly used substances of transgenic field in the blood sample on Friday. You know that there is a factory on the east side of the river and there are plants that are growing everywhere in Altimont, right? They could be all related. Not known by many people, the factory belongs to a very famous company RM Corps and produces transgenic products, mainly a medicine which brought them huge success. As far as I know, HW9870 would only act on the DNAs of plants. This is widely accepted. Unfortunately, that is all I know. There is not too much new information online. Now we know the cause of the symptoms could well be HW9870. If HW9870 could change plants' genes, I suspect it may also change the genes of human, even though it is not supported by currently accepted knowledge and that is all my guess. If HW9870 could change human's genes by my assumption, in the worst case, it may cause tumors or even cancers. We may need to contact an expert in biology and chemistry to require further information to support what I think."

Thinking for a while, Yin said, "I think the cause of those symptoms must be related to this HW9870 and the factory. Everyone has been talking about the plants growing in Altimont and now, those symptoms commonly appear among people. Dr. Karson, we must stop the factory from discharging this substance. I know a professor who works at Bellington State University. I believe he does research in the field of transgenic technology. I will contact him for further information. I will contact you immediately after that, probably tonight or tomorrow."

"Sure. It will be easier and sooner to stop HW9870 if we can find out some supportive evidences and scientific publications." Dr. Karson said. And before Yin and Sgin left his office, Dr. Karson asked Yin to bring Sgin to his office at 6:00 PM on Monday to get an X-ray test.

63

Going back home from Dr. Karson's office, Yin looked up the contact information of Prof. Clifton Wilson at chemistry department of Bellington State University on her notebook and gave him a call. Yin and Clifton Wilson were both alumnus of the same university. They knew each other when they were in the graduate school, in Berkeley, California, but did not talk often after their graduations. Yin knew his current personal phone number, where he worked and what research field he engaged in. Prof. Clifton Wilson, phD in both biology and chemistry, was known by many chemists and biologists for his advanced research in transgenic field. Clifton Wilson picked up the phone, welcomed Yin's call and said he was more than willing to discuss the issue further in person. After hanging up the phone, Finn drove Yin and Sgin to Bellington.

On the way, to Yin's great relief, Sgin's temperature went down to normal, even though he still kept coughing. *Everything will be ok.* Time passed fast as Sgin kept talking to his mother. Three hours later, at around 2 o'clock in the afternoon, they walked into the house of Clifton Wilson. Wilson invited them to sit down and have tea, and then started the topic directly. He asked what had happened in details, including the wild crocus plants, the factory, the common symptoms residents in Altimont had and HW9870. Yin told him what Dr. Karson believed. Then Clifton Wilson brought a research paper from his study which he said was from a friend and which hadn't been published. He showed it to them.

"This is a paper about HW9870, from Prof. Stanley Bussmann in Colorado. He sent his paper to a few professors in the states."

Clifton said, "You may bring it back to Altimont and please read it carefully. Now let me explain what is in the paper." Clifton took a long pause, like thinking what he was going to tell. Yin and Finn tried to be patient, looking at him and waiting for his words. A minute later, Clifton continued, "As most people who took advanced courses in chemistry would know, HW9870 is a chemical substance used in transgenic field to stimulate only plants to change their genes. By the technology of in vitro cell culture or tissue culture, many publications have proved that it is true that HW9870 would not stimulate certain animals' cells to mutate their genes. Yet with large amount of experiments, Prof. Bussmann pointed out that, even though HW9870 would not stimulate some animals' cells to mutate, it would possibly stimulate lung cells to mutate their DNAs."

"So if the symptoms are caused by this HW9870, what disease would it be?" Yin asked.

Finn complemented, "And how serious is that?"

"That is what I am going to talk next." Prof. Wilson again paused for a short while, thinking, and then said, "Generally speaking, when a chemical substance stimulates human cells to mutate their genes, the change could cause abnormally cell division and proliferation, which is to say, the appearance of tumor or, in the worst case, malignant tumor, which is also called cancer. From your descriptions of the common symptoms people have, I think there is a possibility that people have tumors in their lungs."

"Clifton, your explanation is consistent with that of Dr. Karson." Yin looked at Clifton in wide-eyed amazement, "It is very serious. I need to stop the discharge of HW9870 as soon as possible."

Clifton said, "Yes, you may use the paper I just gave to you as a support and if possible, my words. Prof. Bussmann just faxed this paper to me to ask me to repeat the experiments in the paper before it being considered published. Before you came, I just asked him if I could show you the paper and if you could use it and he agreed. I don't know how much an unpublished paper could help though."

They thanked Clifton. Bidding him adieu, they departed his house and drove back to Altimont directly. On the way back, Yin read the paper carefully.

When they got back home, Yin immediately dialed Dr. Karson's phone number and told him what she knew from Clifton. She said that Clifton also suspected the symptoms might possibly be caused by tumors in lungs. She promised to bring the research paper to Dr. Karson tomorrow afternoon when she would bring Sgin to do the cancer check.

Yin and Finn went to work early in the second day morning wanting to speak to Edwin Luptak before work. They waited and met him in the lobby when he walked into the front door. Yin asked for his symptoms again and told him what Dr. Karson and Prof. Clifton Wilson were worried about. Hearing what Yin said, Edwin started to worry. Yin told Edwin the worry was hard to be proven but it could well be the case. She gave Edwin the business card of Dr. Karson and gave advice for him to ask his families and friends and anyone else he knew who had the same symptoms to see the doctor as soon as possible. Edwin said he was going to call the doctor when he arrived to his office.

An hour later, Edwin called Yin's office and told her that he had contacted Dr. Karson just now and that Dr. Karson agreed him to bring people he knew who had the symptoms to go to the doctor's office this afternoon.

When work ended that day, Yin and Finn went back home and prepared dinner. After dinner, Finn said he also worried about the symptoms and wanted to go to the doctor's office with Yin and Sgin. At 6:00 PM, three of them arrived to the doctor's office. In the hallway, they met a group of people. There were around 20 people and Edwin walked in the front.

"We just had X-ray tests. Dr. Karson asked us to wait in the meeting room where he said the door was open." Edwin greeted the three anxiously.

They greeted Edwin and the other people back, walked passing them and knocked the door of Dr. Karson. Dr. Karson was observing the X-rays and went to open the door. Inviting them to come in, quickly he gave Sgin an X-ray test at the lungs and then asked them to join the others in the meeting room. Before they left, Yin handed the research paper to Dr. Karson.

15 minutes later, Dr. Karson walked into the meeting room. He told people that there were more or less shadows in their lungs in the X-ray photos. He thought they were tumors. For the diagnosis of the tumors and to see if they are benign tumors or malignant tumors, further tests needed to be done. Then he asked people to come into his office one by one to explain their specific X-rays and to reschedule for the further cancer tests.

In the meeting room, people started to worry about their health and the entire Altimont.

64

When Yin, Finn and Sgin sat in Dr. Karson's office, he explained to them that the shadow in Sgin's X-ray photo is somehow bigger than those in other X-rays and that itself worried him. Hearing Dr. Karson's explanation of the possibility of cancer, Yin almost cried out. Agitated, afraid and sad, yet she tried to look strong in front of Sgin, in order to avoid his emotions reflecting her bitterness. Dr. Karson scheduled a time on the coming Saturday to do further cancer tests for Sgin. It would take them a few hours to do the tests. Yin and Finn expressed their hope to stop the discharge of HW9870 as soon as possible. Dr. Karson agreed and asked if they were available to go to collect the air samples, the water samples and the plant samples together tomorrow. Before they left, they set up a time to meet Dr. Karson in his office tomorrow afternoon.

It was 4:37 in the afternoon.

Yin and Finn, along with Dr. Karson, arrived to the bank of the river. It was a windy day. The sky went dark earlier than in summer time, which complicated their moods. Dr. Karson handed disposable gloves to Yin and Finn, "We need to keep the air and the water from contamination", put the gloves on and took out three small clear bottles from his big bag. Receiving the bottles and following Dr. Karson's instruction, they carefully opened the bottles, waited for a minute and then covered the bottles. It was to collect the air samples. Dr. Karson took out a marker pen from his bag to write down the location and the time on the bottles and carefully placed the bottles on a bottle holder. Then he handed another three bottles to Yin and Finn. This time, they bent down and contacted the bottles with the water, letting the water flow into the bottles. "Half bottle." Dr. Karson called. With half bottles of water, they stood up and carefully covered the bottles. "Great!" Dr. Karson said, collecting the bottles from Yin and Finn. He took out a cloth from his bag to wipe the water outside of the bottles, again wrote down the location and the time and then put the bottles on another holder. Dr. Karson asked the three of them to go back to their car and drove to the next location. They repeated the action till, finally, they had the collections from five different locations on the riverbank. Then they drove to different locations far from the river and collected another five batches of the air samples. It was 6:20 PM now. The sky was totally dark and the lights on the streets were turned on.

Yin called Finn's home and talked to Helen and Sgin. They just had dinner. Yin told them that she and Finn were collecting samples with Dr. Karson and would not be back until later in the evening. After that, Dr. Karson drove them to eat a quick dinner and then continued to collect the plant samples. By 8:30 PM, finally, they collected all the samples needed. Dr. Karson sent Yin and Finn back home. He knew they needed to spend time with Sgin. Then he directly drove to his office. His assistant arrived at his office at 9 o'clock and was waiting for him. They were going to work for another two hours and check the content of HW9870 in the samples.

Yin received a phone call from Dr. Karson the second day morning when she was at work. The result of the samples came out, indicating that there is HW9870 in the samples. Yin asked Dr.

Karson to write down the data in details and told him she would go to his office to take the report after work.

During lunch hour, Yin talked to Edwin Luptak. She told him the result from checking the content of HW9870 and hoped him to write a complaint these two days about everything he knew about the substance and every person he knew involved. 20 minutes later, Finn arrived to the cafeteria and joined them.

"I bought lunch for you, Finn. Where did you go?" Yin pushed the piece of pizza to Finn, "We were discussing about the result from Dr. Karson."

Finn took a bite of the pizza and said, "I just picked up a call from Emily. She is sick too."

"Emily is sick too?" Yin stopped eating and looked at Finn, "You mean from the same symptoms?"

"Who is Emily?" Edwin Luptak asked.

"A friend of us." Finn said, "Yes, the same symptoms. I gave her the contact information of Dr. Karson and gave advice for her to visit him as soon as possible."

"Seems that many people are sick by this substance." Edwin said, swallowing down the last bite and preparing for leaving, "I will write a complaint tonight and ask people who I know to write complaints too. When are we going to mail these complaints out?"

"By next week, some complaints can be mailed out." Yin paused, thinking, and continued, "We are all waiting for the tumor check these few days. We may know what to add to the complaints after that."

"I will take a day off tomorrow to get the check. I will let you know the result by tomorrow afternoon." Edwin Luptak said, waved to say goodbye and left the cafeteria.

In the cafeteria, Yin tried to persuade Finn to visit Emily after work. If it was not because Yin needed to go to the doctor's office this afternoon and then go back home to take care of Sgin, she would visit Emily herself after work. *It was very important to stop the discharge of HW9870. I need to be quick.*

All these years living in the same house with Yin, Finn sensed that Yin still deeply loved Richard, the married man, even though she never admitted. He was not sure about the future between Yin and Richard. *She has not told Richard that Sgin is his son.* Finn still loved Yin as much as he did before, yet he somehow adjusted himself to accept the fact that Yin would not like him that way. Finn agreed to visit Emily after work today.

65

Sgin still coughed often in the days since he saw Dr. Karson. He still couldn't breathe easily. Helen sent him to school in the morning and picked him up in the afternoon as usual. He loved to learn as much as Yin did when she was a child. On Wednesday, Yin went back home immediately after getting the report from Dr. Karson. She paid attention to Sgin's temperature to observe if he ran a fever again. Looking at her son, she was reminded of Dr. Karson's words that there was a possibility of lung cancer. Yet she still tried to think optimistically and hoped for the best. *Everything will be ok.* On Wednesday evening, after a delicious meal and a long walk, when they went back home, Sgin wanted Yin to read a story for him, specifically, a Chinese ancient story. Sgin was curious about Chinese culture and its stories. Yin had had read enough Chinese ancient stories when she was young. Yet this evening, she just couldn't recall any in details. Maybe deeply in her mind, there was still much worry, beneath all the hopes she kept and her strong looking. She looked up on the internet and found a good story, and then printed it out and read it to Sgin. It talked about how Cao Chong measured the weight of an elephant. Cao Chong was the son of Cao Cao, the leader of the Cao Wei regime in the Three Kingdoms period in Chinese history. Someone sent Cao Cao an elephant as a gift. Cao Cao asked the attendants for ways to measure the weight of the elephant. When everyone couldn't give a good idea, the young Cao Chong stood out and said he had an idea. He asked the attendants to lead the elephant down into a boat and mark the water line and then replace the elephant with stones until the water came up to the same line. Then he asked them to weigh each of the stones and add up the weights. He then pointed out that the sum of the weights of the stones was the weight of the elephant.

Sgin listened carefully and when he heard the whole story, he was amazed at the way Cao Chong weighed the elephant. He asked Yin a lot of questions regarding the story, from the principle of weighing the elephant to the Three Kingdoms period. Yin answered his questions one by one and said she would tell him more about the Three Kingdoms period in the future.

Thursday afternoon was the warmest afternoon in the past few days. Yin opened the window a little bit to get some fresh air. She spent the last hour before 3:30 PM on her newest research paper. She finally could concentrate on her work after talking to Edwin Luptak on the phone.

She spent 20 more minutes in her office after work hours. When she decided to leave and opened her office door, Finn was waiting outside in the hallway. Yin walked out and closed the door, "surprised that you did not knock at my door."

"I usually would, but today I just decided to wait." Finn said, "It seems you focused on work today."

They walked down the hallway and stopped at the elevator. Yin pressed the elevator button and said, "Actually, I talked to Edwin earlier on the phone."

"What did he say?" Finn asked when the elevator door opened and they walked into the elevator.

"Dr. Karson analyzed his X-ray and his sputum and diagnosed it was a small benign lung nodule. It is not a cancer and no treatment is required." Yin repeated her words again, "It is benign. It is not a cancer."

Walking out of the elevator and towards the front building, Finn exhaled a few times and nodded, "We still need to stop the discharge of HW9870."

"Of course." Yin said, "As soon as possible. I will bring Sgin to Dr. Karson's office on Saturday and mail the complaint out next Monday, along with the summary of the paper from Clifton and the data Dr. Karson gave to me."

They walked through the lobby and the front door towards the parking lot. Yin wanted to go back home quickly and tell Sgin everything will be ok.

Things went well before Friday evening on which Sgin's temperature suddenly went up again. It began at half past 7, when everyone was watching TV after dinner, Sgin started to cough frequently which got Yin's attention. She then found out that he was running a fever. Sgin told his mother that he felt sick and it was not as easily for him to breathe. The fear came up to Yin's mind and she immediately made the decision to bring Sgin to hospital. Yin realized the cough and the breathing difficulty could well be caused by the lung tumor, but she also believed the tumor, if there was one and likely there was one, was benign.

Finn drove them to the hospital. In the hospital, they talked to Dr. Ray. Under the recommendation of the doctor, Finn and Yin stayed with Sgin in the hospital that night. More tests were needed to be done to determine if there was a tumor or if there was some disease else as soon as possible. Finn and Yin decided not to go to work tomorrow until the diagnosis came out.

After a few tests, they were requested to go back to the room. Sgin's temperature was under control soon, yet his other symptoms lasted until next day. The collection of Sgin's sputum and the air exhaled from his lungs was also taken to the laboratory for further tests. Yin and Finn did not close their eyes the whole night, waiting for the result. Worried and stressful, Yin felt that she could not breathe as easily too.

At 9:15 AM, someone knocked at the door. Then the door was open. Dr. Ray walked towards them, bringing a few pages in his hands. He looked serious.

66

Dr. Ray stopped in front of Yin, Finn and Sgin, lifted the pages and looked for information in the paper. Sgin just woke up.

"Dr. Ray, is there a tumor in his lung?" Yin asked.

"According to the result of the tests, yes, there is a benign tumor in your son's right lung." Dr. Ray seemed finding the data he wanted and stopped the search in the paper.

Yin made sure the tumor was benign and seemed not as anxious as a couple of minutes ago.

Yet Dr. Ray still looked as serious as when he walked into the room. No ease appeared on his face. He asked Sgin, "Sgin, what do you already know about the disease?"

"There is a benign tumor in my lung." Sgin answered.

"What else do you know?" Dr. Ray asked.

Sgin responded, "Not much."

"We found out that other than the tumor, there is another disease. What do you want to know about the disease?" Dr. Ray asked.

Yin looked at Sgin when he was thinking. Half a minute later, Sgin told Dr. Ray, "Dr. Ray, could you tell me everything about the disease?"

Dr. Ray paused, looked at three of them to confirm they were ready to hear what he was going to tell and then continued, "The tumor itself was benign, but, based on the data from the collection of the air exhaled from your lungs, Sgin, the content of oxygen is higher than the normal standard and the content of carbon dioxide is lower than the normal standard, which is to say, the ability of your lungs to convert oxygen to carbon dioxide is not good. That indicates the likelihood of a disease other than the tumor. We talked to Dr. Karson on the phone a while ago and gained some information from him. Since the benign tumor could well be caused by the chemical substance HW9870, so could this conversion disability. According to the results of other tests, we doctors had a meeting to discuss the cause and we diagnosed you with a very rare genetic disease, namely oxygen conversion disease."

Hearing Dr. Ray's words, Yin felt sudden dizzy that she lost her balance. Finn reached out and took her arm. A huge fear came up to Yin that, for a short moment, it was hard for her to speak.

Half a minute later, Yin asked urgently, "Dr. Ray, what is oxygen conversion disease? Is there a way to cure it?"

"Oxygen conversion disease is a very rare disease. The cause has not been found yet." Dr. Ray repeated, "Unfortunately, there is currently not a way to cure it. It is a terminal illness unless there is a miracle."

Hearing the term "terminal illness", Yin's whole world was turned upside down. She felt dizzy again and leaned against Finn's arm. She just couldn't speak.

"Terminal illness? I have heard that term before. It means I am dying." Sgin said, looking at Dr. Ray, "So what is the miracle that you talked about?"

Dr. Ray was going to tell something supportive, "There was a person who was diagnosed with this disease cured in the history. He was very sick but then his major symptoms were gradually vanishing and eventually cured." Dr. Ray took a pause, seeking for their reaction, and then continued to cheer them up, "Medical treatment would help. Support from families would help. A good faith would help. I believe there should be a way to look for the miracle."

Let's look for the miracle and, meanwhile, stop the discharge of HW9870.

In the evening, Dr. Karson gave Yin a call. They talked on the phone for an hour. In the first place, he expressed his shock of hearing the news about Sgin's disease from Dr. Ray. Then he started to explain that, after talking to Dr. Ray in the morning, he asked Edwin and others to come to his office and he had just finished the work of checking the collection of the air exhaled from their lungs and did not find the data abnormal, that was to say, only Sgin was diagnosed with the oxygen conversion disease among his patients. He recommended Yin to bring Sgin to New York City to get further medical treatment. It was the same as Dr. Ray's recommendation. Yin accepted the recommendation and told Dr. Karson that she was worried about the continuous discharge of HW9870. They made the agreement to try their best to stop HW9870. Yin said what she was going to do first was to write a complaint tomorrow and, together with the other information that she received from Dr. Karson and Prof. Clifton Wilson, mail them out on Monday.

After talking to Dr. Karson, Yin called up Edwin Luptak when he was writing his complaint. Edwin told Yin that he and others would send the complaints to the factory on Monday too. They assumed the factory would stop the discharge of HW9870 immediately after reading their complaints.

Since Cure 5 became a huge success in the treatment of schizophrenia, John Jacobs was with delight daily. *I know I will become the next CEO.* He worked each workday without exception. He would arrive to his office 5 minutes before 9 o'clock in the morning and start his work for the day. At lunch time, he would have meals with his employees and go back to his office after that. He would leave his office at 4 o'clock and directly go back home. It almost became his routine.

On Wednesday morning, John Jacobs did not realize the complaints were waiting for him when he walked in his office. He looked in good spirits. Short after that, a phone call came in and he picked up. It was a call from the human resources department. The issue was that the department received a score of complaints today about a chemical substance they were using. John Jacobs asked the department to send the complaints to his office immediately.

An hour later, he roughly read the complaints. One of the complaints, which got his attention the most, was from Yin Lin, the famous astronomer. He carefully read her complaint and other attachments again. After finishing reading the complaint, he called up Zachary Zoller and other TTAM team 5 members to come to his office to have a meeting immediately. When they arrived to his office and sat down across the huge desk, he gave each of them copies of people's complaints. They started to read them.

Zachary Zoller, after the reading, spoke first, "As we experts all know, HW9870, the chemical substance they talked about, would only act on the process of the mutation of plants' genes. That's a knowledge which almost all the chemistry or biology majors would know. HW9870 has been used for a long time and by many transgenic technology factories, yet no incident has been reported. I read the paper from Prof. Stanley Bussmann. He did some research about HW9870, but the paper itself has not been published yet and was not confirmed by other biologists. On the other hand, only Yin Lin's son was diagnosed with the oxygen conversion disease. No other person was diagnosed with this disease. So it was not reasonable to believe there must be such a connection between HW9870 and the oxygen conversion disease."

Dr. Leonard Morain followed Zachary Zoller and said, "As for Dr. Karson's data, from the collection of the air, the water and the plants samples, it showed that there is HW9870 in the samples. We need to consider if the benign tumors some people have are caused by HW9870."

"Yes, we need to consider it. But like Zachary said, HW9870 has been used for a long time and accepted as not affecting human's health. With only an unpublished paper which was not confirmed yet, I personally don't believe there is a connection between all these – those are not evidences to show the connection. They can't ask us to stop the producing process based on the unpublished paper. But at the mean time, we need to take action. We need to investigate." John Jacobs asked.

"All we now can do is to start an investigation." Zachary Zoller said and then quickly viewed the information again.

After the meeting, Zachary Zoller and others went to eat lunch. John Jacobs started to write the responses to the complaints. He skipped lunch today. With strong doubt that what were in the complaints were related to their factory, John Jacobs decided not to report these complaints to Richard Meier. He didn't want Richard to worry. He felt he could handle the situation well himself. Before 4 o'clock, John Jacobs finished writing all the responses. He asked the assistant to mail them out tomorrow morning and then went back home from work.

67

"Hello." Yin picked up her phone and said "hello" again before she heard the voice of Edwin Luptak. It was late Friday afternoon, at 5:02. Yin was watching TV in the living room when Edwin called her up. Sgin and Finn's families were in the kitchen. Yin was about to help them with preparing the dinner.

"Hi, Yin, how are you?" Edwin said.

"What's up?" Yin asked and turned off the TV.

Not so surprising, Edwin told Yin that he just received the response letter from the factory. Yin said she would call Edwin back in a few minutes, hung up the phone and went to check the mail box. She also received a letter from the factory. She took the letter, went back to the living room, opened and read the letter carefully.

Dear Ms. Lin,

We have received your letter. Sorry to hear about your son's disease. As far as we know, HW9870 has been widely used by factories and no incident has been reported. It is also known as a substance that would not affect human's health. In your case, even though there is no evidence showing that there must be a connection between HW9870 and your son's disease, we are starting an investigation right away. We will inform you about the result as soon as possible.

Best regards,

John Jacobs

The president of the factory

Yin read the letter again but still couldn't find anything that could mitigate her worries. She knew it could be a very long process before any conclusion was made and before that, the factory was still going to continue the discharge of HW9870. She asked Finn to come to the living room and showed him the letter and then dialed Edwin Luptak's phone number. Edwin told her that he and others received a similar letter and that all the action the factory took was to start an investigation. Three of them decided to meet in person tomorrow morning for further discussion and made an agreement to think for a solution tonight. After talking to Edwin Luptak on the phone, Yin called Dr. Karson up and told him about the response letters. Dr. Karson said he would join the discussion tomorrow morning.

During the dinner, Yin was reminded of the recommendations from Dr. Karson and Dr. Ray and the fact that she had made appointments with some doctors in NYC for Sgin's treatment. No matter how difficult it was, she wanted to find the miracle Dr. Ray referred to. She knew Sgin needed the treatment from New York and she really wanted to bring Sgin to New York City herself to get the treatment. She even wanted to depart Altimont as soon as tomorrow. But there was another urgent issue, relating to the entire Altimont. That was to stop the discharge of HW9870. Sgin's oxygen conversion disease, the benign tumors and the common symptoms among people worried Yin, making her hard to swallow down the food. *If HW9870 can't be stopped immediately and residents continuously inhale the air and drink the water which contains HW9870, would the benign tumors eventually become malignant tumors? Would more people get the oxygen conversion disease?*

"We should contact the media." Yin said and barely swallowed down a bite.

"Your meaning is Newspapers? Do you think that will help? I didn't have this idea." Finn said.

"And TV stations." Yin looked at Finn, "There is a chance that the factory will stop the discharge of HW9870 by the press… Maybe not, but it is still another way." Yin and Finn decided to bring up the idea to Edwin Luptak and Dr. Karson tomorrow morning.

Then they talked about Sgin's disease. Yin knew that Marvin and Helen were from New York City and lived there for decades. Yin permitted that they could bring Sgin to New York City first for the treatment and let Finn and herself stay in Altimont to deal with the issue. She said that she would travel to New York City immediately after having the problem solved.

After dinner, Yin booked airline tickets online for Marvin, Helen and Sgin for Monday from Bellington to New York City. Yin and Finn would take a day off on Monday to send them to Bellington Airport.

When Yin and Finn arrived to Edwin's home the second day morning at 9 o'clock, Edwin and Dr. Karson was drinking coffee in the front yard and waiting for them. Edwin invited them to come in the yard and sit down across the table. He poured the hot coffee in the cups from a coffee pot and handed each of Yin and Finn a cup, "So did you guys think for a solution yesterday night? Dr. Karson and I don't have any good idea."

Yin and Finn took a look at each other and nodded. Finn said, "Actually, Yin thinks we should contact the media."

"Contact the media?" Edwin sat down and asked, "Can you explain?"

"Sure." Finn sipped some coffee from the cup and then continued, "We all know that the only action the factory would take now is to investigate and we feel they are not going to stop the discharge anytime soon. Yin thinks we should contact the media such as newspapers and TV stations and tell them what we believe happens. By this way, it is possible that the factory would stop the discharge sooner by the press."

"Oh, that sounds like a good idea, though I don't know if it works." Dr. Karson said.

Yin put her cup on the table and said, "I told Finn that it is another way of trying to deal with the issue and there is a chance to solve the problem."

Finn finished the cup of coffee and asked for a second cup, "By the way, the coffee tastes really delicious."

They continued the discussion before lunch time came, drinking coffee at the same time. At 11:20 AM, Yin suggested it was the time to go back home. Yin and Finn said goodbye to Edwin and Dr. Karson and then walked to their car.

68

Coming back home from sending Finn's parents and Sgin to Bellington Airport, it was almost 5 o'clock in the afternoon. Yin and Finn had a quick dinner and then turned on their laptops. They started their search for the websites of some local newspapers, local TV stations and also some famous ones nationwide, what was the best way to contact them and report to them. By 8 o'clock, they wrote down a list of who they wanted to contact, their email addresses and telephone numbers. 16 newspapers and 18 TV stations were included in the list. The next thing they did was to write emails to these media. They wrote down details in the emails of what they believed happened in Altimont including the rare oxygen conversion disease, the common symptoms and the benign tumors among people and the descriptions of the strange flowers everywhere and attached the data from Dr. Karson and the summary of the unpublished paper. They did not give out people's names, though they had already gotten permissions from people yesterday to use their names in the news reports.

At the mean time, they were waiting for the phone call from Finn's parents. Helen said she would call Yin up when they arrived to New York City, or the next day. When Yin and Finn finished the writing and were ready to send the emails, Yin's phone rang. The phone call was from Helen. She told Yin that three of them just arrived to New York City and that she would bring Sgin to meet with the doctors who Yin contacted for the treatment. Yin thanked Helen. After Yin hung up the phone, she sent the emails out.

On Tuesday, when Yin was at work, she received email responses and phone calls from the media. A few local newspapers and TV stations made an agreement to meet Yin up this afternoon after Yin finished work. The other media assigned reporters traveling to Altimont and talking to Yin in person tomorrow. All of them seemed to give plenty of concern to what happened in Altimont and said they would report or broadcast the incident once they confirmed it. On the one hand, the media got the information from Yin that the factory which discharged the chemical substance which the residents believed was affecting their health belonged to a very famous transgenic company RM Corps; on the other hand, they somehow knew Yin was the well known astronomer who contributed to the field of astronomy a few very important research papers. Yin did not give out any names other than the names of Dr. Karson, Prof. Clifton Wilson, Prof. Stanley Bussmann, Finn and herself, which she had already mentioned in the emails, during the phone calls.

After work, Yin and Finn arrived to the location in a hurry where they should meet the report teams up. Before meeting the report teams, they made an agreement not to tell the report teams about their "fake relationship" which was known by residents of Altimont. In a while, they met the report teams. They first brought them to look around and get to know the fact that the specific crocus grew everywhere in Altimont. Then they brought them to have a look at the factory from across the river. They arrived to the riverbank and the report teams prepared for the recording. When they started to record, Yin pointed at the other side of the river and said, "Can you see the factory? You may also see there are a lot more this kind of crocuses grew densely near the factory. It is clear that this kind of crocus was planted by the factory, maybe for their products, and now the crocus grew everywhere in Altimont."

Yin took a pause. Finn followed her and added, "We and Dr. Karson collected the plant samples and found out that there is HW9870, the chemical substance we talk about, contained in the samples. What's more, this chemical substance also appears in the air samples, the water samples and the blood samples and we believe it could well be the reason which affects people's health."

Reporters nodded, writing their notes, and started to ask questions.

One of the reporters requested, "Ms. Lin, so tell us more about what happened in Altimont."

Yin started to explain, "As you have already seen and I said just now, the same type of crocuses now grow everywhere in Altimont. It all started two months ago when we first saw the crocus and then we got to know there was a factory across the river in the east side. A couple of weeks ago, many people began to have the same kind of symptoms such as coughing, difficulty breathing and running a fever. Later, some of them were diagnosed with benign lung tumors. One child was diagnosed with a very rare genetic disease, the oxygen conversion disease."

After Yin finished her explanation, another reporter asked, "Ms. Lin, did anyone contact the factory yet?"

"Yes, we have written letters to the factory hoping them to stop the discharge of the substance right away." Yin said.

The reporter asked, "So you did write letters to them. And what was their response?"

Yin responded, "They said they would start an investigation immediately, but haven't stopped the discharge of the substance."

"Ok, understand." The reporter said.

The reporters then asked Finn a few questions and Finn tried his best to answer the questions. After the recording, Yin showed the report teams the data from Dr. Karson about the samples of the air, the water and the plants and the unpublished research paper from Prof. Stanley Bussmann about the discovery that HW9870 might possibly mutate the genes of lung cells. Before they left, the reporters said they would bring the recordings back and, hopefully, the news would be released the next two days.

69

Richard finished work an hour earlier than usual on Wendesday. At 3:00 o'clock he walked out of the building of his company and drove his white Ferrari FF car towards uptown direction. Next Thursday would be Thanksgiving Day. Richard felt sudden festive that he seldom felt in the past year and was in blissful ignorance of the stress work brought to him. He wanted to share his feeling with Yin. He planned to buy a couple of gifts for Yin and her son Sgin - that was the reason why he left work a bit earlier today. He was going to a clothing store which he usually visited in the Upper West Side of Mahattan.

30 minutes later, he arrived to the store, parked his car and walked into the store. He took the elevator to the children's clothing floor directly, wanting to choose another winter jacket for Sgin. He remembered that he just bought a winter jacket for Sgin a few months ago. *Did Sgin have the chance to wear the jacket?* Before meeting Yin up, Richard didn't like shopping that much due to his busy schedule in work. He now somehow started to like shopping.

An hour passed quickly. Already spending an hour in the floor, Richard hadn't decided which jacket to buy. He wanted to sit down and rest for a while. He walked to a couch near the hallway and sat down. There was a boy about 6 year old sitting next to him. With the boy were apparently his grandparents. They were talking about something which Richard did not pay attention to. In Richard's mind, he only thought about which jacket to buy. Richard told himself that he would have a whole afternoon and a whole evening to choose gifts for Yin and Sgin. There was no need to rush. Richard took out his wallet from his pocket and checked if he brought his credit card with him. Another five minutes passed. Five minutes later, he wanted to continue his shopping. He stood up and wanted to walk away.

At this moment, the boy called him, "Don't forget your wallet, Sir…"

Richard turned back and saw the boy. He had a pair of big eyes just like his and he looked just like him. Richard was startled that he couldn't speak for a moment, standing there.

At this moment, the boy's grandparents started to pay attention to Richard. They looked at Richard and then there was a flinch appearing on their faces.

"Sir, you forgot your wallet." The boy said again.

"Oh…" Richard walked back to get the wallet, said "thank you" to the boy and left the couch, still with shock. Richard didn't want to get too much attention from the boy's grandparents as they seemed as shocked as Richard himself. It seemed there was doubt in their minds.

Soon Richard picked a jacket and left the store. He drove to a bookstore and picked a CD, which recorded Christmas songs, as a gift for Yin. He bought another same CD for himself. He knew Yin liked music a lot. But one question was still on his mind. That was why this boy looked just like him.

On Wednesday evening, after dinner, Yin and Finn went online and had a video chat with Sgin and Finn's parents. Yin asked Sgin how he was doing. Sgin said everything was fine. Then Yin reminded Helen and Marvin of the doctor appointments for Sgin. The first appointment would be at 10 o'clock tomorrow morning. Helen and Marvin said they would remember to bring Sgin to meet with Dr. Hyde. Then Marvin brought Sgin to watch TV in the living room and left Helen in the study to continue the chat. After the door of the study was closed, Helen started to tell Yin what they saw in the store this afternoon.

"Yin, you said Sgin's father lives in New York City?" Helen asked Yin. She looked wanting to confirm something.

"Yes, he is from New York City." Yin answered but wanted to know why Helen suddenly mentioned Sgin's father.

"Yin, I think we saw him this afternoon." Helen said.

"You saw him?" Yin took an awkward pause, swallowed and repeated again, "You saw him? Are you sure? Where?"

"Did you talk to him and did he tell you that he was Sgin's father?" Finn asked, wanting to know what exactly happened.

Helen began to describe what she saw this afternoon, "We saw the man in the store. He sat next to Sgin and when he left, he forgot his wallet and Sgin called him. He turned back and we saw him. I think he is Sgin's father. He is tall and looked very nice and friendly. I would say he is at least 50 something, but looked like someone in his 40s. The reason I think he is Sgin's father is because Sgin looked just like him."

"So you didn't ask him, right? And what was his reaction when he saw Sgin?" Finn asked.

Helen continued her explanation, "No, Marvin and I didn't have a chance to talk to him. He stood there for a while but then when he found that we paid attention to him, he left quickly. It seems he was somewhat shocked too."

Yin thought they did see Richard. Her mood now became somewhat complicated. She really wanted to know how Richard would feel when he knew he had a son and when he knew his son had the oxygen conversion disease.

263

When he got back home, Richard placed the gifts carefully on the couch. He was going to mail the gifts out tomorrow in the hope that Yin could receive the gifts before Thanksgiving Day. He placed the CD into the CD player and listened to the Christmas songs again and again. All the evening, Richard's mood was complicated. He couldn't erase what happened in the store from his mind. The festive feeling he had earlier turned to be a mixed feeling of confusion and anxiousness. He actually didn't know what happened and what was going to happen.

70

"This is Altimont Television morning news at 5 o'clock. First, let's look at a piece of breaking news. A factory in Altimont was reported by residents on Tuesday that it discharged a chemical substance affecting their health, causing diseases and illnesses among people. Common symptoms that people have include difficulty breathing, cough and fever. Diagnoses include benign lung tumors and a rare genetic disease oxygen conversion disease. According to our sources, the factory belongs to the world-class transgenic factory RM Corps and the chemical substance the residents claimed is called HW9870. Now let's listen to the interview with Yin Lin, the well known astronomer and the resident of Altimont, and her colleague, Finn Kane."

It was Thursday morning, one week ahead of Thanksgiving Day. Yin and Finn turned on TV at 5 o'clock in the morning and were listening to the morning news. The news of the factory and HW9870 was now being first broadcasted by Altimont Television.

Yin believed other news reports would be released a bit later in the day.

Yin was now talking on the TV, explaining what happened in Altimont, "Can you see the factory?..." After Yin's explanation, Finn appeared on the screen and started to talk. The whole interview lasted for 20 minutes. And then the screen was back to the anchor, "We are trying to talk to the representative of the factory and RM Corps. We will bring the newest report to you as soon as possible."

Yin changed the TV channels. Before 7:45 AM, at which she and Finn left for work, there were three more TV channels reported the news.

"Let's buy some newspapers on the way to work." Finn said.

"Ok." Yin responded.

What happened in the store occurred in Richard's mind over and over again before eventually he fell asleep at 3 o'clock on Thursday morning.

When Richard woke up, it was already 8:15 AM, a little bit late for him to arrive to work on time. He got up in a hurry, prepared himself for the day and then went out of his apartment building 12 minutes later. Before he left, he took the CD of the Christmas songs out from the CD player and brought it and the Thanksgiving gifts with him. Usually, he would spend half an hour to 40 minutes to watch local news on TV. No time for him to do so today. Then he drove his car towards downtown direction. He listened to the Christmas songs on the way.

Arriving to the RM Corps building 26 minutes later, out of his expectation, he saw a dozen of cars stopped in front of the building, on the sides of the street. Easily for Richard to tell, those were special cars with installed equipments for TV report. Some reporters held microphones standing in front of the gorgeous front door of the building and seemed ready for their work. Many bystanders stopped on the street to see what happened. Richard had had never seen anything like that before. He was anxious and urgently to know what had happened that probably his company was reported to media.

Richard parked his car and then walked out of the parking lot to the street again. He snaked to the front, wanting to have a listen to what the reporters were trying to say. Of course, no one knew that he was the CEO of RM Corps. The reporters stood a little bit far from him that he couldn't hear clearly what they were talking about. Only one word that he was sure he heard was "Altimont". *Altimont? Yin? What about Altimont?* But when he tried to understand more, the reporter standing nearest to him stopped talking. Waiting there for another five minutes, the reporter still kept silent, seemed waiting for the confirmation from the TV station.

At this moment, two men stood next to Richard started a conversation.

One man said, "Have you watched the news this morning?"

"Yes." The other man responded, "The pollution in Altimont."

Pollution in Altimont?

"The news said the pollution is related to a factory of RM Corps. So that is the reason why the media is here." The first man said.

Factory? Altimont transgenic factory? What are they talking about? I have never heard John Jacobs mentioned anything to me.

"Excuse me." Richard interrupted their conversation, "You just mentioned the pollution in Altimont and a factory of RM Corps. Could you tell me more about what has happened and why the media is here?"

"Sure." The first man jerked his head towards Richard and said, "I happened to watch news this morning. There is a pollution reported to the media. The pollution happened in a town named Altimont. A RM Corps factory, which is also located in Altimont, grows a kind of flowers which are now seen everywhere there. What's more, the factory discharges a chemical substance into the river and the air, causing such pollution."

The first man looked at Richard. Richard took an awkward pause, swallowed and asked, "Why would there be pollution?"

The second man confirmed, "Yes, what he said is correct. I watched the news too. It said that the residents in Altimont got diseases from the pollution, for example, benign lung tumors. One child was diagnosed with a very rare genetic disease."

The first man said, "The news also said that the residents made complaints to the factory but the factory won't stop the discharge of the substance immediately. All they are doing now is to start an investigation."

"What substance are they talking about?" Richard asked, looking at both men.

The first man continued, "Something called HW9870? Not sure. I am not an expert in chemistry."

"HW9870? That is a substance which would not affect human's health." Richard said firmly, "That probably is the reason why the factory does not stop the discharge now. Residents' diseases could be caused by other reasons."

Now Richard had an idea about why the media was here in front of his company. He said "thank you" to the two men and left.

10 minutes later, he opened the door of his office. Victor Dupont was waiting inside his office, looked very anxious too. Not letting him talk, Victor Dupont started the conversation first, "Richard, there is something that I must talk to you now. Did you see the media in front of our company? I didn't watch or read the news, but if you watched news on TV this morning as usual, you probably would know the reason they came here is because there is alleged pollution in Altimont reported to the media. I received many phone calls from them already just now. That is the reason why I would know this news now. They wanted to interview you."

"I know what happened." Richard sat down and placed the Thanksgiving gifts on his desk.

"Oh, you did watch the news in the morning?" Victor asked.

"No, but I just talked to the bystanders downstairs. They told me something they heard from the news." Richard said, "But I need to know more." Richard paused for a couple of seconds and said, "Tell me what you know."

Victor Dupont said, "The Altimont transgenic factory, which produces Cure 5, was reported to the media a couple of days ago that it discharges a chemical substance, specifically, HW9870, which causes pollution in Altimont. Common symptoms, such as difficulty breathing, cough and fever, appeared among people. Some people are diagnosed with benign lung tumors. One child was diagnosed with oxygen conversion disease, a very rare genetic disease. Residents of Altimont thought the diseases were caused by the discharge of HW9870. They first made complaints to the factory but John Jacobs said the factory would not stop the production before they found out the truth or any direct evidences, which can show the connection between HW9870 and the alleged pollution, come out later. Then the residents reported to the media. That is all I know so far."

"Ok, I understand now. Yet I am still confused because HW9870 would not affect human's health. Ask John Jacobs to give me a call now." Richard said.

71

After a short while, John Jacobs called Richard's office. Richard picked up the phone. Richard first told Jacobs what happened he saw and heard this morning and asked further information from Jacobs. After getting confirmation from Jacobs that the chemical substance the residents of Altimont suspected affecting their health was indeed HW9870, Richard said, "John, there must be some misunderstanding from the residents. I was a chemistry major and I know chemistry. HW9870 would not affect human's health."

"You are right, Richard." Jacobs said, "The team leader of TTAM team 5, which created Cure 5, Zachary Zoller told me the same thing. He also said HW9870 has been widely used for a long time and was already accepted as not affecting human's health. That was the reason why I told the residents to wait for our investigation. You know there is no evidence to ask us to stop the production of Cure 5."

Richard said, "You did the right thing, John. I am not blaming you for what happened this morning, but you should have told me about this earlier. Now people all over the world know about the news. It may affect the reputation of our company and Cure 5."

Jacobs apologized and explained that he just did not want Richard to worry. Richard said let him think for a while and he would call John Jacobs a bit later to tell him a solution.

After hanging up the phone, Richard reminded himself of the days he spent in Altimont and how much happiness he gained during those days. The moments he spent with Yin, like it happened yesterday, played on his mind. He still clearly remembered the kiss he first gave to her, the words he shouted on hill Pine that he wanted to be with her forever and what her engagement ring looked like. For 6 years, Richard tried to avoid thinking about Altimont as much as he could, as it would get him very emotional. However, now there was an issue in Altimont that he had to think about it. He could understand why residents in Altimont would suspect HW9870 discharged from Altimont Transgenic Factory affecting their health. But, to Richard, it was very clear, as anyone who had learned advanced chemistry would know, that HW9870 was not such a chemical substance which would affect people' health. *It is impossible that HW9870 would cause tumors and oxygen conversion disease, as the residents claimed. I have to explain this to the residents in person to protect the reputation of RM Corps from damage.* Even though there was much unwillingness for Richard to step into Altimont again, he felt there was a need to go to Altimont himself to give the explanation to the residents.

RM Corps had had gotten excellent reputation worldwide before this morning. Especially after the success of Cure 5, RM Corps became the number 1 in transgenic medicine field. Since he became a professional businessman, Richard was successful in avoiding his own life being reported by the media. Yet now this alleged pollution in Altimont might be hugely impacting the reputation of Cure 5 and RM Corps negatively. If not solved properly, the situation could eventually get out of control and the damage could be uncountable. After thinking for almost an hour, this time, Richard decided to appear in front of the media to give the explanation to the residents, as he was never a coward and would not be one. This would then be his first time to be reported by the media. He knew once it happened, people all over the world would know what the CEO of RM Corps looked like.

He dialed John Jacobs' phone number.

Picking up the phone, John Jacobs asked directly, "Richard, so what is your solution?"

"I decide to go to Altimont in person to give an explanation to the residents and discussed the issue with them." Richard answered.

"You will come in person?" John Jacobs paused for a second and then continued, "Ok. Let me tell the residents and organize the meeting. When will you come?"

Richard took a quick look at his schedule for the next few days, "Um… Let me see." Thinking for 3 minutes, Richard told Jacobs, "I will cancel the international conference held from next Monday to Tuesday and the trip to France next Thursday, so I will be temporarily free from tomorrow to next weekend. I will go to Altimont tomorrow. I know it will take a few days for you to organize the meeting, contacting the residents, and for me to prepare for the meeting. So please hold the meeting with the residents next Thursday." The international conference which would be held in Scotland next Monday and Tuesday was for successful business persons to communicate their experience in doing business. Richard had had agreed the conference committee to attend the conference before the news reports almost brought RM Corps an international scandal. Now he had to cancel it. *Nothing else was as important as the issue in Altimont.*

"Ok. Recall next Thursday will be Thanksgiving Day." John Jacobs said.

"No problem. Just next Thursday." Richard said, "Please invite the media to come that day in the meeting room, too."

"Richard, I thought you did not like to be reported by the media…" John Jacobs said.

"Just organize the meeting as my request." Richard said before he hung up the phone.

72

As the rest of the Thursday, many more TV channels and newspapers reported the news. The Friday morning news said the report teams went to the building of RM Corps in downtown New York City and was waiting for the response from the representative of the headquarter of RM Corps.

When Yin was at work on Friday morning, she received a phone call from an unknown number. She did not pick up the phone immediately, but waited till lunch time to call it back.

"Hello?" Yin said, "I received a phone call from this number earlier today."

"What is your name?" A woman said.

Yin answered, "My name is Yin Lin."

"Hold on." She said.

The phone call was transferred. Half a minute later, a man began to speak, "Is that Ms. Yin Lin, the famous astronomer?"

"Ah?" Yin felt odd to be asked like that and did not know how to give an answer. Paused for a few seconds, she finally said, "Yes, this is Yin Lin, an astronomer from Altimont Astronomy Station, not sure about the famous part."

The man said, "Ms. Lin, this is John Jacobs, the president of Altimont Transgenic Factory of RM Corps and the vice president of RM Corps. We received your letter last week about HW9870."

"Yes. So have you had a conclusion from the investigation yet?" Yin wanted to know the answer. *Maybe he wants to tell me something about the news.*

"Yes." John Jacobs responded immediately, "The owner and CEO of RM Corps wants to give an explanation to the residents of Altimont himself. He will arrive to Altimont later today and there will be a meeting held next Thursday. I am going to give you where the meeting will be held and I would like you to tell the residents who want to attend the meeting about it and give me a name list of who will attend the meeting before next Tuesday." Then John Jacobs gave Yin the address, a meeting room in the factory, and the time the meeting will start. Yin wrote down the meeting details carefully and confirmed them again, "Ok. I will inform the residents about this meeting. I am sure that many people want to attend the meeting."

John Jacobs said, "The meeting room is huge. It has 2500 seats. We will invite many media to come so it will probably take 500 seats. You may invite at most 2000 people to come."

"Ok." Yin said.

John Jacobs continued, "One more request I would like to add is that we want a resident to represent the residents to give a brief talk about his or her side of the story and involve in a discussion with the owner and CEO of RM Corps, during the meeting. I would like you to give me the name of the person before Tuesday, too."

"In front of the media?" Yin asked, writing down the request.

"Yes, and the media has told me that it would be a live meeting. That is to say, people all over the world will know about the meeting immediately." John Jacobs said, "Ms. Lin, I hope you will be the speaker."

"I will consider it." Yin said. Then she confirmed again all the information she just wrote down.

73

It was almost 9 o'clock in the morning. The cabin door of the RM Corps' jet was already closed. In a few minutes, the jet would depart New York City. Sitting on the jet, Richard took a gaze at the window. It was a sunny day. The sunshine illuminated the wing of the jet to be golden color, bringing some warmth to this cold weather. It reminded Richard with the trip he had years ago to Altimont. The difference, after years passed, besides the difference in weather and season, was that Richard had a more complicated mood than before. On the one hand, it was the very important issue that he was going to deal with in Altimont bothering him; on the other hand, once thinking of that the distance between him and the woman he still truly loved would be decreased and that soon they would be in the same town again, his heart started to beat fast.

Seven hours later, at 4:15 PM, Richard, for the first time, sat in the meeting room of the factory with John Jacobs.

"Richard, it was a little bit late today, so let's talk briefly. We can meet again on the weekend or next week before Thursday for a longer talk." John Jacobs said, "This is the meeting room which will be used for the Thursday meeting."

"It is big enough." Richard gave John Jacobs a slight nod, "Have you started to contact the media, John?"

John Jacobs looked at Richard firmly and said, "Yes, I did." Paused for a second, John Jacobs continued, "I contacted, I think is, 34 well known TV stations and 19 newspapers publishers yesterday immediately after I talked to you on the phone. The TV stations all agree to come and telecast the meeting live."

"Good." Richard said, lifting his thumb.

John Jacobs said, "As for the residents who will attend the meeting, I will get the name list next Tuesday. I would say 2000 residents will attend the meeting." Thinking for a few seconds, John Jacobs continued, "I arrange that a resident will represent others to give a talk first, you know, to the media, again, about what they believe happens. And then you may involve in a discussion with him or her. It will be more like a debate. The resident, as we all know, will point out that HW9870 is affecting their health. So all you need to do is to review the knowledge of HW9870 and use it to give a believable explanation that the substance would not have such an impact."

"Definitely, HW9870 is not the reason. So what do you think is the reason that caused the diseases?" Richard asked.

John Jacobs responded, "Something we don't know about. But as you said, definitely not HW9870, as the residents claimed. You know Cure 5 is such a good medicine that is helping a lot of people. Yet the reputation of Cure 5 and the whole RM Corps is now at risk of being totally damaged because of something untrue. They have an unpublished paper about the possibility that HW9870 would affect human's health. We told them that we were starting an investigation. But that is indeed all what we can do. We can't stop producing Cure 5 based on an unpublished paper, without further evidences."

Richard talked to John Jacobs in the meeting room for another 10 minutes and then they left the meeting room and the factory. John Jacobs sent Richard back to the hotel. Before Richard got off the car, John Jacobs told him that he hoped that Richard could meet with the resident representative next Wednesday, a day before the meeting day.

Richard went back to his hotel room. It was the same hotel and the same room which he stayed last time he visited Altimont.

Yin and Finn contacted Dr. Karson, Edwin Luptak, Emily Lawless after work on Friday and told them about the coming meeting. They agreed to attend the meeting and contact people they knew for the information. Yin herself was not very sociable and did not know many people. She contacted a few others she knew and got another few names to the list.

Yin spent the whole Saturday in front of the computer talking to Sgin and Finn's parents. Helen told Yin that Sgin's doctor, Dr. Hyde, would give Yin a call to discuss the treatment before next weekend. Yin thanked Finn's parents and told them about the Thursday meeting. Yin said, "Next Thursday, there will be a meeting held in the factory that will be telecasted live. The owner and CEO of RM Corps will come and talk. The president of the factory hoped me to represent the residents to discuss the issue with the CEO during the meeting."

"We will watch TV." Helen said, "Just hope you can come to New York City as soon as possible."

Yin agreed, "Hopefully, I can persuade the CEO to stop the discharge of HW9870 on Thursday and if then I will go to New York City on Friday."

At the end of the day, before Yin turned off the computer, she told Finn's parents that she would pay attention to the phone call from the doctor next week.

On Sunday, Dr. Karson, Edwin Luptak and Emily Lawless each gave Yin the names of hundreds of people they knew who wanted to attend the meeting. They all hoped that Yin was the person to represent the residents to talk. After years of practicing speaking in front of audience and giving talk all around the country for her research topics, Yin finally had some confidence to talk in front of people. Yet this time, everyone hoped her to debate with the CEO of RM Corps in front of the world. That made her a little bit nervous. But she had decided to accept the task.

On Tuesday morning, Yin called John Jacobs and faxed the name list to him. She said she would be the representative to talk for the residents. John Jacobs hoped Yin to come to the factory on Wednesday afternoon, after work, to meet with the CEO of RM Corps, before Thursday.

After coming back to Altimont, Richard's mood became quite simple. Not as what Victor Dupont had had told him that it would take four five years to have nostalgic ties to the town, the second time Richard came into it, he suddenly had a sentimental attachment to this small town, which he would only have for his hometown. He didn't experience this feeling last time he was in Altimont and this feeling went stronger and stronger within hours. This sentimental attachment, Richard believed, was probably brought by the deep love he had for Yin. Richard even felt he was willing to give up all he gained through his business just to get back to the old days and ask Yin to give him another chance. Just let him talk to her in the morning when she was gone. But he later realized it was just his day dream which would never come true, because now Yin was the wife of another man and the mother of the man's child. *It is better not to meet her.*

The whole weekend, Richard stayed in the hotel room, lying on the bed and tasting the feeling. A voice message from John Jacobs asked again if Richard would be available on Wednesday afternoon to meet with the resident representative, but Richard did not respond the message. Until Wednesday came, he walked out the room and asked the driver of his company to take him to hill Pine.

74

"So Ms. Lin, how is your son?" John Jacobs asked.

It was 4:47 PM, Wednesday. Yin and John Jacobs were the only two sitting in the large meeting room, which would hold the live meeting tomorrow. With them sitting in the front row, the voice of John Jacobs was raised by the voice amplification effect of the room.

"I am seeking treatment for him." Yin answered simply, peering slowly around the meeting room. It was indeed a very large room. Besides the wide stage, on which a dark brown sofa set was placed in the middle with microphones in front of it, the rest of the room contained four sections for the attendants with one section on the second floor.

"I have spoken in rooms similar to this before." Yin said and gave attention back to John Jacobs.

"Good. Don't get nervous when you talk. Try to explain as clearly as you can." John Jacobs took a look at his watch, "Let me make a phone call to my boss."

John Jacobs took out his phone and dialed Richard's phone number. The call went through but it seemed Richard turned off his phone. John Jacobs left a brief message, "This is John. Just would like to know if you still come to meet with the resident representative today." Then he hung up the phone and told Yin that he would call the boss again a little bit later.

From the moment Yin walked into his office earlier, John Jacobs had found that the young lady was indeed very beautiful as described in the gossip. Not only did she have a good looking and a nice smile, it could be deemed that she was also very intelligent from the way she talked. Now that he looked at Yin again. The well known astronomer was sitting in front of him. As everyone in Altimont knew, John Jacobs also heard that, in the early 30s, Yin had already published a few important research papers about the sunspot which were now read and understood by many astronomers worldwide, making her a very young astronomer to make the achievement. She was well known in the field of astronomy. John Jacobs suddenly had strong respect towards Yin.

John Jacobs took a second look at the watch and said, "Tomorrow, when the meeting starts, at 8:30 AM, you will talk about your story. It will take about half an hour. After that, my boss will walk to the stage. You two will sit on the sofa set and start a conversation. He will explain to you and the media and you can discuss details with him."

Yin listened carefully and nodded.

40 minutes later, Richard still didn't come. John Jacobs dialed Richard's phone number but Richard's phone was still turned off. John Jacobs started to worry. He asked Yin to wait in the meeting room, walked to his office alone and found the phone number of the driver who took Richard to places in Altimont this time. He dialed the phone number of the driver. The phone rang. The driver picked up and told John Jacobs that Richard was on hill Pine. John Jacobs asked the driver to remind Richard to call him back later and then walked back to the meeting room.

"Sorry, Ms. Lin. My boss is not here in the factory. I assume he would not be able to come today." John Jacobs paused and said, "It is a little bit late. Let you go home now. Let's see if you will meet with him tomorrow before the meeting, if not, then you will definitely meet during the meeting."

John Jacobs and Yin walked out the meeting room to the gate of the factory. John Jacobs thanked Yin for coming before they said "see you tomorrow" to each other.

Michael Hernandez was among the attendants to the Thursday live meeting. As for many other residents, Thursday morning was a busy morning for him. He woke up at 6:15, prepared himself for the day, ate a quick breakfast for about 20 minutes and then went out from home. Usually residents did not get out to the streets at such an early time. Today it was an exception.

Michael Hernandez drove across the bridge and then turned east and arrived to the gate of the factory at 7:20. Some residents had arrived and talked to each other in front of the gate. Many special cars for TV report stopped near the gate. The report teams were preparing for the coming meeting. Michael Hernandez parked and got out of his car and joined the discussion. They talked about that the owner and CEO of RM Corps would have a discussion with Yin Lin during the live meeting.

10 minutes later, at around 7:40, the report teams were allowed to go into the factory. Residents were asked to wait for another while. Many residents arrived to the gate in the next 20 minutes.

At 8:00 AM, Michael Hernandez, along with many other residents, walked through the gate into the factory. They were directed to walk through the front yard and then the front door of a huge building. They used both the stair and the elevators to get up to the second floor. Walking down the hall, there was a few huge doors. With them walking through the doors, the meeting room appeared.

Michael Hernandez found a seat in the middle of the first row of section 2, right after section 1 which was fully occupied by the report teams.

10 rows ahead, Yin sat in the middle of the first row of section 1, reminding herself with the words she was going to speak during the meeting. Besides her were Finn and John Jacobs. Finn turned his head back, glancing around the back of the meeting room. John Jacobs tried to contact Richard yesterday evening and finally Richard picked up the phone. John Jacobs told Richard the

process of the meeting and that the discussion part would begin at around 9 o'clock. Richard promised to arrive to the meeting for the discussion with the resident representative. Other than that, he did not want to say anything more. John Jacobs sensed the eccentricity Richard kept since he came to Altimont. He understood that it could be from the stress Richard got about the coming meeting, so he did not ask more and hung up the phone. However, this morning, till now, 15 minutes before the meeting begin, Richard still did not come. That made John Jacobs very anxious.

I must find Richard now.

75

The meeting began on time at 8:30. A host walked from the back of the stage to the front, stood in front of the sofa set and announced to the microphone, "Ladies and gentlemen, welcome to the live meeting held in Altimont Transgenic Factory. Today we invite around 2000 residents of Altimont, 34 TV report teams and 19 newspaper publishers to come. People all around the world can follow the live meeting on TV." Paused for a couple of seconds, the host reminded herself that, a few minutes ago, John Jacobs was still waiting for the CEO coming to the factory and so asked her not to announce the coming of the CEO before he actually came, even though, to her, it was clear that people all around the world got the information from the media earlier that the CEO of RM Corps would talk during the meeting. She was a new college graduate and luckily given this opportunity to speak in front of the world. She did not want to make any mistakes. She continued her announcement, "In the past week, there were reports about that a chemical substance, namely, HW9870 which has been used by RM Corps is producing pollution in Altimont, causing residents to have symptoms and diseases. We are going to find out the truth about it during this meeting. First, let's welcome Ms. Yin Lin, the researcher of Altimont Astronomy Station and the resident of Altimont, to speak for other residents about what has happened in Altimont. Ms. Yin Lin has contributed some research papers which are now deemed to have very important status in the study of the sunspot."

Yin stood up, climbed up to the stage, walked to the middle and faced the audience. She received the microphone from the host, swallowed, and started to speak.

Miles away, Richard was on the way to the factory. Richard woke up early today at 6 o'clock, had breakfast and then prepared himself for the meeting. He wore a new black suit chosen for the meeting, black leather shoes and the same cobalt blue tie which Yin had seen, looked very professional. He changed clothes, especially ties, quite often, yet years passed, he still kept the cobalt blue tie.

The same driver was waiting for him downstairs. He left the hotel at 7:26 AM, knowing that he had to arrive to the factory before 9 o'clock. Yet suddenly, before the driver drove him on the way to the factory, he wanted to gather some courage by visiting Yin's apartment once again. He could still clearly remember how to go to Yin's apartment from the hotel. He stood in front of Yin's apartment building for almost half an hour before he left for the factory, which pretty much encouraged him to face the issue.

10 minutes before 9 o'clock, Richard arrived to the factory. John Jacobs was waiting at the gate. "Richard, finally you come. We have to be quick." John Jacobs exhaled multiple times and brought Richard walking through the yard, directly towards the meeting room, "We can't walk into the meeting room now because then everyone will know you are late to the meeting. Let you walk from the back of the stage directly to the front. In that way, no one would know that you are late."

When they arrived to the back of the stage and met the host there, it seemed the resident representative just finished telling her story. *Thankful we are not too late.* John Jacobs introduced Richard Meier to the host in a hurry and asked her to announce the discussion section that the owner and CEO of RM Corps, Mr. Richard Meier, was now going to discuss the issue with the resident representative.

From the back of the stage, Richard and John Jacobs could hear the voice of the host clearly, "Ladies and gentlemen, now it is the discussion section of the meeting, let's welcome the owner and CEO of RM Corps, Mr. Robert Meier."

A mistake! Not Robert, Richard! Richard walked through the door to the front of the stage with a microphone in his hand, blaming the host for mistaking his name. *Anyway, I will make the correction.*

Yin, holding the microphone, sat down on the sofa set with back towards the direction of the door when Richard walked through the door onto the stage. She jerked her head 45 degree, looking at the media and the audience, and felt relieved from the stress she held just now when she spoke, waiting for the CEO to sit down across on the other sofa and join the discussion.

Richard walked a few steps on the stage and then stopped. A silky raven shoulder-length hair appeared in his eyes. Richard could perceive the familiar black hair and the portion of the cheek of the woman.

Yin? Is that her?

Richard's heart started to beat fast. He hesitated for a few seconds, which got the full attention from the audience, and then walked to the sofa. When he passed Yin with his back towards the audience, he tried to give a nice smile to her. Now he could see the woman was indeed Yin. His heart beat faster and faster with emotions coming up to his mind. His eyes were wet by tears. He quickly blinked to dry his eyes, exhaled to be less emotional and sat down on the other sofa, facing Yin.

Richard? Yin was startled to see Richard sitting across from her. *Richard is the owner and CEO of RM Corps who I am going to discuss the issue with? Richard is the owner of the factory which discharges HW9870?* At this moment, it was hard for Yin to speak, same with Richard. They looked into each other's eyes, like communicating by eyes. Emotions came up to both of them. Everyone looked at them two and waited for the discussion, but the odd was that neither of them started to talk.

Finally, a few minutes later, Richard lifted the microphone to his mouth and started to talk, still looking into Yin's eyes, seeking for her reaction, "My name is Richard Meier, the owner and CEO of RM Corps. Sorry, someone just mistook my name. Let's discuss the issue?"

Hearing Richard's voice which she didn't have a chance to hear in the past 6 years, tears came out and filled Yin's eyes. She could no longer hide the fact that Sgin was Richard's son from him, "Did you know you are the father of a child who is dying?"

Noises spread from the audience and then a long silence occupied the meeting room. Everyone was so confused and tried to know what had happened and why Yin Lin would say what she just said.

Richard was very surprised to hear Yin's words. He tried to figure out what Yin exactly meant, reminded himself of the boy he met in the store and finally found the answer. Now he could almost understand everything but except one thing. That was why Yin chose to leave him instead. He asked, "Your meaning is that Sgin is my son? I think I saw him in New York City. Is that him?"

Noises came out from the audience again. Michael Hernandez, sitting on the nearest seat of sections for residents from the stage, couldn't believe what he just heard. He tried to recall what happened during that time that Yin suddenly left Richard in a morning and went for a vacation with Finn. He always couldn't understand it and the reason behind it.

Yin gave Richard a nod, "He was diagnosed with the oxygen conversion disease because what has been discharged from your factory and he is in New York City with Finn's parents for the treatment."

Richard felt a sudden sadness and he totally understood how Yin had felt from what she just told him. He stood up, walked a step further towards Yin, helped wipe her tears and sat back on the sofa, "Why did you leave me that morning?"

What? You know why!

Yin cried out again, "Because I happened to pick up your phone call which was from your wife."

"What?" Richard said firmly, "I didn't have a wife. I was single."

Everyone was confused. Yin was so confused and explained, "There was a woman who said she was your wife and I was the other woman."

Now Richard sensed what happened during that time. *It must be Judy.* Richard said, "You were and are not the other woman. There was something misleading. Why didn't you tell me that? Why chose to flee?"

Tears fell down from Yin's face. Pausing for a few seconds, she said, "I had no choice."

Michael Hernandez, with everyone else, now understood what happened between them and the reason why Yin chose to leave Richard.

Richard again walked to wipe Yin's tears.

Yin looked at Richard and said, "Now I just hope to persuade you to stop the discharge of HW9870 so I can go to New York City tomorrow."

"Let's go to New York City together tomorrow." Richard said in a nice voice, "But please just give me a chance to explain something for HW9870."

Everyone kept silent again, listening to Richard's explanation.

Richard said, "I studied some chemistry courses when I was in college and has been working in transgenic field for 25 years. From the view point of science itself, as almost every chemistry major who studied advanced chemistry courses in a university would know, HW9870 is a chemical substance which would not affect human's health. Also, HW9870 has been used widely for a very long time with no incident reported. I think the diseases residents and our son got have nothing to do with HW9870."

Yin followed Richard and said, "But the symptoms are quite common now. You know, cough, difficulty breathing, fever and the benign lung tumors. And now Sgin was diagnosed with the oxygen conversion disease, a very rare genetic disease. The crocuses which are planted by your factory now grow everywhere in Altimont. Even like what you just said, HW9870 is not the reason causing the pollution, but it is still reasonable to believe there is some connection between the pollution and your factory, even with some unknown reasons. We really can't find the evidence to support it, but, Richard, please temporarily stop the production and find out the truth first."

Pausing and thinking for a minute, Richard totally agreed what Yin just said, "You are right." He looked at Yin, "Let's stop the production temporarily and find out the truth first."

Yin's words succeeded in persuading him to think about the possible connection between the pollution and his factory, even if the reason might be unknown and there was no evidence to support that there was such a connection.

Everything will be ok.

Since Richard came to Altimont again, he had felt that he could give up all he gained from his business for another chance with Yin. Now He finally understood the reason why Yin chose to leave him and there seemed to be hope.

76

The meeting ended in people's huge shock – now the first time people all around the world got to know this rich and handsome CEO, at the same time, they learned the love story between him and the well known beautiful astronomer. But to Yin and Richard, it was a new start. When the meeting ended, they walked down the stage hand in hand.

After the meeting, Richard told John Jacobs to temporarily stop the production of Cure 5 and find out about the truth and solve the problem as soon as possible so that Cure 5 could be produced soon again. An hour later, in the factory, Yin received a phone call from Sgin's doctor, Dr. Hyde, who said he just watched the live meeting and was still in shock. The doctor discussed Sgin's disease and treatment with Yin and Richard through video chat.

"Glad to meet you, Mr. Meier and Ms. Lin, Sgin's parents. My name is Jonathan Hyde, Sgin's doctor. I talked to Ms. Lin earlier on the phone." Dr. Hyde said.

Richard and Yin said, "Glad to meet you, Dr. Hyde." Richard continued, "We will arrive to New York City tomorrow and we can meet in person then. So now tell us more about Sgin's disease."

Dr. Hyde said, "Sgin has the oxygen conversion disease, which is very rare and hard to be cured. Here, I don't use the word 'terminal illness', but rather 'hard being cured', because with proper treatment and the support from families, there is hope to get this disease cured... Um, at least there was a case like that in the history." Dr. Hyde paused, looking at both Richard and Yin, and continued, "As for the disease itself, it is a genetic disease, which is to say, the genes of lung cells has been more or less changed, causing the lungs of the patient have difficulty to absorb oxygen and convert it to carbon dioxide."

"Is there a treatment plan?" Richard asked urgently.

Dr. Hyde said, "As I said just now, it is hard to be cured but not absolutely can't be cured. However, there is no such successful treatment plan developed yet."

"Is it equal to say it is a terminal illness?" Yin asked.

"Not quite," Dr. Hyde said, "What I meant was that there is no a successful treatment plan to cure the disease yet. However, with proper treatment, the development of the disease can be slowed down to some degree. At the mean time, if there is enough luck, the disease may just disappear itself. And, again, there was such a case in the history."

"A miracle!" Yin and Richard said together.

"Yes, a miracle." Pausing for a few seconds, Dr. Hyde said, "Besides the treatment, support from families is very important, too."

Richard said, "We will arrive to New York City tomorrow. Can you tell us the treatment in details then?"

"Sure," Dr. Hyde said, "Just give me a call when you arrive to the city. I can meet you in person and give you more information."

After Yin and Richard talking to Dr. Hyde, Finn drove them to a coffee shop. There they discussed what happened during that time, how they spent the years and removed each other's misunderstanding.

77

When the sky just turned blue from dark, Yin and Richard left Altimont for New York City. Three hours later, they arrived to Bellington. From there, they took the RM Corps' jet to New York City. At 1:14PM, they arrived to LaGuardia Airport in Queens, New York City. Finn's parents would pick them up. Sgin would also come.

In the past 6 hours, on the way to New York City, silence occupied the air between Yin and Richard most of the time, except, a few times, Richard expressed his complicated mood that he was going to see his son again today. They both felt kind of relieved, from the meeting and years of misunderstanding, mixed with unexpressed hope and anxiousness related to Sgin's disease.

20 minutes later, they walked out from the airport with luggage. Sgin saw his mom and dad immediately. "Dad, dad!" Sgin called. Jerking his head towards the direction of the voice, Richard saw Sgin, the same boy he met in the store. *That was him. I know that.* A smile naturally showed on Richard's face. Yet, at this moment, he found himself hard to move due to the ecstasy. This was the first time in his life that he was called "dad". When

he was still in surprise to see Sgin, Sgin ran towards him. "Dad, dad!" Sgin called again. Richard naturally stretched his arms to hold Sgin. He lifted Sgin and hugged him in his embrace for a while. Yin walked a couple of steps further and stood next to them with a smile on her face. Finn's parents walked next to them with a smile on their faces.

"It is really nice, isn't it?" Finn's parents talked to Yin.

Yin nodded, still smiling.

"Your name is Sgin, right?" Richard looked at Sgin with a smile.

"Yes, dad." Sgin said, "S-G-I-N."

"Great." Richard said, "A really cool name. What does it mean?"

"You can ask mom." Sgin answered and looked at Yin.

Richard turned his head towards Yin and asked, "What does it mean, Yin?"

Yin grinned at them and laughed out loud without words.

"What does it mean?" Richard asked again nicely.

"You will know." Yin said.

Richard turned his head back and looked at Sgin, "Sgin, we have met before, right?"

"Yes, in the store." Sgin said, "You forgot your wallet."

Richard laughed out loud, "Yes... Actually I was in the store buying a gift for you. Did you receive the gift?"

Yin immediately said, "Your gift arrived on Tuesday and Sgin was in New York City, so… I brought the gift."

"Oh, ok." Richard said and gave a smile to Sgin, "Your mom will give you daddy's Christmas gift later."

After a while, they decided to go back home. They walked towards the car. Yin insisted to live in the home of Finn's parents, "Richard, Sgin and I will live in Helen and Marvin's home. We will send you back to your home first. We can surely meet tomorrow or Sunday if you will be available. How is that?"

Richard nodded, "Can we bring Sgin to look around New York City tomorrow and eat lunch together?"

"Sure." Yin paused for a few seconds and said, "But remember, we will have to call Dr. Hyde to discuss about the treatment, too."

Richard said, "Of course. I will contact Dr. Hyde when I get back home. Can we meet again later today with Dr. Hyde? I mean, if he can take a couple of hours to meet with us today."

"Sure. Just give me a call after you contact him." Yin said.

They sent Richard back home and then drove back to Helen and Marvin's home.

78

Not long after Finn's parents brought Yin and Sgin to their home, Richard called Yin and told her that Dr. Hyde agreed to meet with them in an hour. Richard then picked Yin up and drove her to Dr. Hyde's office. There, they discussed in details with Dr. Hyde. Dr. Hyde explained the symptoms, diagnosis and treatment of the disease and gave them encouragement to face the problem.

Hopefully, everything will be ok.

After the talking to Dr. Hyde, Richard drove Yin back to Helen and Marvin's home. With the temporary stop of the factory production, Yin somehow got a little bit relief, from where, but then, she got more and more worried about Sgin's disease, on the way to New York City. After listening to the explanation of Dr. Hyde, Yin understood the oxygen conversion disease better and gained more confidence to seek the miracle doctors referred to. So on the way back, through the car's windows, she finally could concentrate on the streets and the buildings of New York City.

New York City looked so different from her previous imagination – the streets were busier; the buildings were taller; there were more stores and restaurants. At 7:40, the sky already turned dark in this early winter day. The millions of steady aureolin lights from the windows decorated the dark facades of the buildings, making them look grandiose and quiet. Yin remembered, years ago, when she agreed to move to New York City with Richard, she once was worried about that going to a big city like New York could get her lose the simple happiness she gained in Altimont. Yet tonight, with the apparent difference from Altimont, the city brought her the same kind of peaceful sentiment which always kept her calm and happy when she was in Altimont. Yin couldn't figure out the reason why such a big city would also keep her in such a simple mood as Altimont did.

When they arrived to Helen and Marvin's apartment building, Richard again invited Yin to bring Sgin to look around New York City tomorrow. Yin agreed.

When Yin woke up the next day, Richard already arrived and waited downstairs. Half an hour later, Yin brought Sgin to go downstairs and sit in Richard's very expensive white Ferrari FF car.

"Good morning, Sgin." Richard turned his head back and looked at Sgin with a smile. He then said, "Good morning, Yin."

Yin smiled and gazed at the outside of the car's window, "Good morning."

"Good morning, Dad." Sgin said, "Where are we going?"

Richard said, "How about driving to Columbus Circle, where my apartment was located at? And from there, we can walk into Central Park. Do you want to visit Central Park, Sgin?"

"Yes." Sgin nodded.

Richard drove along Broadway. 18 minutes later, they arrived to 59th Street and Columbus Circle. Richard parked the car in the parking lot of his apartment building and then brought Yin and Sgin walking into Central Park. He started to introduce Central Park to them, "Central Park is an urban park located in the center of Manhattan, from 59th street to 110th street. It is the most visited urban park in the states and one of the most famous parks in the world. Those are what you would know from looking up any book providing an introduction of Central Park. I grew up in New York City and often visited Central Park. Like tourists, New Yorkers like Central Park as much. You would see people walking, running or riding bikes in the park during the day…"

Based on Richard's introduction, Yin paid attention to the scenery of the park. It was a sunny day. The weather was nice, like a 62 degree. Sunshine fell down on the trees, to the ground, warming up the cool air. Except the branches of the trees, partly without leaves, which would reminded them of that winter was coming, the weather and the park gave them an illusion that it was indeed a spring day. With them walking along the small footpath, at the end of it, more footpaths and roads stretched therefrom. Yin now saw the bike riders Richard talked about. On the road, the cyclists were riding bikes in high speed passing them from the front. They waited for the crosswalk light to turn white to cross the road. Then along another footpath, they saw some benches on the side of it. They stopped for a rest and sat down on a bench.

"Do you like Central Park, Sgin?" Richard asked Sgin.

"Yes, very much." Sgin said, "How about you, mom?"

Pausing for a few seconds, Yin said, "Yeah, I do like it. And the weather is really nice today, not like a winter day."

"The weather in New York changes a lot." Richard said, "Sometimes you would see warm temperatures in winter, just like today. Sometimes a winter can be much warmer or colder than the previous one. Every year is different. That is just how the weather is in New York."

They kept silent for a minute, thinking about what Richard just told them about New York City, before Richard started to talk again, "We will spend another hour in the park and after that, I will bring you to eat lunch at around 33rd street, near the Empire State Building. After lunch, we can take the elevator to the top of the building and, from there, we can view the panorama of the city."

After a while, they kept walking in the park and listening to Richard's introduction of the park and the city. An hour later, they walked out from the park. Richard went back to the parking lot of his apartment building to get his car and drove them to 33rd street. They ate lunch in a restaurant on 33rd street and 5th Avenue. Across the street located the Empire State Building. After lunch, they went across the street and into the building and took the elevator to the top of the building. A beautiful panorama of the city spread out before them. They saw Central Park, like a green rectangle, from a distance. It was surrounded by many tall buildings from each side.

40 minutes later, they took the elevator to the ground and left the Empire State Building. From there, Richard drove them to downtown where they spent an hour walking on the streets. Richard invited them to eat dinner together, but Yin wanted to bring Sgin back to Helen and Marvin's home before dinner time. So Richard drove them back to Helen and Marvin's home.

79

Half a year passed. It was the last few days of May. June was coming. A day ago, Richard Meier and Judy Kahn's divorce became final.

Half a year ago, after the live meeting was held and Yin went to New York City with Richard, she made the decision to resign from Altimont Astronomy Station and stay in New York

City to look for the miracle and get Sgin's disease cured. She wrote a letter of resign and mailed it to Finn. Then Finn helped her hand the letter in to the station. Soon the resign request was approved. Ms. Frost expressed her wish that Sgin's disease could be cured in the letter responding to Yin's letter of resign.

After Yin got unemployed, under the help of Richard, Sgin continued his education in a local school and Yin found herself another job in New York City. It was a part time research teaching job in New York University. Yin needed to spend more time with Sgin, take care of him and bring him to the doctor's office three times per week for the treatment. With the feeling that she did like the city, however, Yin hadn't decided to live in New York City forever. Actually she was busy all the time, spending most of her free time thinking about Sgin's treatment, leaving no time to think about where to settle down in the future. She went to the university on Mondays, Tuesdays and Friday mornings and brought Sgin to the doctor's office on the afternoons of Wednesdays, Thursdays and Fridays, after picking Sgin up from his school. Coming back to Helen and Marvin's home from the university on Mondays and Tuesdays, she cooked dinner for Sgin and Finn's parents. For that purpose, she learned different recipes online including Indian recipes and Thai recipes. Wednesdays and Thursdays' meals would be prepared by Helen because dinner time would arrive when Yin brought Sgin back from Dr. Hyde's office. On the weekends, Yin brought Sgin going out for dinner and met up with Richard.

In the month after Sgin began receiving the treatment, his symptoms were somehow controlled and mitigated that sometimes he felt easily breathing with less cough. At the mean time, Yin gradually accepted New York City as her temporary home.

After the live meeting on Thursday, the whole production of Cure 5 was asked to stop. John Jacobs and the whole factory were assigned to find out the true reason causing the pollution. Everyone of TTAM team 5 watched the live meeting. With the progress of the live meeting that they learned the shocking story between their boss and the astronomer whose name they often heard of during the days in Altimont, they agreed with each other that what Yin Lin said was right and that Mr. Meier made a correct decision. The next day, on Friday, John Jacobs had a meeting with TTAM team 5 members to discuss the cause and the solution.

"I believe that you all watched the meeting held yesterday." John Jacobs looked at the team members and they all nodded. John Jacobs asked them, "Can anyone tell me what you think about the decision that Mr. Meier made?"

"He made the right decision. We agree with Yin Lin." Zachary Zoller responded, "Before, when the residents made the complaints to us, we didn't believe what they said was true because we were sure that HW9870 would not affect people's health and so it was not the reason to request us to stop the production. After hearing Yin Lin's words yesterday, I think we should learn how to care for people and the environment, not just put the profit to the first place all the time, you know. Even though we can reject their request because there is not yet evidence to support that there is the connection between the alleged pollution and our factory, based on Lin's logic, before any evidence comes out, we need to stop the production because there may well be such a connection. We need to realize the production may possibly be causing people sick. Then how can we still continue the production knowing all these? Why can't we stop and check first?"

"Ok." John Jacobs paused for a second and asked, "Does anyone have an idea what might be causing the pollution?"

Dr. Morain said, "I thought for a whole evening yesterday. Apparently, anything used by us as an ingredient should not be the cause. What I assume is that what is or are produced by the ingredients, which we may or may not have knowledge of, caused the pollution. You know, we used transgenic technology in the process, so something new could be produced."

"Yeah, I think Dr. Morain is correct." Zachary Zoller agreed.

In the next hour, John Jacobs asked about the method to find out the cause. Everyone spoke for their own method. Zachary Zoller recommended doing experiments imitating the process of the Cure 5 production, collecting the air and water discharged from the experiments and analyzed the components. His method was agreed by all other members and John Jacobs himself.

A day later, on Saturday, Richard called John Jacobs and asked him to spend money on helping the residents cure their diseases, weeding the crocuses which grew everywhere in Altimont and improving the quality of the air and the water. Receiving the demand, John Jacobs spent the whole Sunday making up a plan of helping people and improving the environment and, again, held a meeting with TTAM team 5 on Monday to discuss the plan.

In the next month, when TTAM team 5 tried their best to find out the cause of the pollution, John Jacobs' plan of helping people and improving the environment was put into action - the common symptoms among people were mitigated and the crocuses were weeded. Another few weeks later, TTAM team 5 found out the cause. It was from a new substance produced in the production process which they did not have knowledge of. From there, in the next month, they developed the method and improved the machines to prevent this substance from discharging to the environment.

Three months later after the live meeting, John Jacobs reported their achievement to Richard through the phone, "Richard, by your request, we tried our best to help the residents and change the environment to that of before. Now common symptoms among people finally disappeared and the environment was improved to barely like before. We will continue the progress. At the mean time, TTAM team 5 found out the cause of the pollution and solved the problem so the production of Cure 5 can now start again."

One day after five months' treatment, Sgin did not have any symptoms that day. Yin reported this to Dr. Hyde, which was deemed by him as a good sign of the cure. In the following weeks, the symptoms did not come back. Dr. Hyde did a check of the oxygen conversion disease and found out that everything became normal, which indicated that Sgin's disease was cured.

Finally, we found the miracle.

Yin was extremely happy when she heard that Sgin's disease was cured. She thanked Dr. Hyde multiple times and called Richard and told him about the good news immediately. Dr. Hyde was quite happy too that Sgin's case became the second case in the history and his first case that the oxygen conversion disease was cured. He told Yin that he decided to develop his treatment method to help more people who suffered the disease.

Cure 5 began to be produced again two months ago, under the supervision of the whole factory, to make sure there was no more discharge of the substance which had had caused the pollution. Meanwhile, TTAM team 5 collected the air samples and the water samples and analyzed the quality of them routinely. Since the production, no more incident or pollution was reported. Altimont restored to what it was like before.

Altimont saved Yin and she saved the town.

80

In the past half a year, since the live meeting was held and Yin left Altimont for New York City, Finn went back to the life he had before, riding his bicycle to work as usual on weekdays, cooking dinners for himself and watching TV alone in the evenings. During the weekends, he went for walks in the park and went shopping in the malls as he did before. What was the difference, to him, was that, after watching the live meeting in person, seeing Yin leave for New York City, helping her resign from Altimont Astronomy Station and seeing Altimont restored to that of before, Finn now understood the significance of keeping a simple life in the complexity, which he couldn't figure out years ago. In the first years working in Altimont, the town gained him a new feeling, a simple happiness, which he had had never experienced before. Yet during that time, the feeling was just a feeling. The simple happiness was just something he enjoyed without a deeper understanding of the wisdom behind it. When he first time had the feeling of the simple happiness was when he didn't understand the complexity of the world. After he experienced the complexity which tended to make him lose the feeling, he could now again gain the feeling back because experiences and understanding would also gain him wisdom on why him needed to keep his life simple.

As for his love towards Yin, it already changed to a deep friendship. Finn now understood that Yin left Richard and tried not to get back together with Richard throughout the years because of a piece of misleading information. *I wish her the best.*

Emily Lawless' symptoms were mitigated and eventually cured. On this Saturday afternoon, at 4 o'clock, while she was making the advertisement for her nails salon, she received a phone call from Finn Kane. Finn said he just went back home from work and invited her for a walk in the park for which she agreed.

A while later, Finn drove his car and arrived to Emily's home. Today Emily wore a light blue T-shirt, a pair of champagne pink shorts and a pair of fashionable silver sandals, looked very beautiful. She sat in Finn's car and Finn drove her to the park where he and Yin had had often visited before.

When they got out of the car and walked into the park, Finn started the conversation, "Altimont now looks like what it was before. I remember last fall when Yin and I walked in this park, there were a lot of crocuses, you know, everywhere. Now they are all gone." Finn laughed out.

"You still like her? I mean love." Emily wanted to know.

Finn took a quick look at Emily's eyes, seeking for her intent behind the question, and then responded, "Didn't you watch the meeting, the live meeting, last Thanksgiving Day?"

"Yes, I did." Emily, as many others in Altimont, would not forget what happened during the meeting, "Finally knew who the man was."

"You mean Richard, the man who engaged to Yin? He still loves Yin." Finn said and kept walking.

"I am sure he does and I think Yin also loves him." Emily said. She hesitated but decided to ask Finn again, "How about you, Finn? Do you still love Yin?"

Finn stopped and looked at Emily, as to confirm his true feeling. They kept silent for half a minute before Finn started to walk and talk again, "Emily, there is something I want to tell you. That is that... Um... I eventually can lay down my emotions towards Yin. Now I consider her as just a friend."

Emily followed Finn and started to walk. She waited for 10 years to hear what Finn just said. Yet when she finally heard the words, she didn't know if it was because she was too happy that she couldn't even figure out what her reaction should be. She didn't smile nor cry, but kept walking and finally said, "Finn, so what is your plan for the future?"

Finn paused for 10 seconds and responded, "I think you also know that Yin resigned from Altimont Astronomy Station and moved to New York City. I got the news from Yin a couple of weeks ago that her son's oxygen conversion disease was cured. She is now making decision on where to settle down for the future, too. My parents live in New York City. I would like to visit them next week. I will have a meal with Yin and her son. When I come back from New York City, I will then decide what to do next. But I think I will stay in Altimont... Um..."

"Great! I hope you have a good trip." Emily interrupted, "What did you want to say?"

Finn hesitated, "Nothing. Let's keep walking." Through the conversation, Finn started to appreciate the beauty of Emily and realized that he gradually developed feeling for her.

When they walked to the end of the footpath, a fountain appeared in front of them with water poured into the basin. The grass, decorated by colorful flowers, embraced them.

"Emily," Finn suddenly turned towards Emily, "Would you like to go to New York City with me?"

Emily looked at Finn, smiled and said, "Sure."

81

8 years passed since Yin first met Richard. 8 years ago, she was just a young researcher known in Altimont for her potential. In her mind there was only her ambition. Now she turned out to be a great scientist and a good mother. She changed a lot to be more matured and sensible. She often asked herself a question since she stayed in New York City. That was what brought her happiness? Before when she lived in Altimont, she thought it was from a kind

of peaceful sentiment the environment and the relatively isolated location provided and the niceness of the residents. She was worried that going to a big city like New York could ruin such happiness. Yet when she arrived to New York City the first time, she found that it was not the case. She still found the simple happiness from New York City.

So what brings me happiness?

Today, Richard invited Yin to go out alone for a talk. During the talk, he told Yin that he just got divorced and asked her to marry him. Yin agreed. They were engaged.

Richard said, "I have decided to retire from RM Corps and move to Altimont with you."

Yin said, "Richard, you really don't need to. I can settle down in New York City so that you can continue your work. We don't need to choose to move back to Altimont because I also like the city here."

Richard said, after all the experiences, he didn't want to continue to the stressful work. He said what he truly wanted now was just a family and a peaceful life.

Yin nodded and nodded.

After a long conversation, the couple decided to move to upstate New York, where they could buy a land and build an astronomy station. Yin would work as an astronomer again and Richard would start to build up his interests in astronomy. There, they could teach Sgin some astronomy knowledge. It was great that it would be easier for Richard to visit his mother. They decided to move as soon as the beginning of next month.

The day before Yin, Richard and Sgin left New York City, Finn and Emily arrived to the city. They planned to stay in the city for two days. Finn called Yin up, wanting to give her a surprise, "Hi, Yin, guess what, I am in the same city as you." Yin did receive the surprise and told Finn that they were leaving the city. Finn asked their plan in details and then invited them out for dinner, "This may be the last meal we can eat together within the year. After that, You, Richard and Sgin would go upstate direction while Emily and I would go back to the south. I know you are busy now, but please come and meet us up." Yin agreed.

4 hours later, Richard, Yin, Sgin, Emily and Finn, they all sat around the same table in a restaurant downtown and agreed to eat more. Richard helped request the food and Yin requested her favorite ice green tea lemonade for them all.

"It is surprising knowing that you are visiting New York City, Finn. Welcome, Emily!" Yin said, smiling, "When you called me at noon today, I thought you were in Altimont."

Finn said, "I wanted to give you the surprise so I didn't tell you before we arrived to the city. But then I got to know something equally surprising, that you, Richard and Sgin are leaving the city. I didn't ask on the phone, but I am still curious. Why did you decide to leave? I thought Richard worked in the city."

"He is retiring from the company. Work was too stressful." Yin responded.

Finn asked, "Then why moving to upstate New York? Don't you want to go back to Altimont?"

Yin said, "That is the decision. I worked for Altimont Astronomy Station for 11 years and now it's the time to have my own astronomy station. The reason I didn't want to leave Altimont was because I was worried of losing the happiness I gained from the town once I left for another place. But now I am happy, truly happy, you know, so I can go anywhere. Maybe you can work in my astronomy station in the future, Finn. Consider it."

Everyone laughed out loud.

"Sure, great idea." Finn said.

They stayed in the restaurant until three hours later. When it was time to say goodbye, Yin and Finn told each other that they would keep in touch often.

The second day morning, Richard drove Yin and Sgin towards upstate direction. On the way, Yin gazed at the scenery outside of the car windows. It was the beginning of June, the beginning of the summer season. The Sun stretched its face out from the horizon, coloring the sky and the earth to be golden. The fields next to the highway quietly stood tall green trees, like that they were enjoying the sunshine and the fresh air. The serene scenery reminded her of the simple and peaceful life in Altimont - from her home, she passed the quiet residential area, crossed the clear river, went through the peaceful wood and finally took herself to the place where she chased her dream. Secretly, the question she kept since she came to New York City again appeared in her mind, *what brings me happiness?* She slight thought. The scenery and her deep memory of her life in Altimont inspired her. A moment later, she found herself with the answer.

It is love that brings me happiness and Altimont is such a great town teaching me how to love. The niceness between residents, the friendship between friends, the care between families, the romance between lovers, the sincerity towards career and the gratitude to the environment makes Altimont a town full of love. There, you experience love. There, you learn to love. Then you can go anywhere.

50455530R00176

Made in the USA
Middletown, DE
25 June 2019